A
HEARTFELT
CHRISTMAS
PROMISE

Also by Nancy Naigle

Christmas Joy

Hope at Christmas

Dear Santa

Christmas Angels

Visit www.NancyNaigle.com for a list of all Nancy's novels.

A
HEARTFELT
CHRISTMAS
PROMISE

Nancy Naigle

ST. MARTIN'S GRIFFIN
NEW YORK

First published in the United States by St. Martin's Griffin, an imprint of St. Martin's Publishing Group

A HEARTFELT CHRISTMAS PROMISE. Copyright © 2020 by Nancy Naigle. All rights reserved. Printed in the United States of America. For information, address St. Martin's Publishing Group, 120 Broadway, New York, NY 10271.

www.stmartins.com

Library of Congress Cataloging-in-Publication Data

Names: Naigle, Nancy, author.
Title: A heartfelt Christmas promise / Nancy Naigle.
Description: First edition. | New York: St. Martin's Griffin, 2020.
Identifiers: LCCN 2020019360 | ISBN 9781250312648 (trade paperback) | ISBN 9781250312655 (ebook)
Subjects: LCSH: Christmas stories. | GSAFD: Love stories.
Classification: LCC PS3614.A545 H43 2020 | DDC 813/.6—dc23
LC record available at https://lccn.loc.gov/2020019360

Our books may be purchased in bulk for promotional, educational, or business use. Please contact your local bookseller or the Macmillan Corporate and Premium Sales Department at 1-800-221-7945, extension 5442, or by email at MacmillanSpecialMarkets@macmillan.com.

First Edition: 2020

10 9 8 7 6 5 4 3 2 1

Wishing you all a few small-town slow-down days.
Merry Christmas.

ACKNOWLEDGMENTS

Thank you to the incredible team at St. Martin's Press. Eileen Rothschild, I couldn't ask for a better editor. I love the extra push you give me and my craft is so much better for it. Tiffany, Natalie, Marissa, DJ, you bring the whole picture together, and keep all the parts moving. Thank you so much for the attention to those details.

Thank you, Kevan Lyon, my agent, for believing in me and getting my stories into the right hands. I appreciate your tenacity, patience, and skilled negotiations, and all the cheers along the way. I never would have written the first Christmas book had it not been for you, and they sure have brought me joy.

Thank you, Rolling Hills Percheron Farm in Winston Salem, specifically, Jeremy Hancock, for showing me around your farm and letting me know when the colts were born. This book has been in my head ever since that first visit.

Thank you, Jennifer Siegenthaler, for sharing your experiences and pulling Jeremy away from chores, or let's get serious . . . the college basketball game, long enough to answer my questions that you couldn't about the horses and hitch process. I'm so inspired by those beautiful gentle-spirited animals and the work it takes to run that farm.

Thanks, Andrew, for your patience, support, prayers, and for always making me laugh. You are my balance when things start stressing me out. Thanks, too, for sharing your team hitch experiences, and for helping me bring a real horseman's point of view to the story. You're my real-life hero.

Last, but not least, thank you to my friends and family. No story is written alone. There are beta readers, brainstormers, people I see doing something that inspires me, the "get real" gang that'll talk me off the ledge or tell me I'm flat-out crazy, and the readers who remind me why I ever sat down to write that first book in the first place. I had one simple goal:

Write one book, to help one gal through one lousy day.

Writing this novel would not have been nearly as satisfying without your help and fellowship.

Thank You!

A
Heartfelt
Christmas
Promise

CHAPTER ONE

Vanessa slid her hand along the slick wooden banister as she climbed the stairs. The warmth of the wood softened the appearance of the decorative black wrought-iron balusters—a real statement of strength and beauty.

As a young girl, she'd dreamed of living in an elegant house like this, and this one wasn't that far from her office in downtown Chicago, either.

Walking through the guest rooms, she could picture one of them decorated with a colorful handmade quilt atop inviting crisp white sheets. Fluffy feather pillows, soft and firm ones, piled like a cloud for a heavenly night's rest. A small upholstered chair would be perfect by the window overlooking the mature trees in the backyard. Except for the evergreens, almost everything was already winter-bare.

It would be so beautiful blanketed in snow. She could fill brightly colored bird feeders for the red cardinals that just flitted from the bushes at the fence edge to a limb right in front of the window. *The only birds outside my windows at my condo are pigeons and all they do is leave a mess on the windowsill.* This was definitely a step up, and so quiet compared to the city.

Vanessa walked back downstairs knowing this was the home she'd been searching for. "I love this house." She joined her Realtor, Sally, in the living room. "My friends kept telling me when I found the right one, I'd know it. Now I understand what they meant." Excitement swirled in her stomach like blowing snow in a frosty blizzard.

This is it. Home.

"I can't believe it." Vanessa pulled her hands close to her heart. "Finally. Did you keep count of how many houses we've looked at?"

"I could do the math, but you don't really want to know."

"It's been nearly a year of house hunting."

"Your travel schedule didn't help."

"True," Vanessa said. "I was beginning to think I'd have to give up the idea of a house with a yard close to work altogether."

"I told you I'd find you the perfect house, and Sally Fields always delivers."

Every time Sally talked about herself it was with first and last name, and usually followed by "no relation to the actress." Not that anyone would think so. The actress didn't have an "s" at the end of her name, for one. Plus, Sally the Realtor was a good foot taller than the talented actress with the infectious smile.

Sally strutted through the house like a peacock. "At least you knew what you wanted from day one."

"I usually do." Vanessa walked over to the windows that overlooked the deck. "That's not always a good thing, though."

As a little girl, she'd loved the rope swing at her cousin Anna's house. Anna was Mom's cousin. Anna and Mom had been inseparable until the day Mom died. Swallowing back the sorrow, she concentrated on the trees on this property. The biggest, a huge oak she'd never be able to wrap her arms around, could easily hold a swing.

Vanessa had spent many hours with Anna while Dad worked. They'd swing for hours in the backyard. Vanessa remembered lifting her toes toward the tallest branches, soaring high and hoping to reach heaven, and catch a glimpse of Mom with angel wings. Mom seemed so close on those days.

Maybe I'll have two so Anna and I can swing at the same time. People never outgrow swinging, do they?

Sally rattled on. ". . . and the closets are wonderful. So much storage. You just don't find this kind of house every day. It's a kitchen a chef would kill for, commercial equipment and everything, but it's done so nicely that it's still homey." She stepped beside Vanessa.

Vanessa tipped her chin up. Sally towered over her at every bit of six feet tall in the too-high heels that were her trademark. "It's very pretty, but you know I don't cook." *But Anna does. She'd probably really love it.*

"Right. Yes, but the in-law suite is nicely set apart with a den. Just like you wanted." Sally curled the listing sheet in her hand as if she were going to pop a fly on the noggin with it. Or maybe it was more likely that Sally would hit her if she didn't quickly jump on this deal.

Hesitation and second thoughts consumed her. Now that she'd found what she wanted, was it stupid to buy a house this big when technically it could be just her? She'd tried to talk Anna into moving in with her before with no luck. But now that Anna had retired, how could she turn her down? There was plenty of room here for long visits, if she couldn't convince her to move in at first. Vanessa hugged her arms around herself. That's what she truly wanted.

"Wasn't easy to find everything on your list." Sally looked quite proud of herself. "This one even has the fence for the dog you don't have yet."

"But you did find it. Thank you." She opened her arms wide, taking in the fresh spa colors of the great room. "This was totally worth the wait."

Sally lifted a finger in the air. "Well, there is one teensy hitch."

The glow in Vanessa's heart faded. "Don't tell me this is over my budget." She tried to maintain her cool, but with her teeth clenched and her fists now too, she was probably far from looking calm. She'd never had a good poker face. "I told you not to show me *anything* over the budget. I hate it when Realtors pull that, and I left work to meet you today with no notice. Let it be anything but that."

Her finger and thumb about an inch apart, Sally said, "Just a smidge over." She winked and expanded the space between her fingers a little more.

That wink about pushed Vanessa over the edge. "You called me away from work to see this house, and it's over my budget? Really? I had meetings scheduled. You said it was urgent."

"It's a sweet deal. It's going to go quick. We can come in under the listing price, but the agent said they are expecting other offers."

Don't they always say that? The house *was* perfect. "How much over budget are we talking here?"

Sally handed her the listing she'd been twisting in her hands.

Vanessa pulled the paper straight and scanned the information. Her jaw pulsed. This wasn't teensy at all. "This is a hundred thousand dollars over my budget."

"But you qualified for—"

Swallowing back what she really wanted to say, she responded simply with a "No ma'am. I set my budget. Not the lender. Period." Trying to maintain her temper, she turned and walked out. She took her frustration out on the car door, which she slammed twice as hard as necessary. The clock showed she'd just fallen in love with that house in record time. On a good note, she could probably get back to the office for the acquisition and merger meeting.

Sally still stood in the doorway as Vanessa backed down the long winding driveway.

What a waste of time.

She pressed the accelerator and headed for the highway without another look back. Once on the interstate, she pushed the buttons to start the heated massage feature on the driver's seat.

A quick glance in the rearview mirror highlighted a deep line on her forehead. The one that always appeared when she was stressed out. She rubbed her finger across it, and opened her eyes wide, trying to force herself to relax.

"I need to focus on work. There are never any surprises there. Just the way I like it." She patted the steering wheel as if she expected it to repeat words of confirmation back. "Forget the house. Even if it *was* perfect. That'll have to be a project for another time. Another year."

Suddenly, for no apparent reason at all, the traffic snarled to a standstill—cars nose-to-tail for as far as she could see. "Of course."

The car idled at a stop. Her phone rang, and she cringed. Sally would be begging her to reconsider. Just as she was about to silence the ringer, she noticed the caller ID. It wasn't Sally; it was Anna. Her mood lifted instantaneously.

"Anna? How do you always know when I'm out of sorts, and need a friend?"

"It's my superpower, cuz."

Anna might have been joking, but she honestly had an uncanny ability to arrive at every godmother-appropriate point in Vanessa's life. They were first cousins once removed, or was that the same as being second cousins? She never could figure that stuff out. No one knew genealogy like Mom. All Vanessa really cared about was that Anna was like family, blood relatives or not.

Anna had always called Vanessa "cuz," even though she'd been more like a much, much older sister all Vanessa's life. "Anna, it's so good to hear from you."

"We are way overdue, aren't we?"

Anna was so much better about calling than she was. "I've been meaning to call."

"I know you're busy. How have you been? You're still working too much, aren't you?"

Vanessa groaned. "Actually, I took a little personal time this morning. I'm on my way to the office now."

"Music to my ears!"

"I may have made that sound better than it really was. It was just a big waste of time."

"Now, why would you say that. Any time off is a blessing."

"I wasted my morning looking at a house that wasn't in my budget. Now I'm sitting in traffic, and late for a meeting."

"It's barely nine o'clock. I'm sure the tide will turn before you even break for lunch."

"If only I ever took one."

"You've got to eat. You need to take care of yourself. We've had this talk before." Anna's voice held that tone that only mothers could usually get away with.

"I know. I know. If I take a break for a healthy lunch, I'll get that time back in productivity later."

"That's not just me talking," Anna said. "It's a proven fact. Maybe you'd deal better with the stress, too. Couldn't hurt, right?"

"Hearing your voice has reduced my stress level already."

"Great. So, catch me up. How're things going? What's new? If you and Robert are looking at houses you two must be talking marriage again?"

"He actually doesn't know I've been house shopping."

"What? You're going to have to let that man into your life at some point."

Vanessa laid out the whole story on the house, and how it was perfect, but not. "And Robert's been acting like he's about to pop the question."

"I've been holding back saying this for a long time, but you keep dodging marriage with him. You've got to decide if you're going to marry him, or just let him move on."

"Well, I—"

"I'm not asking for an explanation. This is something only you can decide, but you two have been together longer than some marriages last these days. It's not fair to either one of you to let this drag on status quo."

She blew out a breath. "Anna, I know we look like the perfect couple on paper. He's nice. Successful. Handsome. Generous. Dependable. The only thing we don't agree on is he loves living in his rooftop condo, and I'm ready to be out of the city to have a house with a yard, but that's not the reason."

"Then what?"

"I don't love him, Anna. I've tried so hard. I like him a lot. I'm just not in love with him." It frustrated her so much. "Maybe I'm not capable of that kind of love."

"Of love? Everyone is capable of love, Vanessa. Follow your instincts. I think you know what you need to do."

"It's not going to be easy to break it off. But you're right." She sat there feeling a little numb. Why had she let this go on so long? "Anna, I miss you, and these talks."

"I miss you too. I'm always here for you. We're family."

"I know, but wouldn't it be nice if we lived closer? I was thinking you could even come up here and live with me now that you're retired."

"Things happen for a reason. Sometimes you just have to open your heart, and trust it will all work out the way it's supposed to rather than trying to manage every detail."

Vanessa laughed. "You know how I hate surprises. I don't see that happening."

"Ultimately, the journey will be wonderful. I promise."

Anna was always saying stuff like that. Even to people she didn't know. It used to embarrass Vanessa, but now it seemed sweet. "If you say so."

"I do say so. And who knows. Maybe one day we'll live closer, but nothing is stopping us from more frequent visits. We can always fly."

"We'll do better next year."

"Yes, we will. Now, the reason I was calling was that I'd

really love it if we could make plans together for the holidays. You could come here. I'll cook and spoil you rotten."

"I don't—"

"Don't you dare say no. I'll fly to you in Chicago if I have to, even if it is bitter cold and damp. Get your calendar out and ink me in. Somewhere. You name the place. I really want to see you."

Vanessa was already going down a list of things in her mind. "Wait. Everything's okay, right?"

"Of course. You're like the daughter I never had, and you're so much like your mother. I miss her too, you know. We've let too much time slip by. Let's have a family Christmas this year. You and me."

Mom had always known how to do it up right. Christmas hadn't been the same since she passed. Her absence left a gaping hole in everything special. Without her it never seemed worth doing, but spending Christmas with Anna was definitely the next best thing.

"Anna, I'd love to spend the holidays together. Yes. We will absolutely do it."

"This is the best Christmas gift ever."

Vanessa's eyes glossed. "This is going to be perfect. I just pulled in at the office. I've got that meeting this morning where I'll be getting my next assignment. The good news is you might *not* have to come to freezing Chicago for Christmas. All that hard work I've put in over the past few years has me positioned for the pick of the projects. I may very well be working in Paris, France—"

"Paris? Wow. AGC has been really good to you."

It was true, but she worked hard for everything she got. "Or Leavenworth, Washington, which doesn't sound all that fancy, but from what I hear it's the best place in the whole country to spend Christmas. Fluffy, white snow glistens from every building, and a million holiday lights decorate the entire Bavarian-style town. It's like being in a snow globe of the North Pole. They even have reindeer."

"Sounds like the company acquired Santa's summer home."

"I hope not. They told me it was a ski resort and vineyard. Year-round destination."

"Anyplace we go is fine with me," Anna assured her.

"This trip will be my treat. No argument, especially since we have to accommodate my schedule, but I promise it will be less work and more play."

"Your mom would love what a successful businesswoman you've become."

Anna hadn't mentioned Dad. They both knew he'd never admit he was proud of her ... even if he was. Vanessa had vied for his approval for as long as she could remember. *Why can't I let my need for his acknowledgment go?*

"And I'm proud of you."

Anna's delicate and comforting voice, like silver bells, left her feeling lighter, and loved.

"Remember when you were six?" Anna asked. "Barely old enough to Magic Marker a poster, but you did and then sold more cookies by yourself than the church did at the Christmas Festival. And when you were in the sixth grade you had more fashion sense than I did, and figured out how to make money using it."

"You funded the start-up for that business."

"Vanessa's Fine Vintage Frills."

"You always believed in me."

"Of course I did."

"I loved going to the flea markets with you, sifting through old jewelry to find just the right pieces for my kiosk. Every Saturday on the driveway."

"I remember. You've always had a head for business," she said. "You were quite the entrepreneur. I thought you'd own a boutique one day, but I guess I wasn't dreaming big enough. You've done so well. And now you're picking the projects you want to do. That's quite an accomplishment."

There wasn't anything entrepreneurial about her job now. It was simply making the decisions the executives made become reality. But she was good at it, and she'd moved up quickly. "It's been a hard road and lots of work, but yes, I'm in an excellent position now."

"In your career. Yes, I'd agree," said Anna. "But your personal life could use a major do-over, and spending Christmas together is a good first step."

"I'll call you after this meeting, when I get my assignment and know where we're going. Fingers crossed for Paris!"

Chapter Two

Vanessa rushed into the elevator just before the doors closed. "Eleven, please."

Why was it that when she was in a hurry this elevator seemed to stop at every floor? Good thing she didn't work in a building with more floors. Finally, when she was the only person left, it lurched to a stop, and the doors opened.

The front-desk receptionist lifted her head and offered a good-morning.

"Good morning." Vanessa checked the time, then picked up her pace to drop off her handbag in her office.

Kendra, her assistant was waiting on her. "I have all the paperwork for the meeting right here for you," she said, trading the documents for Vanessa's purse. "You're a little late, but not horribly so. You're near the bottom of the agenda."

"Great." She'd reviewed everything yesterday, so she was already prepared. She rushed down the hall, then paused in front of the conference room door to catch her breath, before quietly opening the door and entering with an air of confidence.

Never apologize.

She took her seat at the fourteen-foot table. Gleaming wood and fine leather chairs filled the room. There were normally at least another ten people on the phone.

Offering a simple nod and grin to her boss, who nodded back, she turned her attention to Roland McAdo, who was droning on about the status of his merger down in Miami. He was the Chicken Little of the bunch, and Vanessa usually just tuned him out, knowing full well that no matter how dismal a picture he painted, he'd pull it off with great success as he always did.

Roland sat down and pushed the agenda between him and Vanessa.

"I've got one. Thank you." She flipped open the folder Kendra had prepared for her. Glancing over it, she saw that she hadn't missed much. Just some recaps on older projects.

Down the list toward the bottom were the discussions about the two latest acquisitions. The ones she'd already expressed interest in. Paris, because who wouldn't want to work in Paris for a while, and the one in Leavenworth that included a hefty bonus. Which, come to think of it, could mean that the house she fell in love with this morning wouldn't really be out of her budget after all.

She shifted in her seat, excited about how things were coming together. She patted her damp palms on a page in her notebook, determined to look calm.

The meeting would go on for at least another hour and a half. If she got the Paris project, she'd meet with the director immediately following this. If she was assigned Leavenworth, she'd owe Sally a phone call. It would be a long day for her and Kendra, but a good one either way.

No time for lunch today, Anna. I'll do better tomorrow.

Each project was reviewed. If it wasn't in green status, then a get-to-green plan was discussed before they moved to the next. One of the big acquisitions was an East Coast sporting-goods chain. They were in desperate need of warehouse space to accommodate a huge deal with Outdoor Sports Pro that could mean millions. Since she didn't have any properties open to offer from her portfolio, she excused herself for a quick break.

When she got to her office, Kendra leapt up from behind her desk.

"How's it going? Do you know which project we're getting next?" Kendra had been her assistant for more than four years now. They were so in sync that Vanessa never worried about anything falling through the cracks.

"No. Not yet. There's a big discussion going on about Gary's East Coast sporting-goods megachain. They just landed some huge exclusive deal and need warehouse space ready by the beginning of the year."

"That'll slow down the meeting," Kendra said.

"I know. Thought I'd use it to my advantage and grab a cup of coffee and check messages."

Kendra handed her a stack of messages. "I put hash marks under the ones from Sally. That lady thinks you're dodging her calls or something. I told her I'd have you call her as soon as you got out, but that your calendar is packed."

"Hmm. Yeah, we had a difference of opinion on that house this morning."

"I wondered. I take it the place was horrible."

"No. Not horrible at all," Vanessa said. "In fact, it was perfect."

"Then what's the problem?"

"It was over budget. I'll tell you while we're celebrating our new project later."

Kendra clapped her hands together. "I can't wait. I've already researched both locations."

"That doesn't surprise me. I have too. It's going to be great." Vanessa breezed out of her office and stepped back in the conference room. One of her coworkers, Micky Cooper, was pleading the case for a warehouse project to get moved to one in his portfolio in North Carolina. Something that had been on his books for a long time. It must not be making big profits lately, else why would he offer it up?

She took her seat.

"Porter's has two huge warehouse spaces. Plus, the surrounding area has plenty of space for expansion. It'd be tight to do a shutdown and get ready by January first, but the right person could get it done."

Vanessa politely smiled, rocking in her chair as she swung back around toward her boss, Edward Grayson. Yeah, it could be done, but Micky wasn't the guy to do it. He was always running late on his projects. He was really much better on the front-end negotiations than the execution of things like this.

Edward's bushy eyebrows wiggled like restless caterpillars. "You're right, Micky."

Micky gave a cocky nod and leaned back in his chair.

"Only this can't slip. Not one day." Edward's glasses slid farther down his nose as he swiveled his gaze across the team sitting at his table today, and then his focus landed on Vanessa.

As in a disastrous game of spin the bottle, Vanessa's insides flipped.

"Porter's is a small town. I went out there personally when we closed that deal. It's the best option we've got in our portfolio to make this happen in the short time frame. Execution has to be flawless. Vanessa—"

"No." She hadn't meant to say that out loud. Trying to cover, she said, "Edward, there are plenty of good people on this team who can handle that assignment, and Thanksgiving is next week."

"I need *you* to handle it."

"Sir, with all due respect." She lowered her voice and leaned in closer to him. "Paris? Leavenworth? I've earned those." The words hung like peanut butter in the back of her throat.

"You're right," he said. "You have."

She raised her chin, hoping he'd change his mind.

But Edward looked down the table again and with not an ounce of remorse announced, "I need you in Fraser Hills, North Carolina, on Monday. It'll be quick, and I promise I'll give you the next big thing that comes through this door. This has to go right. It's important."

Her throat tightened. "Yes, sir."

Micky leaned forward with a sly grin. "I'll send you the files on Porter's."

She nodded as she sat there trying to hold herself together as the agenda moved on.

When they got to the two projects she'd been vying for, she could barely breathe while her dream projects were assigned. Micky and his brother Gary were assigned the Paris project as a team. None other than McAdo landed Leavenworth.

"That's it for today." Edward pushed himself up from his chair.

Vanessa was thankful Micky and Gary, full of enthusiasm, had cornered Edward so she didn't even have to make eye contact with him. She pasted a smile on her face and headed straight to her office.

"What's our holiday going to be? Christmas lights in Leavenworth or pastries in Pah-rhee?" Even in the worst French accent ever, Kendra's enthusiasm was endearing, if poorly timed.

"I need a minute." Vanessa waited until Kendra backed out and closed the door. She gathered her thoughts. Being a team player was important to Vanessa . . . usually. She just never was the one who had to change her plans for the team. This had come from left field.

A new email popped up on her computer screen. It was the Porter's file from Micky. With a sigh, she sat down and started scrolling through the documents.

"A fruitcake factory?" Even worse than she'd thought. She now remembered when they acquired this one. They were already running a pretty lean staff. It shouldn't take that much time. Get in, get out, and pick up a long-term, big-city megacompany project that she could really sink her teeth into for a while.

At least she'd be closer to Anna for the holidays.

She picked up the phone and dialed Edward's office.

"Hey, Becky. Is Edward available? I need a few minutes with him."

"He just got back. Come on over."

"Thank you."

She stood, straightening the bottom of her jacket and smoothing her skirt. "I'll be back in a few minutes," she said to Kendra with a fake smile. "Have to chat with Edward."

Kendra looked like she was about to throw confetti. *If she only knew.*

*

Vanessa rolled the dialogue over and over in her mind. Becky was away from her desk, so Vanessa knocked and walked into Edward's office.

"I can always count on you," he said.

"Yes. Yes, you can, but I was counting on Paris. Or actually Leavenworth. That bonus could help me with the house I want to buy. Instead, I get fruitcake? Really? Someone should have shut that down when we took it on. It's bringing in a pittance. Leave it to Micky to leave the work on the table and take the easy way." She sat in the chair across from him.

"I know you're upset," Edward said.

"Why can't I team up with McAdo on the Porter's closure, then take over Leavenworth when it's done? I can do both. You know I can."

"I need you focused on Porter's. This deal will fall through if we don't have adequate warehouse space in time. It's big money."

"What about Rick Gula or Patsy Jennings? They're both great at shutdowns."

"They moved on last summer. No one likes the shutdowns. I get it. I wouldn't have assigned this to you if I had another option."

"I gave you another option."

He shook his head. "I tell you what, I'll match the amount of the Leavenworth bonus if you get yourself to Fraser Hills on Monday morning and get that fruitcake factory shut down by January first."

That was unexpected, but it wasn't what she really wanted.

With her hesitation, Edward threw his hands up in the air. "Fine. I'll double it."

Double? That added up to one big bonus.

"And I'll still give you your pick of the next projects."

"Are you going to put that in writing?"

He cocked his head, his neck beginning to turn an odd shade of pink.

"Strike that. Your word is good with me." She stood. She could be only so mad with that kind of bonus for such a short assignment. "I'd better get to my office and get Kendra working on those reservations."

"I think that's an excellent plan."

Vanessa walked back to her office dreading having to burst Kendra's bubble. It would have been such a nice reward to let her come to Paris to help get things started. She was going to be disappointed.

I'll make it up to her on the next project.

But when Vanessa walked in, Kendra stood with two flutes of French champagne. "Let's celebrate. I can't wait!"

Vanessa took the bubbling glass and raised it to her. With a high-pitched clink, they both sipped.

"Okay," said Vanessa, taking another sip. "Thank you, this is nice, but I've got bad news."

Kendra lowered her glass.

"I'm sorry to say we will not be in Washington or Paris."

Confusion flooded Kendra's features. "Where, then?"

"I'll be in the mountains of North Carolina for a quick shutdown."

"North Carolina?"

"I can't believe it either. I'll be closing down a tiny fruit-cake factory and clearing space for a sporting-goods company to warehouse inventory. And it's a tight timeline."

"Over Christmas?"

"By January first."

"If that isn't heartless." Kendra drained her glass. "Do those people even know what's coming?"

"They must. We are always very clear at acquisition that things can change down the road. It is rotten timing, but it can't be helped."

Kendra poured more champagne in both of their glasses. "Mm-hmm. That's always what the big company line is. Just business, right?"

"Well, yeah. I mean, everyone will be well taken care of. That's never a problem." Vanessa tried not to think of the individuals involved when she handled shutdowns. It had been a long while since she had done one of these, and somehow, she'd never had to do a shutdown over the holidays. "I'm disappointed too, but our next project will be something wonderful. Edward promised."

"Christmas in Paris would have been amazing, but I feel worse for the workers in North Carolina than for us."

Vanessa plunked down in her chair. "Edward thinks he needs me on this one. I plan to make the best of the situation."

"Of course you do." Kendra slugged back the champagne. "You're right. It's our job, and at least *we'll* have paychecks next year."

Ouch. If that wasn't like a kick to the gut.

"I know you have plenty of vacation built up," Vanessa reminded Kendra. "There's no need for you to spend your

Christmas in Fraser Hills with me. Just let me know what days you'd like to take off and I'll approve them."

"Thank goodness," Kendra said. "I don't mean any disrespect, but I don't think that town is going to be very festive this Christmas. I'd rather be in a happy place."

"Let's hope when Porter's doors close, even better opportunities await them with the new warehouse opening," Vanessa said. "They'll need employees. That's something."

"Yeah, you're right." Kendra lifted her glass. "New jobs for everyone."

If only I could guarantee that.

CHAPTER THREE

In Fraser Hills, North Carolina, Mike Marshall stood at the edge of the practice ring behind his barn with one dusty leather boot propped on the bottom fence rail. Watching his daughter, Misty, work the horses always made him miss Olivia. After eleven years, you'd think a man might be able to deal better, but the older Misty got, the more she reminded him of Olivia. Even the mannerisms echoed her mother's, although Misty had been so young when she died. She probably didn't recognize the similarities herself.

He scrubbed the stubble on his chin. The team of shining Percherons moved around the ring, their equipment jingle-jangling as Misty navigated the hitch in perfect unison past him. All six horses performed flawlessly at her lead.

There weren't many sixteen-year-olds that could handle a six-hitch better than his daughter. She'd already won more blue ribbons than most would in a lifetime. Pride swelled inside him as he looked on.

Her love for these animals was as big as his own, and the way she'd dedicated herself to learn the niche skill still blew him away. It was hard work, and it required patience, focus, and stamina that most adults didn't even have.

She circled the heavy wagon in a figure eight and then completed an impeccable execution of "spin the top," a tricky move that required the driver to spin her team of horses and wagon without moving one back wheel.

He applauded as she came out of that spin. The melodic pound of horse hooves passed by him again.

Misty's grin told him she was happy with the workout too. This team was ready, and it was the direct result of her hard work this year. Some of these horses were young, only three years old, but Misty had trained them tirelessly. She was determined, and her efforts were paying off.

"Great job!" Mike walked over, giving each horse a pat as he passed by. "I honestly think this team might be our best one. It took me years to become that good."

"Thanks, Dad, but everyone knows you're the best. You have the trophies to prove it."

"Yours are coming, little girl." He held out his hand to help her down from the wagon, then pulled her in for a hug. "How about you let me cool these guys down and get them unhitched and put away? You don't want to miss the football game tonight."

"Yeah, but I can't let you do that. It's my responsi—"

"Why not? I offered. My favorite girl."

"Your only girl."

"Go. Have fun."

She eyed him curiously. "There's a roast in the Crock-Pot."

"I know. I might have already snagged a nibble."

"Like you always do?" She pointed an accusing finger in his direction.

"Yeah, but I can fend for myself."

"You'll eat cereal."

"I happen to like cereal. Now quit back-talking me, and get on out of here and have some fun."

"Are you sure?"

"Positive. Zack is finishing up in the barn. He'll help me."

"Thank you, Daddy!" She wrapped her arms around his neck. "You're the best." She ran to the side of the arena, climbed the fence, and then disappeared around the barn toward the house.

Zack was a good kid, and he'd learned fast. When he came looking for a job, he didn't know a darn thing about horses or barn upkeep. He was from the next town over and was desperate for work when he'd seen the posting for help at the feed and seed store. The kid could carry big bags of feed with no problem. When Mike learned that Zack had been kicked out of his parents' house for dropping out of school, he'd offered him the job with one condition. That he graduate that summer. He'd get a paycheck and a place to live in the old trailer on the back of the property.

Zack turned out to be a great hire. He studied and worked twice as hard as anyone Mike had ever had work for him. He was lucky to have Zack working for him, but he also knew one of these days he would find a girl, have kids of his own, and probably move on. Chances were that little place Mike and Olivia had lived in while Mike built the house wouldn't be a young couple's dream house for long these days.

The thought of this farm without Misty or Zack around brought back an unwelcome feeling. The same one that had practically crippled him when he'd lost Olivia.

He sucked in a deep breath, pushing those thoughts away. He got down to work unhitching the team. Patting the front left horse, he unfastened the hold-back straps and then unbuckled all the girth straps, moving through the process with barely a second thought, he'd done it so many times.

"Good boy," he muttered as he moved quickly. These horses knew exactly how many steps it took to unhitch, not even attempting to move until given the signal. He worked silently, removing the gear, putting it away, and brushing down the horses before turning them out to cool down.

Zack came through the gate. "All done inside. Got the puppies all back in the stall with their momma. That little Scooter pup seems to be getting stronger every day."

"Thanks for keeping an eye on that little guy. I thought you and Misty were going to need a miracle to get him on his feet, but he's doing pretty good."

"Me too, but Rein is paying attention to him now."

"That's great," said Mike. Rein, his black Lab, was a good mother. "She's had several litters over the years. She knows when something isn't right before we do. That she's taken the pup back in is a big step forward."

"I was hoping that was the case. Let me help you with the horses." Zack reached up and removed the harness from the next horse and set it in the wagon.

"Thanks. You can brush this one down, then turn him out." Mike handed off the horse he'd just unhitched to Zack.

Zack walked the horse to the side of the arena, tying him

to the post with his name on it. "I heard Misty leave in the dually."

"I told her she could go to the football game tonight," Mike said. "She needs more than these horses in her life. At least that's what the women in this town keep telling me."

"I don't think she has any complaints."

"I hope not. We have such a good routine keeping things going around here, but I need to be sure she has some balance."

"She's such an asset with all her competition wins. The number of parade invites seems to really have picked up."

"It has," Mike agreed. "You've become a great asset too, Zack."

"Thanks for giving me the chance. I told you I'd never let you down."

"A man is only as good as his word. I had no worries."

"Misty is a horse person to the core," Zack said. "I don't think you have to worry about her, but then what do I know?"

"Sometimes I think she's more worried about me than I am about her. She needs to be a teenager too. I know they're right about that part."

"Guess you're right. Having kids seems like a lot to worry about."

Mike laughed. "It's worth it."

Can't stop them from growing up.

"Miss Lilene dropped off the final details on the Christmas parade for next week," Zack said. "I put the envelope on your desk in the barn office."

"Good. I can't believe Thanksgiving is next Thursday. Somehow it doesn't seem like Christmas should already be here again, but here we are planning to give Santa a ride."

"Yeah and instead of eight tiny reindeer, he'll have six huge horses pulling him from town."

"Better than reindeer. No flying, though," Mike teased.

"It would take some mighty big wings to get these horses off the ground."

"Oh yeah, but they have more power than flying reindeer, so Santa can carry bigger toys."

"Good, because I was kind of hoping for a four-wheeler for Christmas this year."

"It could happen." Mike might even grant that wish himself.

"Misty said she's going to be riding next to you in the Christmas parade."

"Partially true. She'll be driving the wagon, and I'll be riding next to *her*."

"No one would believe that a teenage girl the size of her could handle these giants." He curled a set of reins. "Multiple sets of these at once? That's not for the weak."

"No, it's not." If he could be grateful for anything it was that his baby girl could take care of herself.

Even with Zack's help it was after eight by the time Mike got back in the house.

He showered, letting the hot water hit his tired and aching muscles until it ran cool. He toweled off and changed into a pair of sweatpants, then padded barefoot into the kitchen to serve up a huge bowl of pot roast for himself.

He settled on the couch and turned the television to the Western Channel. He'd never been one to sit and watch hours of sports on television, but this channel held his attention. Before the episode of *Maverick* was over, he'd put away a second helping of dinner and stretched out on the couch.

The rumbling diesel of the Ford F-450 woke him. He glanced at the clock. Only nine thirty. He must have been more tired than he'd realized. He sat up and put his feet on the floor.

Misty burst through the front door. "Hi, Daddy."

"Hey. How was the game?"

"We were winning by a mile when I left." She peered around the corner to see what he was watching. "*Lonesome Dove*? We love this movie. Can I watch?"

"Yes—wait, no. It's a school night. I can't keep football nights straight now that y'all play on Thursdays."

"Thursday-night ball games are stupid. I liked Fridays better."

"I'm sure they had a good reason. You've got school tomorrow," he said. "Better get in bed, and get a good night's sleep. We've got it on DVR anyway."

"True." She walked over and gave him a hug. "Love you."

"Love you too."

He leaned back on the couch. With Misty getting older, he wondered what it might be like to share his home with someone else. It was too quiet in this house when Misty wasn't around.

The problem was, he couldn't picture himself with anyone but Olivia. Still. Besides, he knew all the women in this town, and they were friends. Nothing more than that.

He picked up the remote and flipped over to the local news channel. The weather was already taking a turn toward winter.

Time to pull out the long johns from the cedar chest at the end of the bed.

With the cooler temperatures, a big pot of soup was always a welcome meal around here. He got up and cleaned up the pots and pans from dinner, then sliced the leftover pot roast into chunks and tossed them into the Crock-Pot. As he chopped celery, carrots, and russet potatoes, the colors started looking like a vibrant fall day. He poured in a large container of beef stock, a can of tomato paste, then gave everything a good stir.

He loved cooking for Misty, although she'd become a better cook than him recently. While dicing an onion to add to the soup, his eyes teared, and he couldn't deny that it might not just be the onion, but the fact that his little girl was growing up so fast. These next couple of years were going to fly by.

A few spices and the onion made a hearty-looking meal. He placed the Crock-Pot in the refrigerator. In the morning he'd turn it on low and let it simmer all day. There'd be plenty enough for Zack to take some home too.

He put his boots back on and walked outside to the barn to get the paperwork Lilene had dropped off.

In the distance a coyote howled. Bad news for most livestock owners. He was glad his horses and those pups were kept safe inside each night.

Gripping the handle on the wide barn door, he slid it across the heavy rails.

The sweet smell of hay never got old. The horses shifted in their stalls, their giant horseshoe-clad feet tapping with curiosity. Ben, the alpha in the herd, nickered and then let out a deep fluttering breath through his nostrils, letting the others know there was no reason to be concerned.

If only people were as easy to deal with as these horses.

These sounds felt like home to Mike. He picked up the papers that Zack had left on his desk, then took a peek in on Rein and did a quick head count on her litter. All present and accounted for . . . for a change. The little yellow troublemaker was snuggled at the very edge of the puddle of black puppies. His head and neck sprawled over the legs of one of the others.

He dimmed the lights and walked outside. The distinctive call of the barred owl that lived in a tree just beyond the barn filled the night. Mike had only caught a glimpse of him once. His wingspan had been easily every bit of three feet wide. There were others. He'd heard them, but had never seen them.

Mike slid the door closed and strolled back toward the house, enjoying the calls of nature. Something scurried in the dirt behind him. He swung around. Scooter sat down on his haunches.

"Caught you. How did you get out without me seeing you?"

The puppy danced in a circle and then lifted his paw and patted at Mike's pant leg.

"You're too cute for your own good. And too little to be out here. Do you want to end up an owl feast?" He swept the puppy into his arms. He had half a mind to bring him into the house for the night, but once you gave in there was no undoing it.

He took the puppy back to the barn and, rather than put him in the stall, scooted him inside the door and closed him in.

In the distance, all the lights in Zack's trailer went out.

A high-pitched bark from the barn broke the silence, but quickly quieted down following a grunt and sigh. He could picture Scooter flopping on the cool floor of the barn in dramatic defeat.

It shouldn't take but a couple more weeks for all of those puppies to be ready to move to their forever homes. Three had already been spoken for.

Mike went to the house. Warmth washed over him as he walked back inside. He sat down and opened the envelope from Lilene containing the parade maps. On the top of the first page there was a sticky note in Lilene's writing inviting he and Misty to dinner on Thanksgiving. If not dinner, then at least dessert at four.

Lilene had been his mom's best friend for as long as he could remember. The ladies of this town had always been so good to him and Misty. He was very thankful for their help, and there was no reason to turn her down. She always fed a crowd, and made great food. As had become tradition, he'd make a batch of fresh deviled eggs to take over. Those six laying hens of his, Henny, Penny, Jenny, Oprah Henfrey, Sophia Lor-Hen, and Eggatha Christie, kept Mike in more than enough brown eggs for all of his friends and neighbors.

Chapter Four

It had been one long day, and Vanessa was glad to just go to bed and be done with it.

She rubbed lotion between her hands, then smoothed it along her arms and legs before drawing back the white sheets to snuggle with her laptop and the Porter's files for a little nighttime reading.

This ought to put me to sleep.

She read through the dashboard, and the summary page of the most recent P and L. Surprisingly, Porter's wasn't in that bad a standing. In fact, if it weren't for the outrageous size of their footprint they were calculating the profit against, they'd be in really good shape. They turned a decent profit, considering the number of employees. And if you rolled in the fact that they were producing fruitcake, it was an amazing amount of revenue. A surprise, because really who intentionally bought fruitcake? She'd always thought of the bricklike concoction as a gag gift. But how many gag gifts can you sell to the same customers year after year? Eventually the humor in that wears off.

The turnover of employees was almost nonexistent. She'd wondered if the small town would be able to handle a larger workforce. If they could reskill some of the staff, then there shouldn't be much of a problem.

She tried to remember all the talk about this buyout when it happened. It had been a while back. She flipped through the past few years' numbers. They'd been consistent. The box indicating that the venture was initiated by the customer was checked. She wondered what had made Porter's approach AGC in the first place. Financially, they'd been pretty strong. At least on paper. Of course, things weren't always as they seemed on paper.

She flipped to the contract and terms. AGC paid handsomely for Porter's. Micky was usually good at negotiations, known for practically stealing companies, but this had been a very fair deal for Porter's, which made her more interested in seeing this for herself.

It wasn't a typical AGC buy. She couldn't find anything in the file explaining the motivation for the original purchase. Then again . . . it was fruitcake.

How does someone decide to open a fruitcake factory in the first place?

She was pretty certain she'd never even tried the only cake with a bad reputation, but the thought of the dense, sticky cake made her stomach go all queasy. *Do I really need to try fruitcake to know I'm not a fan?*

She put the paperwork aside and shook her head. No. She would make it through the next five weeks without even a nibble. She hoped it at least smelled good in the factory.

Kendra had already sent her a new project template. As they continued to refine the tool for each project, she made the plan even more robust based on lessons learned.

When Vanessa opened the template, she smiled. Kendra had even updated the colors to a Christmas theme.

Basically, she had five weeks to shut down the factory and clear out the warehouse space. They could probably run the excess inventory through the storefront through middle to late January if needed, since that wasn't needed for the transition.

She made clearing the warehouse space the priority, and filled in some of the preliminary assessments she'd need to complete next week.

A second email from Kendra included the building layout and inventory of the factory.

It didn't look like there was much big equipment to clear. The ovens were all commercial, but not huge. The number of pieces to auction or sell off wasn't that great either. Probably a one-day sale, if properly advertised, would do the trick.

Of course, those pieces would sell low. They always did. Someone would be having a merry Christmas even if it wasn't the people in Fraser Hills.

She dimmed her bedside lamp and slunk beneath the covers praying the next big project was going to be amazing, because this job was not going to leave her joyful. *One more "paying my dues" project.*

But there was that bonus, and she could already picture herself in her dream house. She picked up her phone and called Sally. Her heart fluttered in excitement as she told her she'd be interested in that house if they could stall until after the holidays. Sally seemed to think they could buy a little time.

Euphoria replaced her bitterness about the Fraser Hills

project. At least it would be good for something. Now to hope and pray that no one else was shopping for a house like that one, and then break it to Anna that the big Christmas assignment was in North Carolina ... not Paris. What a disappointment.

She took her arms out from under the covers, then let out a long slow breath and laid her arms by her sides, trying to relax.

Don't stress. Get in. Do the job. Get out. The quicker the better. Relax.

And Anna will be there. It's going to be fine.

*

Friday morning Vanessa hit the gym feeling better about the Fraser Hills assignment, and that her dream was now within reach because of it. Almost guaranteed.

She pounded out mile after mile on the treadmill; her ponytail swept across her back as she ramped up into a high-intensity interval, staring out the window that faced the busy street below. She'd grown oblivious to the traffic and the hustle of the people below on the sidewalk.

Call Sally to make an offer or wait? It was a gamble. If she called today, she'd be rewarding Sally's bad behavior for showing her a house over her budget. But if she didn't call, someone could sweep her dream house right out from under her.

Only the truth of the situation was, she was going to have to trust that the right thing would happen and wait until she got to North Carolina and got down to work on that project. For two reasons really. If she couldn't pull off the shutdown and ready the warehouse space on time, there'd be no bonus. And if she put in a successful bid on her dream house too early, she'd be up to her ears in mortgage paperwork, and she didn't have time to be dragging out old tax returns and statements while working on the Porter's project. It would be too big a distraction. And today her priority was packing and preparing to get out of Chicago and be on site in Fraser Hills by Monday.

She mentally set Sally aside.

She'd done a search on Fraser Hills, but aside from fruitcake, horses, and Christmas trees there wasn't much to read about.

Either way, it would be good with Anna along for the stay. She'd get things moving on the project, and then she'd book a flight for Anna to join her.

She slowed her pace, to catch her breath and cool down. She pulled the hand towel from her waistband and dabbed the sweat from her face. When she looked up, Robert was stepping up on the treadmill next to her.

"Good morning," he said, tossing his towel over the rail of the treadmill.

She took the right earbud from her ear and let it drop against her tank top. "Hey. You're late."

"You're early." He stepped on the machine and started a slow jog. "I called you yesterday."

"Oh gosh, it was a crazy day. I didn't want to drag you into all the drama."

"Probably for the best. I was busy too, but I wanted to share some news with you."

"Oh? What's up?" He was an attorney. Good news to him wasn't always that good to her, but she feigned excitement. "Tell me."

"Well, it doesn't really matter now. It was yesterday's news. We don't seem to be talking as much lately."

"We're a typical two-career couple," she said. "Time is a premium. We've got priorities. Right?"

"Yeah, but I do expect you to be there for me when I've had a tough day."

"Umm. Yeah, of course." But when she had a tough day, she really preferred to handle it alone. She'd always handled it alone. It was one of the things she liked about Robert. Low maintenance. Well, at least about most things, but lately he'd been pushing for more time, more commitment. And staying away seemed easier than talking about it. What was wrong with how things were?

"You've canceled or rescheduled half of our dates over the past three months to accommodate your projects." He reached over and put his hand on her arm. "I want to spend time with you."

She smiled gently, unsure of how to respond without lying or leading him on.

"I told my folks that we'd spend the holidays with them this year."

Vanessa stumbled over her own feet. Swatting at the control board, she steadied herself and slowed the pace. "What?"

"Christmas is magical there. Okay, maybe a little over-the-top old-fashioned, but it's fun. And you'll love my parents. They're going to love you as much as I do."

Her heart rate jumped and she was only at a walk now. "I can't."

"Why not? It's just a couple of days. Everyone takes time off for Christmas."

"I told you I'd probably be working through the holidays. I've got an end-of-year deadline. There's no time to take off at Christmas. It'll be a quick project. We can go visit them in the new year."

"But it's Christmas. You've never met my parents or sister.

You need to make this relationship the priority instead of work . . . for once."

She stepped off the treadmill and pulled her hands to her hips. What kind of comment was that? An ultimatum? "Or what?"

"Or . . . or . . . it's not going to work." He lifted his chin, his nostrils flaring a bit, and she didn't think that was from the slow jog on the treadmill. "It's Christmas, Vanessa. Everyone spends Christmas with family. It's tradition."

"I don't have traditions, or family for that matter." Well, she had Anna, but Anna understood. She never complained about not spending Christmas together. "Even when my parents were around, we didn't have family traditions. They were always working. It's the reason for the season, not where you are, that makes Christmas special."

"I do. And you and I will be family. We need to pick out a tree. Bake cookies. Have a snowball fight. I don't know, make something special and unique just between the two of us to do each year. Our own family traditions."

He really is the perfect guy. Why can't I love him? Her heart ached. "I have a commitment to this project, and only six weeks to get it done. We'll do Christmas in January. That can be our tradition."

"That's ridiculous," Robert muttered.

Break it off. He deserves someone who will love him. Who can love him. That's not me. But he looked so disappointed. "I tell you what. You can come down to Fraser Hills, North Carolina, and we'll get a tree there. See, I can compromise." Only she hated herself for it right now. Anna's voice echoed in her head. *It's time you decide if you're going to marry him, or just let him move on.*

"I can't be in North Carolina to get a tree and back home

in Connecticut by Christmas day for the festivities." His words were short and clipped.

He stepped off his treadmill, toe-to-toe with her. "Vanessa, I want to spend Christmas with my family . . . as a couple. You and me. I really don't think it's asking too much." He took her hand in his.

She shook her head. *Please don't ask me.*

"You know, we could plan to get married at my folks' place over the holidays, and you could look for a new job next year. One that isn't so demanding on your time. Or take a year off. Would that be so bad?"

"You know I love my job. I've never even considered not working."

"Why not? Do you like being so busy that there's no room in your life for anything else?"

"Well, yes I like being busy, and I love working to a budget and deadline. So, I'm a little competitive. What's wrong with that?" His job was certainly the same way. "I make a good living, Robert. I don't want a different job." And she didn't want to spend any time she did take off on her best behavior singing carols with people she'd never met. *I should send them a fruitcake.*

"So, you're saying you're not going to spend Christmas with me?"

He was a good man and this gym was full of people they both knew. Most of whom were already listening in on their conversation. She didn't want to embarrass him. She glanced away.

He shook his head, disappointment on his face. "I guess I have my answer. Merry Christmas."

She dabbed at her skin with the towel, hoping most of the people hadn't caught the full gist of the conversation.

He headed to the locker room without a word.

"I'm sorry," she said—too quietly for him to hear, not that it mattered. She got back on her treadmill and pounded out a seven-minute mile, but no matter how far or fast she ran there wasn't an easy answer.

Robert walked out of the gym just as she was grabbing the locker room door. He hadn't given her a second glance. He was mad, and she couldn't blame him.

In her car, she dialed the office. "Hi, Kendra. Do I have anything on my calendar?"

"Not a thing. I've got your airline reservations done. Do you want me to schedule a town car to take you to town, or would you rather rent a car on this one? It's a couple-hour drive."

"Town car. If I need a car, I'll rent one there." Something for her local assistant to work on until Vanessa had time to outline everything that needed to be done. "Where am I staying?"

"Mr. Grayson sent down information about a corporate apartment on the premises."

"Good old Edward. Always saving a dime."

"I know, but in this case, it might work out for the best," Kendra said. "There's not a hotel closer than thirty miles. That wouldn't be convenient."

"Not even one?"

"Not a one."

"Corporate apartment it is."

"I've got your itinerary almost ready. I'll leave it on your desk for you."

"Thanks, Kendra. Call me if I'm needed. I'm going to take care of things at home today, and probably do a little shopping.

The winter clothes I bought for Paris might not really work in Fraser Hills, North Carolina."

"Mmm. Population one thousand nine hundred and eighty-seven," Kendra said.

Only 2.5 million less than here. "Sounds quiet."

CHAPTER FIVE

"Dial Anna." Vanessa's phone connected the call, and then Anna's voice came over the speakers in her car.

"So, where will we be spending Christmas! I'm so excited."

"There's been an unexpected turn of events."

"Oh, Vanessa. Don't you dare cancel on me. We've let way too much time pass."

"I'm not. I promise. Only it's not going to be quite as exciting as I'd thought either." *That's what I deserve for being overconfident in my position at AGC.* Switching projects happened often. But this was the first time she'd been caught in that predicament, and that stung.

"I don't care where we go. Paris? Sure, that would have been pretty amazing, but I don't know a word of French. Who knows what I'd end up ordering for dinner? Or how I'd find the ladies' room. Besides, that Bavarian town in Washington sounds wonderful too. Nothing better than a small-town Christmas."

"Well, it's going to be way smaller than Leavenworth."

Anna's laugh tinkled across the line, making Vanessa relax. "As long as we don't have to camp it'll be fine."

"From what I understand I'll have a corporate apartment, but at this point that's all I know about Fraser Hills, North Carolina. Well, and that it's in the mountains."

"Sounds lovely. And better yet, I can drive."

"I'll fly you up. I don't want you driving in the mountains."

"I've got more than twenty years' more driving experience than you do, Vanessa. Quit treating me like an old lady. I'm your cousin, not your grandma."

"I know. I didn't mean it like that but it could be cruddy weather this time of year. Better safe than sorry. I've got Kendra working on pulling together some information on the town for us. There have to be some fun Christmas events planned in the area. As soon as I get settled in and have all that, I'll forward it to you and we'll plan on when you can come."

"I'm completely open. You are my priority this holiday so you just give me an address and I'll be there. The longer the visit the better."

She had a lot of work ahead of her, and Anna would definitely be a distraction. She'd have to delegate more than usual to have spare time, but the last thing she wanted was to hurt Anna, or worse, ruin her Christmas. "I hope the accommodations are decent."

"Fraser Hills. I'm excited just saying the words. It's where we're meant to be. I can feel it. Promise me we'll get a little Christmas tree."

The thought of a tree with Robert had unnerved her, but with Anna it was different—joyful even. The people of Fraser Hills probably wouldn't be feeling much joy knowing their only factory was going to be shut down. Then again, there'd be tons of warehouse positions, so it wouldn't be like they'd be out of work. A win-win.

"Is there something else going on? You don't sound like yourself. Are you disappointed about not getting the project you wanted?"

"A little, but that's not it. Robert and I had it out this morning. He wasn't happy about me not joining him with his folks over the holiday. He gave me an ultimatum."

"Oh? I don't want to cause a problem—"

"No. It wasn't you. I'd already told him I'd probably be working. When the project in North Carolina popped up it completely reinforced what I'd already told him. I honestly think he was trying to force my hand."

"He's tired of spending time without you," Anna said.

"That's what he said. He even suggested we get married at his folks' house at Christmas." Her laugh came out stuttered.

"That's not a horrible idea. I mean, if you are ever going to marry him."

"No. I'm not marrying him. He even had the gall to suggest once we were married, I could quit my job and find one that was less demanding of my time or, get this, not work at all for a year." She hadn't intended to share that with Anna until they were together, but as soon as she got started the words just poured out.

"Oh?" Anna didn't offer anything else. "Well, your job is very demanding. I guess a little life balance wouldn't hurt, but not work at all?"

"Exactly! Not work? Me? I'm not that kind of girl."

Anna's hearty laugh filled the line. "I don't think 'I'm not that kind of girl' applies to that situation, but I see your point. I can't imagine you in an apron, putting stain remover on his shirt necklines, and making dinner every night."

"Never."

"I'm sure he thought he was being supportive. Generous even."

"Pfft. Sounds controlling to me."

A long sigh came from Anna's end of the line.

"He's a very nice guy. He's smart—"

"How does he make you feel?"

"At this moment?" Vanessa wasn't sure. "Aggravated."

"How long have you two been dating?"

"A while. Two—well, almost three years. Actually, three and a half."

"And I haven't even met him," Anna said. "What is it you really want from Robert?"

Vanessa took in a breath. "Nothing more than we have. Dates for parties? I can take care of myself. I mean, he's good company. He's a good man."

"I'm sure he is, but that's not love. You marry for love, Vanessa."

"Mom married for love and look how that turned out."

"Your mother never regretted any of her decisions. I know you and your father have not had a good relationship since she passed, but I promise you he was a very different man before your mother died. I'll say this. Being married to the wrong man is never better than being alone."

"I knew I should've broken it off, but he was so upset about Christmas."

"Do you really think he is going to be any happier to be with a woman who doesn't truly love him? You're stealing his opportunity to find true love with someone who can't wait to do the things important to him."

"Like Christmas with his parents?"

"Exactly. Or stay home for a year. Forever maybe."

"I hadn't really thought about it that way."

"I'm not here to judge, but it's something to consider. If you really weren't torn about work, and how to make things right with Robert, then I think you might already have your answer."

"We probably should have had this discussion a long time ago."

"I'm always here for you. I don't think you were ready for this talk before."

"You're right. As usual." She sighed. "I really liked the idea of being in love, and he was so perfect, but there was never that spark."

"Vanessa, you can't make the spark. It happens on its own. But you also don't want to work your way through the best days of your life. Succeeding in your career is awesome, but not at the expense of a life well lived. You don't even get to enjoy the places you travel to for work."

"The schedules are tight."

"You could make it work. You've got to put yourself out there—heart and all. Believe me, you will find even more happiness in both if you do."

"It's not going to be easy to break it off with Robert."

"Matters of the heart never are, even between friends."

"Thank you, Anna. I've got to take care of some personal business before I do some shopping and pack for this trip. They expect me Monday morning."

"That's quick."

"And I have a lot to do before January first."

"Call me when you get settled in. I'll be right there. I might even treat myself to a train ride instead of driving. I've always wanted to do that."

"I'd be happy to send a plane or train ticket. I'll call you next week from my new home away from home, and we'll figure it all out."

Vanessa hung up the phone feeling better and worse. Better about the holidays, but dreading the discussion with Robert. She did care about him. Although, stepping back and looking at the relationship, he probably could use a talk like she just had with Anna too. They were friends. Comfortable and convenient friends. There never had been any butterflies or passionate romance. The occasional night out. Pizza in the office—hers or his. Someone to celebrate Valentine's Day with. A partner to dance with at a coworker's wedding reception, the ball drop on New Year's, or the annual 4th of July party, which happened to be the only fireworks between them.

I'll miss him if we break off and can't be friends.

Food for thought for her afternoon of shopping. She stopped by the office on her way home. Kendra had her itinerary and information about Fraser Hills packaged nicely along with print copies of the original contracts for Porter's and the warehouse deal. It was a thick packet. *I have my work cut out for me.*

Kendra had already left for the day, so Vanessa left a quick thank-you note on her desk.

Robert was already mad, and she hadn't even told him she'd be out of town for Thanksgiving for work too. It had kind of become their tradition to go to the club for their buffet.

Nice, but not like the family gatherings Mom had always hosted on Thanksgiving Day. A big turkey, ham, and all the fixings. There'd be so many things cooking at once that the kitchen was more like a sauna. Dad would set up card tables in each room, while Mom ran around with dish towels over her shoulder and somehow perfectly timed ten dishes to all be ready and hot at the same time. And yeast rolls. Mom would put those pans in the laundry room with a little heater keeping the room warm for them to rise so big they looked like they might float right out of the pans.

Mom would open all the doors to let cool air in. No one even seemed to mind.

The whole day was clouded by nostalgia. By the time she finished running errands, it was too late to go to her favorite boutique. That would have to wait until tomorrow.

Back home, she ordered Chinese takeout and sat on the floor in front of the coffee table watching television. It had been so long since she'd watched TV that she didn't even recognize most of the programs on the network channels.

She wasn't sure if it was her mood or the selection of shows on at the time, but none of them held her attention. Tired of clicking through the channels, she picked up her phone and scrolled through her messages. Robert hadn't called.

She toyed with the idea of calling him. He was probably still at the office.

Instead, she turned off the ringer, put her phone on the charger in the living room, and called it a night. Tomorrow she'd pick up those pieces.

CHAPTER SIX

✦

The next morning Vanessa went to her favorite boutique. The girls there knew her by name and quickly helped her pick out a comfortable small-town-casual mix-and-match wardrobe for her trip. On her way back to her car, she noticed a new store. A Kindred Spirit Gift Shoppe. The front window was filled with Christmas décor. As she walked by, someone exited carrying three glossy red bags followed by a waft of cinnamon.

She put her things in the car and went back to peruse the store. Bells jingled when she walked inside, and there was that smell again. Almost like the smell of home when she was a little girl. Cinnamon, sweet sugary cookies, and pine.

She meandered through the aisles. All kinds of Christmas things were displayed on Christmas-tree-shaped shelving. She found herself smiling as she lifted a baby snow angel, then an unusual sterling silver bell. When she waggled it in the air it made the prettiest sound. Like the beginning of "Jingle Bells." She set it down and started to walk away, then went back and carried it with her. Beautiful cross-stitched Christmas stockings hung from a reclaimed fireplace mantel against the exposed brick wall.

She lifted one of them, the heavy fabric with the intricate detailed design of a black lab on a sled, and another running alongside made her think of all the years she'd asked Santa for a dog. The only dog in her life had been Anna's old brown mutt, Sam. He stank to high heaven most of the time, and kisses, Lordy he'd practically wash her face. She laughed. It had seemed so gross, but she'd loved it at the same time. *I'm going to have a dog someday.*

"Can I help you with that?"

Vanessa turned to see a portly older woman wearing a white frilly apron with A GRATEFUL HEART IS A HAPPY HEART embroidered across the front. "This is so lovely."

"Handmade," she said. "You just don't find nice stuff like that around much anymore. A local lady makes them for us. Heirloom quality, don't you think?"

"It's gorgeous."

"We can embroider a name at the top while you wait if you'd like."

"I'd love that." Vanessa held the stocking close. "This one for Anna. A-n-n-a." She reached over and picked out another. "I'll take the snowy cottage scene for myself."

"That's my favorite one. Doesn't it look inviting?"

"It does." For all the house hunting she'd done, she wished she already had a home to call her own. "Can you put 'Vanessa' on this one?"

"We sure can. Why don't you enjoy a cup of coffee and

shop around? This won't take but a few minutes." The woman toddled off with the stockings, and Vanessa began lifting the tops from candles. Winter Garland. Home Sweet Home. Christmas Morning, which smelled like peppermint and pine. An interesting combination, but it worked.

With the stockings, bell, two ornaments for Anna, and two candles to take to Fraser Hills packed thoughtfully in a Christmas bag, she left happy with the extra presents.

By the time she got home, she was more at ease about everything going on, even if none of it was the way she would have planned it.

She gathered her suitcase and laid in a stack of pantsuits, still in the dry-cleaner bags. A few winter essentials. Heels. Sensible shoes for the warehouse floor. Tennis shoes for jogging. One pair of jeans and workout clothes, along with her splurges from earlier today. Hopefully that little town had a dry cleaner locally.

With her clothes packed, she tossed all the can't-live-without-'em local snacks, like Kay's Candies chocolate-dipped pretzels and Vitner's Crunchy Kurls, into a smaller bag. She slid the zipper closed on her suitcase, and dragged it to the door.

She wasn't flying out until Monday, but she was ready to go.

Ready except for talking to Robert, and putting that to rest.

How was she supposed tell him what was on her mind? She'd rather not, but she couldn't leave it hanging over the holidays either.

He hadn't called since the incident at the gym. Maybe he'd be relieved to have the relationship cleanly dissolved. *Another closing. My specialty.*

She dialed his number and waited for him to answer.

"Hello." He finally answered on the fifth ring, as if he didn't know who it was, but he knew. The flat tone of his voice still clung to the irritation he'd displayed at the gym.

"Hi, Robert."

"I wondered if you were going to call."

His snippiness made what she had to say easier. Sometimes he could be kind of a jerk when things didn't go exactly his way. "Are you home?"

"No, I'm at the office."

"Can we get together?" He didn't jump on the opportunity. Anxious, she added, "To talk."

"That depends. When?"

"I'm available now. So, whenever is good for you . . ."

"Oh. Okay." He sounded surprised, or more like hopeful. "I can meet you at six o'clock for dinner downstairs at Bistro 2520."

"Tonight?" She'd hoped he would meet now. She shouldn't have been so accommodating. He was taking full advantage of that now.

"Sure. I'll make the reservation."

Of course he would. "Thanks, that'll work. I'll see you then." Vanessa hung up the phone, and let out a heavy whoosh of relief. *I can do this.*

She was already packed. All she had on her plate today was getting this done with Robert. And now that was nearly six hours away.

Never one to take a lazy day, she decided to burn some time with a long nap. She set her alarm, although it was totally unlikely she would nap that long.

She lay across the bed in the sunny spot. The comforter was so warm. It was like lying in front of a fireplace. *Maybe I could get used to this.* She closed her eyes and relaxed.

When she woke up, that sunshine had moved too high in the sky to shine through her window any longer and the room had cooled down dramatically. To her surprise, she'd slept nearly two hours.

I must have been tired.

She showered and got dressed. Time droned on, and she was getting more anxious about meeting with Robert.

From her condo windows she overlooked one of the busiest streets in the city. Traffic was piling up below. She'd played out scenarios in her mind between red-light cycles. *Fifty ways to leave your lover.*

Bistro 2520 wasn't far. Walking distance on a clear day, but she was getting more nervous by the minute. She grabbed her purse and left, trying to pace herself to pass more time along the way, even stopping to look at this week's special cupcakes and goodies in the bakery window that opened a few weeks back. They were like artwork.

Normally she rushed down this street on her way to the office. It had been a long time since she'd taken pause to appreciate the architecture, and were the storefront windows decorated like this yesterday? Today each boasted upcoming Black Friday sales.

When she stepped inside the bistro, she was still ten minutes early.

"May I seat you?"

So nervous she could barely swallow, she said, "I'm actually waiting for someone. Maybe something quiet. In the corner?"

The maître d' offered a playful grin, clearly recognizing her. "I can seat you now," he said, motioning her to follow.

He pulled out her chair. At least from here she had a clear view of the front door. "Someone will be right with you to take your order from the bar."

"Thank you."

A waiter she didn't recognize approached. "I'm Dash. Can I get you something from the bar?"

"I'd better stick to water. Straight up," she joked. "With lemon, please. It's been a lemon of a day."

"When life hands you lemons, make lemonade, right?" His smile revealed a row of perfect teeth.

"Better make it a double lemonade then."

"I can make that happen." He laughed as he scribbled on his pad. "Sure you don't want some vodka in that to make you feel better?"

"Positive. You can bring it in a pretty glass with a fancy garnish, though."

"You got it."

"Thanks."

Robert walked in, just as the waiter walked away. Dark suit, white shirt so starched it still crackled at the end of the day, a fantastic tie, and shiny leather shoes. Except for the vibrant collection of snappy ties, he always dressed the same. She was in blue jeans, boots, and a cable-knit sweater. It was a warmish fifty degrees out. Nice for this time of year.

He took the seat across from her as the waiter came back with her lemonade. His brow rose.

The waiter acknowledged him. "Would you like something from the bar?"

"I'll have a bourbon. Neat." His eyes darted at the curvy glass in front of her. "What are you drinking?"

"Lemonade," she said. "Thanks for coming."

"Sure." He didn't look as handsome with the sour-grapes look on his face.

"I don't know where to start." The waiter set down Robert's drink and backed away exchanging an awkward smile with Vanessa. She pushed her hair over her ear. "Robert, I have to know something. Do you really love me?"

He leaned back, as if looking for an answer floating in the room. "We've been together for almost four years. We've talked about marriage. Yes, I love you."

"Why?"

"What? Why is this coming up now?" He took a long sip. "You're not going to turn this around on me."

"No. That's not what I'm doing. I've been thinking."

"That I don't love you?"

"No." She looked down at her hands in her lap. This wasn't going well. "You're a great guy. Smart, handsome, and it's wonderful how we can be there for each other's work events . . ."

"I agree. We fit. You're pretty. Intellectual enough to carry on a conversation with my partners or clients without embarrassing me. I like doing things with you."

Really? "Smart enough" is his go-to line? "I was thinking about what I'd do if I weren't so busy."

He leaned forward, arms on the table. "What did you come up with? Come to Christmas with me and my family?"

"No." She'd said it too fast, but that was not where she was going . . . at all. "If I weren't so busy, I'd like to hike."

"Hike? Like in the woods?"

"Yes. Anywhere. We could backpack and camp out under the stars."

"How about the penthouse with a star view from the balcony?"

"Not the same." She crossed her legs. "I don't even know your favorite football team. I should know that."

"The Green Bay Packers. Since I was seven."

"Seriously? Hmm." She'd never have pegged him as a cheesehead. He wasn't the type. Or was he?

"Do you know mine?" she asked.

"Do you have one?"

She cocked her head. "When was the last time you told me you loved me?"

He drained his glass. "I don't know. Is this what all this is about? You want me to say it more often. Fine. I love you."

"Robert, I'm not *in* love with you. Not the way I should be. If I was, I wouldn't have found it so easy to reschedule dates, and . . ."

"Let me down on the holidays?"

"Yes. That. I guess so." She shrugged. "When I see you across the room, I don't get butterflies in my stomach. When you kiss me goodbye . . . no sparks."

"We're not twelve," he said, but his voice was softer. "I wanted to talk about this over Christmas." He reached into his coat pocket.

"Don't." Her heart pounded so loud she wasn't sure if she'd uttered the words or not, but he paused.

"I'm not arguing about the trip. I've already told them you're busy. I'll go alone this year, but I'd like you to be there with me." He pulled out a small square box. "From now on." He raised the lid revealing a beautiful ring. "This was my grandmother's. It's been appraised at—"

"It's lovely, and I'm sure it's worth a small fortune, but I can't marry you. You deserve someone better. Someone who will want to do all the things you want to do. Someone who will drop everything as soon as you call, because she can't wait to see you. I'm not that girl."

"We're perfect for each other."

"No. We're content. If I do get married, it'll be for the right reasons. I thought we were on the same page. I apologize it took me so long to figure this out." She set her hand on top of the ring box and pushed it back toward him. "I'm so sorry. I do treasure our friendship. I hope you'll be able to accept my apology so we can still be friends. I understand if not today. But someday."

"When you realize what you're missing out on . . . you've got my number." He cupped the box in his hand and stood. "I wish you well, Vanessa. If you have a change of heart, call me." He patted her shoulder as he walked out.

She sipped her lemonade.

The waiter stopped at her table. "You'll be dining alone?"

"I think I'll just take the drink check. Thank you." An audible sigh of relief escaped as she set her glass down.

She texted Anna.

> **Vanessa:** Robert proposed. I said no.
>
> **Anna:** How are you?
>
> **Vanessa:** Relieved.
>
> **Anna:** Very well then. Trust the journey. I'll see you soon.

Yes, you will.

Even though she knew she'd done the right thing, a dark emptiness hung inside.

She walked home wondering what she'd do the next time there was a work party. Anna would say something like, *Maybe you'll meet someone now that you're not tied to the wrong man.*

I don't think I'm ready to try that again. I'll concentrate on having fun with Anna over the holidays, and work. Work is always good, or it used to be.

On a brighter note, now she could avoid the distraction of the numerous phone calls from Robert trying to convince her to change her mind about meeting him at his parents' while she was shutting down Porter's. That was a plus, because this assignment was going to be hard enough as it was.

Relationships might not be her specialty, but she'd done the kind of job required for the Porter's project a dozen times. This she knew how to handle.

Chapter Seven

The morning was brisk. Mike pulled his collar up. Vapor clouded from the nostrils of the large black horse with each stroke of the brush. This quiet time he spent with each horse was part of their personal bond. Some loved it more than others, but it was a good way to get his hands on every inch of the animal and check for problems, while giving them the reward of something that required nothing of them.

Big Ben and Mike had this down to a science.

"It's okay, Ben. There you go, old buddy." Ben was the first Percheron Mike ever purchased by himself. He'd saved for two years to buy this horse, and they'd been together a long, long time. His oldest draft horse, Ben stood 18.2 hands and last time they'd weighed him he came in at 2,540 pounds. Just shy of the weight of Mike's first car, a sporty Ford Mustang that he and his dad had restored together.

"Your age is showing." He rubbed his hand along the graying hair under Ben's chin. "Don't feel bad. So is mine."

The horse dipped his head down close to Mike's face, blowing a puff of air from his vocals. Mike hugged his neck.

Ben might be old, but he'd come to Mike with years of experience. He was the best horse he owned. Every horse they trained was held up to the standard of this one, and with that they'd built a reputation for breeding excellent show Percherons.

There wasn't anything like a team of solid black Percherons pulling a wagon. Sure, the Clydesdales were popular, but Mike wouldn't trade his team of Percherons for all the beer-wagon horses in the world.

"Hey, Dad." Misty picked up a brush and headed for one of the stalls. "I'll get Box."

"Thanks. No homework tonight?"

"Not much. I've got time to help."

"Are you okay? You seem a little quiet lately."

She shrugged and muttered "I'm okay" as she led Box out into the alley and tied his lead rope to the outside of the stall. She brushed with long sweeping motions, settling her other palm on the side of the horse's neck as she poured soothing comments with every stroke.

Mike finished up with Ben and led him over to his stall door. As Ben ambled in, Mike handed him an apple. Ben brayed a thank-you.

Mike looked around the barn, thankful for all he'd been able to do here. These horses, and Misty, were his team.

"I hope you're hungry," Mike said. "I used the leftover pot roast to make my vegetable beef soup. Your favorite."

"That sounds perfect. I love soup nights. I can make some fried corn bread to go with it."

"I was hoping you'd say that." They exchanged a quick smile. They worked quietly through the rest of the team, and then Mike swept out the alleyway in the barn until Misty got done.

She led her horse to his stall.

Mike walked over to her. "What's going on? You're never this quiet."

"Nothing really. I just have this feeling." She used the back of her hand to brush back her bangs. "I love my job at Porter's."

"That's a good thing. It's been in the family forever."

"I know, but I overheard Lilene talking. Someone from corporate is coming to town."

"Why?"

"I don't know, but after all the fuss when we got bought out, we really haven't heard a thing from corporate. Now out of the blue someone is coming. Like tomorrow."

"They promised nothing would change. There hasn't been any announcement to the contrary, has there?"

"No. But it seems like odd timing. We're so busy. No one has time to deal with someone looking over our shoulders right now. You don't think they'll close Porter's, do you?"

"No way."

"What if they realize how young I am and fire me so they can hire someone older and more experienced to manage the retail store?"

She was quickly outgrowing the title of his little girl. Wise beyond her years, she made him proud and panicky at the same time. "Misty, you might be young, but you're doing a great job. You showed me your reports. You're responsible for the lift in sales last year since the new layout of the store. You've saved them a great deal of money, and profits are at an all-time high. You're a natural. No one is going to replace you. Your good work stands for itself."

"You really think so?"

"I do. Don't worry about things you have no control over. Enjoy being a teenager. There's no sense in worrying about all that stuff right now."

"I know, but I'd be heartbroken if anything happened to my job at Porter's. I love being there. It makes me still feel close to Mom."

He hugged her close. "Which is probably why you're so good at it." A day didn't go by that he didn't curse his grandfather for selling out. Sure, the corporation had promised they'd leave everything "as is" with Porter's, but didn't they all say that? "You know you don't have to work all those hours. If you had more time with your friends, or study group, that wouldn't be the worst thing in the world. Maybe you're stressed because you're so busy."

"I'm getting all A's, Dad. I don't need more time to study, and I see my friends at the store too." The horse she'd just put up leaned forward, hanging his head out of the stall and resting his chin on the top of her head. "Ewww." She lifted his chin and stepped aside, rubbing his jawline. "Now that you've *un*successfully dodged my question, what do you really think this corporate exec wants with us?"

Mike wrapped his arm around her shoulder. "It's anyone's guess. Let's not worry until we know if there's something to worry about."

"I'll try, Daddy." She paused, then glanced up at him.

They walked out of the barn and Mike slid the barn door closed behind them.

"Wouldn't be the worst thing if you could forgive Great-Grandpa either," Misty said. "He said he had a good reason for selling Porter's."

"That," he said, tapping his finger to her nose, "isn't your worry. Let's get some supper." Had she been spending time with his grandfather again? The last time they'd discussed it he'd gotten way too mad. He still regretted yelling at her. It wasn't her war. She had every right to see the crotchety old fool if she wanted to, but he didn't have to like it.

As he shrugged off his coat and coveralls in the mudroom and washed the day's work from his hands, Misty made her way to the kitchen. The quick *shwoof* of the gas stove was followed by the clang of the cast-iron pan hitting the stove grates. He was salivating by the time the eggs cracked for that corn bread—Olivia's recipe.

He took two big soup bowls down from the cabinet and dished out two hefty servings. The soup and corn bread filled the air with a stomach-growling aroma.

"I did the quickie kind," Misty said, flipping a corn bread griddle cake onto a small plate for herself, and three onto a plate for him.

"Works for me." He grabbed the butter and they walked into the dining room to eat. Mike had promised Olivia that he and Misty would always eat at the table together when she was gone. He loved her for asking that of him, because every night at mealtime, Olivia was still in this home. Still a family.

They both dug in. Finally, Misty broke the silence. "Umm, I

do have something to ask you." She laid her spoon down, and put her hands in her lap, looking serious.

He gripped his spoon tighter. "Okay."

"Luke asked me to go to the winter dance with him."

He was thankful it wasn't something bad. "Luke Harrison? Drew and April's boy?"

"Yes, sir."

"He did, did he? I thought you weren't interested in anyone." He shoveled a big bite into his mouth.

"I'm not. Not really. I mean, it's just a dance. Well, the football game will be Thursday and we're going in a group, like we always do. The dance is on Friday night."

Mike continued to chew, buying time to think reasonably about how to respond. Luke was a good kid, though. Kind of a goofball sometimes, like his father, but harmless.

He wished Olivia was really here tonight. Formal dances were definitely out of his wheelhouse. It seemed too much like a date. He wasn't ready for that.

"Please let me go." Her eyes were full of hope.

He put his spoon down and folded his hands. "I took your mom to every dance all through high school. I remember the first time. Mom told me to go down to Dixie's Flower Shop and buy a corsage. I can't even say for certain what kind of flowers were in it, just that they were blue. Light blue as pretty as her eyes. Your mom didn't tell me until years after we were married that the corsage was supposed to match her dress . . . not her eyes."

"That's sweet. I never knew about that."

"Then our senior year she wore a strapless dress. Totally screwed me up. I thought I had it all covered with the corsage that time, but there wasn't anywhere to put the darn thing."

"What did you do?"

"Improvised."

Misty started laughing. "Oh no. I know what it means when you improvise. Did this involve baling twine or fence wire?"

"Maybe," he said with a serious look.

Misty's mouth dropped wide. "Oh, no!"

He laughed. "Yep. I went to my truck and pulled out a couple pieces of baling twine, then laid that pretty little bunch of flowers on her arm and wrapped it around her wrist and over the flowers with a bunch of half-hitch knots with that twine and then tied it in a bow. Worked like a charm."

"I hope I don't get a corsage like that."

"If you do, I hope you'll be as gracious as your mother was that night." He could still see her face. "She flaunted it like it was the best corsage in town."

"She didn't want to hurt your feelings."

"At the time, I really thought she was impressed. But no. I'm sure you're right. Your mom was a very nice girl. It didn't take much to make her smile." Just the thought still made his insides go gushy. "I loved her smile."

"You're getting all googly-eyed again. I hope someday somebody looks like that when they talk about me."

"Don't rush it. I'm not ready for that."

"I know, Dad. I'll always be your little girl. Don't you worry."

She got up and came around the table and hugged him. "So, I'm going to need a really pretty dress."

"I don't know the first thing about buying a dress. Do you think Lilene or one of the ladies at Porter's could help you?"

"Probably, but please don't make me have them help. I'll end up with a poofy old-lady dress."

Visions of his little girl all dressed up made his heart knot.

"If you'll trust me with your credit card, I can buy one on-line. That's what all the girls are doing."

"All the girls?"

"Yes, but I promise to clear it with you first."

For a while there he'd thought she believed it when he said she couldn't date until she was thirty. That wild hope was about to get kicked to the curb.

He leaned forward in his chair and pulled his wallet from his back pocket. "This is a big step. I'm trusting you to be responsible with this." He flipped his platinum card down on the table in front of her. "I want to see the dress before you enter that credit card number." It almost broke his heart to think she was going to go to her first dance, a date no matter how you framed it, without Olivia.

She squealed so loud he flinched.

"I guess that means you're happy. Or my soup is already giving you some serious gas pains. Too many jalapeños in it?"

She swatted him. "Stop that. You know I'm happy. You're the best dad in the world. I promise you can trust me with your credit card."

"There'll be a curfew."

"No problem." She jumped from her chair. "This is so awesome. I have to go upstairs and call Brandy." She did a half squat. "Can I be excused? I'm too excited to eat one more bite."

He nodded toward the stairs, and she fled past him carrying the red plastic card pinched between her fingers with a grip so tight it looked as if she were afraid it was going to fly away.

Our little girl, Olivia. She's growing up.

CHAPTER EIGHT

Vanessa sat in the back of the car reviewing the reports on Porter's. She looked up from her computer. More trees. "How much farther?"

The driver lifted his eyes to the rearview mirror. "About another twenty minutes."

She glanced at the time on her phone. "I guess that would make Fraser Hills about two hours from nowhere."

Did he just snicker? He focused back on the road. He was probably thinking the same thing.

This was the longest Monday morning.

The farther they drove, the more the land rolled, making her a bit queasy. She reached for her tote bag for a bottle of water. Hopefully a few sips would settle her stomach.

On this winding road, she couldn't stand to look at the staffing worksheet another minute. She'd seen enough though. Several had been working there since Porter's first opened its doors. The average years of service was fifteen, and that would've been even higher if it weren't for the influx of new hires over the past two years.

She'd done a lot of job hopping when she first got out of college. It was the only way to quickly increase her salary. She was proud of her current salary, but her goal was to be comfortably retired by the time she was fifty.

They passed the first sign with FRASER HILLS on it. Three miles away. Finally.

The driver hit the blinker and slowed down to take the turn.

Vanessa slipped her shoes back on and tucked her laptop into her bag.

They rode by sprawling acres of green grass and livestock. Pretty barns with painted barn quilts above the vast doors gave the landscape an unexpected pop of color that was otherwise pretty much gone since all the autumn leaves had already fallen.

On the right, Christmas trees lined up like toy soldiers up a steep hillside, ready to grace living rooms over the holidays.

In the center median a sign read WELCOME TO FRASER HILLS. A white oval hung below it with HOME TO PORTER'S ~ THE BEST FRUITCAKE IN THE USA printed on it.

How can they make the claim of best in the USA? Who decided? And why? Hiring someone to taste all the fruitcake in the nation to pick one and call it the best would have to be the worst job in the world, or at least the USA.

She reached into her purse and jotted a note to add the removal of the Porter's sign in the closure plans.

Staring out the window, a train track ran adjacent. Her stomach clenched with each climb of the road. *Possible rail access. That could be another positive asset for the warehouse.*

"We're here," announced the driver. "Fraser Hills."

Main Street looked like something out of a story book. There were shops on each side of the road, and small houses dotted the roads off to the right and left. Main street was wide, with no median. Instead, bright white parking lines slashed the blacktop like a giant game of tic-tac-toe: nose-to-nose parking between the northbound and southbound lanes. Parallel parking in front of each store blocked her view of some of the shops as they drove by.

With fewer than two thousand people living in the town, Vanessa had feared there'd be nothing more than a bank, a grocery store, and a gas station—and Porter's, of course. But this town was charming, and alive.

Each storefront had its own look, painted in bright colors that somehow worked together although there was clearly no planned scheme. Pastels next to jewel tones next to a school-bus-yellow pizza shop. It was like they'd tried to include every crayon in the box—making it kind of whimsical. It was an appealing location. Professional buildings next to retail shops. Among them, antiques, boutiques, candles, gift shops, and an old pharmacy that even boasted a soda shop. She wondered if the soda jerk wore a garter on his sleeve while concocting real phosphate soda recipes like the one her grandpa had taken her to the summer before she went into first grade. *Anna and I will definitely have to check that out.*

Pleasantly surprised by the size and multitude of welcoming shops, she mused about how much Anna would enjoy visiting here too.

Several people walked along the sidewalks. Rolls of bright red and green wrapping paper poked out of the top of one woman's shopping bag as she strolled down Main Street.

"This is Porter's." The driver pulled to a stop in front of the building at the corner of Main and Porter House Road.

She peered out the window. It was nothing like she'd imagined. The brick building stood three stories tall, towering over the two-story buildings around it, and its dark red brick gave it an appearance of strength. Rather than opening onto either street, the front doors faced the intersection on an angle at least ten feet wide where the building's corner had been flattened to create a covered main entrance. Three steps led from the sidewalk up to tall double glass-front doors with black shutters on each side. White columns flanked the steps, carrying the weight of the glossy white roof that covered the entryway; above the portico, huge shiny black-and-white-painted letters spelled PORTER'S vertically down the face of the building.

"Can you wait here for a few minutes? I need to pick up the key to the apartment, and get directions."

"As long as you need."

"Thank you. I shouldn't be too long." She stepped out of the car, and closed the door.

Something loud came from behind her down the street. It sounded as if it was getting closer. She spun around, catching sight of shiny black horses clip-clopping her way. A breath caught in her throat as she leapt from the street to the sidewalk.

The earth seemed to vibrate as their hoofbeats got closer. Their muscles flexed like those of a bodybuilder oiled up and ready to compete for the big title.

The man sitting on the wagon looked strong and fit too. She swept her hand through her hair as she watched him approach. His shoulders were broad; his hair was a little long below the brim of his Western hat.

Anna is not going to believe this. She raised her phone and took a picture. Then another as the horses slowed near the four-way stop at the corner.

Six horses in all. The shiny black wagon they pulled was stacked high with big bales of hay.

She stood there nearly breathless, in awe of the scene before her. Tracing the horses with her eyes, then lifting her gaze toward the man. She smiled wide, then touched her fingers to her lips.

One of the horses sputtered and snorted as he passed, all six moving like a single unit.

"Amazing." She lifted her chin.

He nodded. "Good afternoon."

His voice was deep and strong. So captivating that she stared impolitely for a long moment before she finally managed a finger wave. "You too."

He lifted his hand to his hat and smiled.

*

Vanessa took a picture, then watched until the horses and wagon turned at the next road.

She forwarded the photo to Anna.

> **Vanessa:** This was my first sighting in Fraser Hills.
>
> **Anna:** Now, that's what I call a welcome.

Until that moment she'd been so captivated by the horses that she hadn't even noticed the sweet aroma that hung in the air. It smelled like warm bread, and sugar and spices. Her mouth watered, reminding her she hadn't eaten yet today. Not that fruitcake was on her list of favorites.

The Porter's building seemed to occupy the whole block—much bigger than she'd expected even after seeing the plans.

Playful green-and-white-striped awnings softened the dark red brick exterior around the retail-store windows to either side of the entrance. The Porter's logo—a black silhouette of a horse-drawn carriage riding past snow-topped Fraser firs—shone from the old glass inserts. A deep red ribbon scrolled around PORTER'S in green script. Very classy, actually, if a little outdated. *Although a horse-drawn carriage did just drive by.*

Vanessa's cheeks stung from the crisp air. She briskly climbed the stairs and grasped the shiny brass door handle. A whoosh of warm air washed over her like a hug, as a set of gleaming brass bells on a leather strap jangled against the heavy door.

"Welcome to Porter's." A young lady wearing a black-and-white-striped vest bearing the Porter's logo waved from a long wooden counter. "Let me know if I can help you find anything."

"Thank you."

The space was warm and inviting. Nice wide aisles of shelving, not the metal kind, but furniture-quality, tastefully decorated for the holidays. The old building was clean and spacious.

The heavenly smell was even stronger in here. She walked through the retail space, enjoying the anonymity that wouldn't last long once people knew she'd arrived from AGC headquarters.

"Welcome to Porter's." An older woman also wearing a striped vest, with BETTIE on her name tag, approached Vanessa with a platter. "Samples are always free. Take one." Her voice dropped to a whisper. "Or two, I'll never tell."

"No, thank you." Vanessa turned and started for the next aisle, but the woman caught her attention again.

" 'No, thank you'?" Bettie eyed Vanessa. "You've never had our fruitcake, have you?"

Vanessa turned back to face the woman. "Well, no." She waved a hand. "I'm not really a fan of fruitcake."

"Ours isn't like any other. Trust me. You'll like ours. Just try it." Bettie pushed the platter closer to her. She had to be every bit of seventy, and she was so cheery it was hard to say no.

Bettie's blue eyes twinkled.

"Umm. Okay, but only a small piece." She took one of the little paper wrappers and braced herself as she placed the piece of cake in her mouth just to be polite. *Please don't let me gag.*

She pasted a smile on her face, prepared to give it a good show at the very least. As she chewed, the flavors tickled her taste buds. The texture was light and silky. With her hand still at her lips, she slowly made eye contact with Bettie.

"You want another bite, don't you?" Bettie beamed.

"This can't be fruitcake."

"This is Porter's fruitcake."

"Wow. That *is* really good."

"You're not telling me anything I didn't already know. I wouldn't take a job offering samples of just any old thing. I'm not that good of a liar." She stepped closer and tucked three more pieces of fruitcake into the top of Vanessa's purse. "For later," she said in a hushed voice followed by a wink. "You'll thank me the next time you see me." She squeezed Vanessa's forearm and then swept over to the other side of the store where a couple had just walked inside to offer them a free sample too.

Vanessa licked her lips. Anna was not going to believe this.

Fruitcake in all sorts of containers and sizes was for sale ready-to-ship, but there was a whole counter, more like a bakery, where you could pick out exactly what you wanted in an assortment box.

There were fruitcake cookies, fruitcake pops with sticks, fruitcake muffins in plain or bran and gluten-free too. Even a rack of do-it-yourself kits, and books on how to preserve your fruitcake. A book she didn't plan to read, because no matter how absolutely delicious that cake tasted, she'd never understood the appeal of fruitcake preserved for one year, much less several.

On the other side of the store there were dozens of branded items. Everything from shirts and koozies to jackets and snow globes. Even handmade scarves, and Christmas ornaments and cards by local artisans.

She picked up one of the ornaments. *Fairly priced too.*

She didn't have time for all of this right now, though. Vanessa walked over to the cash register.

"What can I do for you?" the young lady asked.

"Hi." She glanced at the girl's name tag. "Misty. I'm supposed to pick up an envelope that Lilene left here for me. My name is—"

"Vanessa Larkin?"

"Yes."

"I've got it right here." The girl lifted the tray in the cash register and withdrew a card.

Vanessa accepted it and flipped it over in her hand to be sure this was indeed addressed to her. "So it is. Thank you."

"You're welcome. Can I pack you up a muffin or tea to go?"

"Umm. No. Thank you, that's very sweet of you. I think I'm good." A quick finger wave and Vanessa was back out in the town car. "Whew."

She handed the directions to the driver, then pulled out one of the samples that Bettie had given to her. "You have to try this."

He took the cake and hesitated before he put it into his mouth. "Is this fruitcake?"

She patted him on the shoulder from the backseat. "I know. I had the same reaction. Go ahead. Don't be a wimp."

He broke the small piece into two and lifted a half piece of cake to his mouth. She was pretty sure he was holding his breath. But once he began to chew, his eyes got wide. "That's *not* fruitcake. No way," the driver said.

"I know. It's great. Right?"

"It tastes like more." He popped the rest of the piece into his mouth without hesitation.

"You're welcome." She slid her finger beneath the back flap of the bright envelope and took out the card as he pulled away from the curb.

The card had a pretty straw basket filled with flowers and baked goods on the front. WELCOME TO FRASER HILLS was artfully inked around the artwork. Inside it read, *Please let us know if we can make your stay more comfortable. You can reach one of us at Porter's any day of the week.* It was signed by Dave, Jenny, Bettie, and Misty. Below that, *Welcome Vanessa, My office is upstairs, first door on the right. Next to yours. See you soon, Lilene.*

She tucked the card into her purse, patting it. Her mom would have done something like that.

The driver pulled in front of a tired-looking old warehouse on the outskirts of town. "This is the address," he announced. "You sure this is right?"

"Oh? Well, I'm not quite sure. I've never seen it before."

The hulk of a man twisted in his seat. "Want me to go check it out for you first?"

"No. I'll go." She opened the car door. "Could you wait a minute, though? I'll need help with my luggage." She stepped out onto the dirt and gravel parking area.

She looked at the number on the building. It was the right address. She held the key in her hand. Hoping for the best, she walked to the door, which thankfully looked new.

If the apartment was too bad, she'd find a house somewhere nearby to rent instead. That would be a waste of good money, though. She wouldn't be here that long. Just a matter of weeks, and the chance of a lifetime. *Keep your eye on the prize.* What was a few weeks in less than desirable conditions when her dream home would be in reach when she got back to Chicago?

Gravel crunched under the tires of a tan compact car as it sped through the lot and slid to a stop by the town car. A slight woman hopped out, wearing an oversize forest-green sweater with a cornucopia appliquéd across the front.

"Welcome!" The woman raced to her side. "You must be Ms. Larkin. It's so nice to meet you. I'm Lilene. Oh, I see you got the card."

"Lilene? Yes. Nice to meet you. Yes. I got it. That was so thoughtful. Thank you."

"We wanted you to feel welcome." She grabbed the key from Vanessa's hands. "Glad I caught ya. This key can be a little tricky if you don't know what you're doing." She pushed it into the keyhole, then tippy-toed as she lifted the handle, and then twisted the doorknob. Lilene gave the door a little kick with her black all-weather boot and the door swung open. "If you don't do that little lift before you turn, you'll never get in."

"Thank you. I'll remember that." Vanessa took the key. At first glance, or maybe it was her energy, Lilene had appeared to be about her age. Now Vanessa could see she was probably older. The old-style haircut didn't help either.

Lilene hit a panel of switches just inside the door. "It's dusty down here, but we didn't get much notice about you coming. We'll get this cleaned up this week. I promise the apartment upstairs is sparkling clean. I took care of that myself."

"Okay." Vanessa followed her to the stairs that led to a second story overlooking the warehouse floor. "This is part of Porter's?"

"Mm-hmm. Haven't used it in a long time. We found the warehouse behind the retail shop to be much more convenient, but then found a way to consolidate into the one building. Plus, there's a good parking lot at the other space. In the winter you can get stuck over here."

Great.

"We won't let you get stuck."

"I'm not driving, so I should be fine."

"Oh, you won't have a car?" Her lips puckered.

"I'll just Uber over."

Lilene shook her head.

"Or taxi."

Lilene paled. "I guess I could set up something with Jimmy. He's our only taxi driver, but he works another job during the day. Oh, but we do have a bicycle you can use." She gestured to a seafoam-green Schwinn with a basket on the front of it.

"The only bike I've ridden lately is the stationary one in the gym. Let's come up with a schedule for Jimmy, or you could pick me up."

"I could. Yes!" Lilene exclaimed. "I'd be happy to drive you around. I'm here to do whatever you need. We could do coffee in the mornings together. I'll be your personal assistant while you're in town. How long will that be, by the way?"

That was a peculiar question. "Well, I guess we'll see how things go."

"We installed a new code on the apartment door for you." She stood to the side and demonstrated. "Just push 0729 and enter."

"That'll be easy enough to remember. That's my birthday." Vanessa laughed at the coincidence.

Lilene's eyes widened. "Oh, I know. I did that on purpose. I looked you up on Facebook. I wanted it to be super-duper easy for you."

"Thank you." *I think.*

Lilene opened the door to the apartment. "Here you go."

It was actually quite nice, with great light, and now that she could get a better look at Lilene she realized she was probably in her late fifties. No doubt one of the employees who'd been with the company a lifetime.

A wall of windows overlooked pretty black board fence and pastures for as far as she could see in one direction, and trees in the other. A nice vintage executive desk with hand-carved legs sat right in front of the windows.

"Is there internet?"

"Yes. We have you all set up. The passcode is written on a sticker next to the printer in this armoire over here. The bedroom is through that door straight ahead, and the bathroom is off of that. Over this way you have a sitting area with a gas fireplace, and the kitchenette. I think you'll find it very comfortable."

"Yes, it'll do quite nicely." It would do for now—perfect for a corporate apartment, but a little too small for her and Anna to enjoy the holidays in together.

"I stocked the refrigerator with some basics to get you through a few days while you settle in. Coffee too. Well, you'll find everything."

Vanessa walked toward the door hoping Lilene would take the hint and follow. "Yes. I'll be fine. Thank you for making the trip out here to help me settle in. I'm going to have the driver bring up my luggage, and we'll get down to work tomorrow."

"Right. Yes. I'm ready." Her voice bubbled over.

Vanessa herded Lilene out.

"Nice to meet you." As soon as Lilene stepped outside, the town car driver came up with Vanessa's luggage. She pointed him upstairs and she waved goodbye to Lilene from the door.

"You can leave them on the landing there," she said from the bottom of the stairs.

He walked back downstairs, and headed for the door.

Lilene almost tumbled inside trying to balance a huge basket covered in clear plastic in her arms.

"Whoa." The driver sidestepped Lilene.

She peered around the basket. "Sorry. I got so anxious when I saw that you beat me here, I forgot this was in my car. I meant to bring this over earlier to surprise you." She pasted a nervous smile on her face. "Surprise?"

Lilene was already climbing the stairs toward the apartment, rattling on. ". . . my famous chocolate-dipped fruitcake squares. I'm kind of known for them. It's not an official Porter's thing, but people do love them. There's also some chocolate peanut butter fudge. You're not allergic to peanuts, are you?" Without even waiting for an answer, she continued, "And a zucchini bread with chocolate chips. Can you tell I like chocolate?"

Vanessa smiled, as she opened the apartment door.

Lilene set the basket down on the kitchenette counter. "Thanksgiving is this Thursday. If you're not flying back home for the holiday you are welcome to join us. I always make way too much food, and the more the merrier anyway. You don't have to bring a thing. Just your appetite."

"I couldn't. I've got a—"

"I'll let you just think about it, but I already had my grandchildren help me make the place cards and there's one with your name on it," she sang out. "Here." She pushed an envelope toward Vanessa. "I set up the meeting with the employees for tomorrow night."

"Thank you. That'll work out nicely. Can you have Jimmy on standby to take me home immediately following?"

"Yes, ma'am. I sure can. The meeting will be at the elementary school in the cafeteria. They have a nice stage there. That's where we hold all of our town meetings and large business gatherings. We can talk it over tomorrow. I'm sure you'd like some peace and quiet after your trip to town."

Would I ever!

Lilene ran her fingers across her lips like a zipper. "I'm going to just leave you for now." Stage-whispering, she said, "You call me and let me know when you need that ride. I can be here in two jifs, or send Jimmy over."

Vanessa held her breath until she heard Lilene take the last step and the main warehouse door slam. From the window, she watched the car turn onto the road.

She's enthusiastic. I'll give her that.

She glanced over the papers that Lilene had left. She

seemed very competent, and eager to please, but she'd made a typo. Her five thirty P.M. meeting was communicated as *eight* thirty. Hopefully, the actual email and posting to the factory workers went out correctly. She'd have to check on that in the morning.

She'd made announcements in some strange places before, but never in an elementary school cafeteria. She thought back to when she was a student at Kempsville Elementary. Rows of tables with teeny chairs. It seemed like a mean joke to have adults hunched up in teensy chairs with their chins on their knees as she discussed the big changes planned for Porter's.

CHAPTER NINE

The next morning, Vanessa had to admit she'd be way more motivated to get out of bed right now if the Eiffel Tower were outside her window instead of the North Carolina mountains.

Stretching, she reluctantly got up and went over to the window, lifting the shades in one quick tug. Thick clouds hung low across the mountains like a mystical storyland, making the reason these mountains were called the Blue Ridge Mountains make complete sense. The range truly appeared blue and somehow silent. *Could a massive structure of cast iron and steel really be more impressive than nature's architecture?*

Invigorated, she took in a deep breath and stretched her arms over her head.

It really is majestic.

The downside of not staying at a hotel was there was no gym to get the day started. She'd been on the track team in high school and back then they ran rain or shine all year round. The whole team would run for miles, pounding the pavement around the football field until her legs were like gelatin.

She'd probably burn more calories in this cold weather, and that wouldn't hurt, based on the looks of those goodies Lilene had left.

She changed into her workout gear, then took the stairs at a quick clip. A calypso of clangs echoed through the empty building.

Outside, the air was crisp, but the sun shimmered on the dew that still moistened the leaves and grass. She stretched, then started an easy jog around the building, careful not to twist an ankle on the uneven gravel lot.

She wished now that she'd paid more attention on the drive over yesterday. If memory served her, turning left would take her back to town. She reset her fitness tracker.

Out of habit, she looked both ways down the empty, quiet road before taking off to the right.

The air seemed so fresh. The incline tested her muscles. The gentle roll of the land was more demanding than it appeared. Finding a comfortable pace, she let her mind clear, getting lost in the rhythm.

A bright red cardinal darted across the road and tried to disappear into a tumble of vines and reeds, quickly followed by a muted tan colored bird. *Probably his mate.* The male looked like a Christmas ornament against the winter-bare vegetation that had given in to dormancy until spring.

Black fence lined this stretch of road for as far as she could see.

Her fitness tracker chirped. She stopped, pivoted, and started heading back.

A thunderlike reverberation overlaid the sound of her shoes

against the pavement. Through the trees, on the other side of that black board fence, three huge horses ran by. Their manes loose and flowing, they looked as if they could run forever if not contained.

She surrendered her breath to their beauty. Slowing to a stop, as the horses passed—mighty and beautiful.

Wow.

In a moment they were out of sight, as if they'd been nothing but a figment of her imagination. She jogged in place, hoping they'd return, but they didn't. She ran back, glad that she recognized the curve in the road as the warehouse came into view.

A car that looked like Lilene's was parked near the door. She slowed to a walk as she got closer. Lilene sat messing with her phone in the driver's seat.

Vanessa tapped on the car window. "Hello. Good morning."

Lilene screamed, pulling both fists to her chest. "Oh, I didn't want to bother you." She lowered her window. "You scared me to death." She panted, still holding her heart. "Mercy. I forgot to ask if you were an early bird. Which apparently you are."

"I am." Vanessa caught the enticing aroma of something savory coming from the car. In that instant her plan for a smoothie went right out the window.

"I'm your ride to the office. I wanted to be sure I was available when you were ready, but I didn't want to text or call if you were sleeping."

"I won't be long. Do you want to come up and wait? I'm sure I have something to offer you." She laughed, since Lilene knew better than she did what was in the apartment.

"I can do ya one better," Lilene said. "I made something for you. Fresh from the oven."

Lilene scooched out from behind the wheel balancing a

casserole dish wrapped in a festive burgundy and gold towel with a stressed-out turkey on it, leaving her purse sitting on the seat of the car.

"Come on. Let's enjoy it while it's hot."

"You didn't have to do that. But it does smell good."

"It is. It's a family recipe."

If this is what they mean by Southern hospitality, I could get used to it. "Can I carry that for you?"

"No. I've got it. Did you have a good run?"

"Yes. It's beautiful here."

"Mmm. The natural beauty of the Blue Ridge Mountains is always changing." Lilene paused in front of the warehouse, a serene smile on her face as she glanced over her shoulder toward the mountains. "It's like redecorating your house just by leaving the curtains open. You really have to experience Fraser Hills to appreciate it. I know we don't have all the fancy stuff you're probably used to, but it's full of good people with a real sense of community. It works."

"That's good." Vanessa jogged ahead and opened the door for Lilene, then raced up the stairs ahead of her. "Come on in. I'm going to grab a quick shower and get dressed."

"Sure. You go ahead and I'll get some fresh coffee going for you. We can eat and then head to the office together."

When Vanessa came back out after her shower, Lilene had two places set at the tiny dining table.

"This is above and beyond," she said to Lilene as she sat down across from her. As Vanessa picked up her fork, Lilene cleared her throat and bowed her head.

Vanessa followed suit.

Lilene said a quick prayer for the meal, and an extra one for their work together through the assessment of Porter's.

Vanessa managed an "amen" as she swallowed hard. The knot in her throat made it almost impossible to swallow the forkful of the egg casserole she'd just put in her mouth. But she did and the flavor was rich, savory with the perfect amount of spice. "Mm. This is so good."

"It's a leaner version of the Southern breakfast casserole. When my Norman had his little cholesterol scare a couple of years ago, I started cutting him back. He never even knew. Well, he knows now because when he goes turkey hunting, I make him make the sausage for us. Nothing better than fresh turkey sausage."

"This is turkey?"

"Sure is."

It was delicious, but somehow the thought of a huge feathered turkey hanging by his feet over some big guy's shoulder as he trekked through the woods was a little harder to swallow than that of pre-formed sausage patties in the grocery case.

Lilene's face squinched. "Too much information for you?"

Vanessa swallowed. "Yeah. A little." She slugged back some coffee, and tried to wash away that image so she could finish.

"Just rewind that. Pretend I never said anything. Oh goodness, I do sometimes ramble on."

"Thank you for breakfast," Vanessa said. "It was a nice surprise. And delicious."

"Well, it was kind of two birds with one stone really. One, I wasn't sure when you'd need a ride and wanted to show you that I'd be here for you. Two, I figured if I proved I was a good cook you'd come to Thanksgiving dinner." She raised her hand. "I know. Norm said, 'Lilene, don't be pushy.' But I have to tell you it just really bothers me to think of anyone not getting a dose of family on Thanksgiving." She patted her chest. "I really hope you'll come."

"Don't count on it. I have a lot to do, and who knows, I may even ride down to Georgia to visit my cousin for the holiday. I'll be fine. I promise."

"The invitation stands." Lilene's shoulders drooped as she headed for the door. "I put the rest of the casserole in the refrigerator. It'll be just as tasty when you heat it up later."

Vanessa followed Lilene out to the car, reminding herself to not become emotionally invested in these people. She was here to do a job. There was no time for anything else.

It was a short drive to Main Street, and it was already buzzing with traffic and people opening their stores. Lilene turned onto Porter House Road and went around to park in the lot behind Porter's.

"This is where all the employees park." She took her key out of the ignition.

Vanessa followed her to the back entrance. The brick steps were steep; it was a wonder someone hadn't complained. Vanessa grabbed the handrail, steadying herself as they went inside.

"This is where the factory team punches in and out every day. None of us are supposed to use the front door. It's strictly enforced. I mean, you didn't know, but from now on you probably should come through here. It keeps the store from getting unnecessary traffic." Lilene blushed. "I'm sorry. You can, of course, do whatever you like."

"So, the factory workers clock in over here and then go back across the street to the factory?"

"No. There's nothing in that building."

"The plans showed the factory across the street in the other building."

"Not anymore. The factory is down that hall now."

She'd have to check into that. "Never mind. Show me the way to my office."

"From the back entrance we're at the other end. Your office is right next to mine," Lilene said, while Vanessa mouthed the words in her mind.

She followed Lilene upstairs and down a long corridor.

Just beyond the stairs, Lilene stopped. "Those stairs come up from the retail area. This is my office. You're in the next one down. It overlooks Main Street."

"Thank you." Vanessa walked by Lilene, who was putting her coat on a rack next to her desk.

Vanessa was pleased with her office, even if it was temporary. Leather chairs were positioned across from a masculine desk of walnut or mahogany with a timeless look to it. The ornate carved legs and edge of the desktop looked hand-done. A matching credenza held a nice bronze of a horse and carriage, similar to the one on the logo. Floor-to-ceiling built-ins held rows of awards and certificates. In the far corner of the room, a Christmas tree held years and years of collectible annual Porter's ornaments.

She swept her fingers over the dusty branches of the Christmas tree, then rubbed her hands together to get rid of the residue.

It only took a few minutes to set up her computer and sync her calendar with the latest meeting updates from Chicago. Edward had scheduled a meeting for the top of the hour. That was only five minutes away. She unpacked her things and then called him.

"Vanessa. Good morning. You're all settled in by now I'm sure?" his voice boomed.

A pang of guilt shot through her about breakfast with Lilene. Normally she kept her distance from the workers and got right down to work. She'd have already been knee deep into the project plan by now. "Yes, sir. I've got a meeting with the employees tonight." She jotted a note on the pad next to her to ask Lilene about the time discrepancy. "I need to check with Micky. I don't have the latest plans and inventory. Where we have the factory located on our plat is now a vacant building. I'm not sure exactly what we're looking at here. I'm going to need a few days to get the inspections we need to ensure it can be updated in time."

"Make it happen, Vanessa. That's why I sent you. Budget doesn't matter at this point. We've got the right footprint there. The location was approved this morning. Get it done. No matter what it takes."

"Yes, sir. I'll get workers reassigned immediately."

"And shut down Porter's. No sense in having to deal with all of that as we renovate and reposition for January first."

"That may not be necessary," she said. "I'll le—"

"Don't make it more complicated than it has to be. We can take the loss with the increased revenue from this project. Gotta run. I'll look for an update by the beginning of next week."

She hung up the phone and pulled up the reassignment plan she'd put together over the weekend. She pressed the button labeled LILENE on the old phone system. "Lilene, can you come in here, please?"

"Yes, ma'am. On my way."

A moment later Lilene was perched in the chair in front of Vanessa's desk with a steno pad and pen in hand like a scene out of an old black-and-white film. "You know you don't have to call me 'ma'am.' 'Vanessa' is fine."

"Yes, ma'am. Thank you. Sorry. I'm just being polite."

"Right. I need to go over the details for the meeting this evening. The time was wrong."

"Yes, m— Well, I had to change a couple of teensy details. I didn't realize it was pep rally night when you sent the information over." She shrugged. "But I've got that all squared away."

"Pep rally?"

"The rally is being held this afternoon right after the kids get out of classes. The Falcons are scrimmaging the Colts. Since Thanksgiving is this Thursday, they're playing the game tonight at six. I had to move your meeting to *after* the game?"

"Seriously?"

"Yes. If you'd tried to meet with everyone at five thirty you would've been in an empty room." Her eyes went wide. "Well, I'd have been there, of course, but you know what I mean. But don't worry. I handled it all." Lilene was clearly proud of herself. Had it not occurred to her that the employees of Porter's should be accommodating her . . . not the other way around?

"So, that wasn't a typo in the report you gave me?"

"No. I set the meeting for eight thirty, but it'll depend on the game. They're archrivals. Sometimes they go into overtime. If it does, it'll be right after that."

Her jaw tightened. Where were these people's priorities? "Fine," she managed politely. She should've handled this herself. She walked over to the printer and pulled off a list of employees. "I'll need to meet with all of these people tomorrow morning at seven o'clock. We're going to walk to the building across the street."

"The one we aren't using that you asked about this morning?"

"Yes. Where the factory used to be."

"Oo-kay." Lilene jotted it on her pad with a bewildered look.

"And take all of those employees off the work schedule for the rest of the week. I'll be assigning them special projects."

Lilene flipped the piece of paper in her hand, and propped a hand on her hip. "What kind of projects?"

"I'll discuss that with them. What I need from you today is to contact each of these people and let them know about the reassignment."

"Is it temporary?"

All of this is temporary. "Is there a problem with you being able to complete this task?"

"No," she said quietly. "But John here on the list, he takes his daughter to school every morning. She fell off the bus last year. Bless her heart, she won't ride that thing anymore. She's terrified. He won't be able to make it at seven. And there's Lewis. I don't know what you need him to do, but he doesn't much like change. He can be a little hard to talk to. Don't get me wrong, he's an excellent worker. He can fix anything, but he—"

"That's precisely why I need him on this project."

"Oo-ka-ay."

Thankfully, Vanessa's phone interrupted the conversation. She took the call and Lilene left the room.

Since her big meeting was now on-the-fly because of the local football game, she had plenty of time to get a few things done before she met with the employees tonight.

Lilene had left for lunch, thankfully, when Vanessa picked

up the huge wad of keys they'd given her to go do a quick inspection of the factory floor.

She walked to the end of the hall, then followed the yellow line to where each worker swiped their badge to clock in and out. They'd implemented several mistake-proofing processes. Impressive. Blue arrows led her to a catwalk above the kitchen area. Everyone wore white, and there wasn't one person out of compliance from what she could see. Things seemed to be moving like a well-oiled machine. Too bad this would all be gone in a few weeks.

She did a quick count from up here of all the equipment on the floor. She typed notes in her phone and took a few pictures to reference back later.

She took the stairs back down to the main level, grabbed her coat from her office, and then walked back out to the parking lot. A large truck rumbled down the road.

She crossed the street to the former factory. It took up practically the whole next block of Porter House Road. There was more than enough space for the warehouse project to not disrupt Porter's. She noted the wooden doors would need to be updated to metal and glass. Dry leaves had piled in one corner of the stoop.

Not a single key on the huge ring she'd been given fit the door. She walked around to the back. The doors at the docks were in pretty shabby shape. She pulled a tape on them, noting the measurements. Easy enough to put in some good commercial metal rolling doors. The same contractor could probably handle all of that work. She'd just have to wait until the maintenance manager could help her get inside tomorrow morning when they all met at seven.

She hated being in a holding pattern, but she could at least get some bids working on the doors today.

A few hours later she'd garnered a list of reputable companies who could do the work, and called with the requirements for bids. It was always faster to pick up the phone, rather than wait for a response on an emailed RFP.

By the end of the day, she was weary of having to hang around town until after the football game. If she went to the apartment, she'd have to arrange a ride back. She gathered her things to explore the restaurant choices while she had some time on her hands.

As she stepped outside, her phone rang. Seeing Anna's name on the display pushed her frustration down a notch. "Hi, Anna."

"How's it going?"

"All settled in. Although folks around here don't seem to have much sense of urgency." She walked across Porter House Road on Main.

Anna's giggle came across the line. "Perhaps, Vanessa, that's a sign you should reduce yours a little. It is practically Thanksgiving, after all."

"Yes, but you'll never believe this. They rescheduled my meeting with all the workers to introduce myself and let them know what I'm here to do to accommodate their local football game."

"That sounds okay. What's so bad about taking an evening to have a nice dinner and join in the festivities around the football game? Relive those cheerleader days. You were pretty good as I remember."

"Oh my gosh. Don't remind me."

"I won't keep you. I know you're busy. I just wanted to know you got settled in and were doing okay. Call me at the end of the week when you get the chance. Have some fun."

Why not? Vanessa disconnected the call. Standing on the sidewalk in front of the butcher shop on Main Street, she raised a fist in the air, pretending it was a pom-pom. "Go!" She kicked one heel up behind her then headed to find out the details about tonight's big game. "This one's for you, Anna."

CHAPTER TEN

Vanessa pulled her coat tighter across her body to guard against the cold. It probably wouldn't be considered fun in Anna's book, but Vanessa did need to check out the local restaurants. She wasn't much of a cook, so finding somewhere with a decent menu near the office was necessary if she didn't want to live on frozen dinners the whole time she was here. It was on the company dime anyway.

"Hello," a smiling woman said, grasping the gloved hand of a toddler as she swung a brightly colored shopping bag from her other hand.

Before Vanessa could respond, the woman had already passed her by.

A man tacked a flyer to the power pole on the corner. "Good afternoon. Don't miss out on the sale down at the boutique." He gave her a little half salute and jogged back to his truck.

"Thank you." She stopped and read the advertisement, then

moved along. The mail carrier walked out of the insurance office. With his satchel over his shoulder, he carried a handful of letters in his hand. "Good afternoon," he said.

"Thanks." It wasn't long before she found herself offering a smile and head nod to the next people walking by. She felt like someone new. Laughing, she purposefully slowed down.

Why am I in such a hurry to nowhere right now?

In front of her, a blackboard balanced on a windowsill flaunted the daily specials in brightly colored chalk. Double-dipped fried chicken, crispy catfish, and fried chicken livers, taters, and home-made gravy. Under desserts: homemade banana pudding and chocolate skillet cake.

My pants feel tighter just reading the menu.

She sucked in her gut.

That banana pudding sounds good, though.

She forced herself to move along in search of something a little less fried, but if that restaurant was open on the walk back, banana pudding to go was definitely going to happen.

A woman with two sniffly red-nosed children tumbled out of the door of the Fraser Hills Family Medical Practice. An attorney's office took up the next few spaces. She tried to picture Robert practicing law in a town this size.

Suddenly, knowing there was no one back at home waiting for her, she felt a little lost. A little alone. She and Robert had been introduced at the AGC Christmas party three years ago. Had she wanted from the beginning for things with him to work out so badly that she'd overlooked the most important part? The part where her heart was supposed to be involved? Or had things changed along the way?

She stopped in front of the window display at a flower shop called The Stalk Market. Twinkle lights sparkled among the petals of bright red poinsettias, and a snowman made of flowers almost reached the top of the space. She hadn't seen anything this elaborate since she went to Pasadena for the Rose Parade. Of course, those floats were twenty times the size, but this definitely showed an artistic eye, and clever use of natural goods. *Is that pipe made out of lavender seeds? Ingenious.*

Vanessa admired the techniques.

"Hi. How are you?"

She swung around. A woman about her age, wearing a brightly colored floral apron over her black outfit and a wreath of baby's breath balanced atop her short black pixieish haircut, stood there smiling. "I'm Diane."

Somehow the woman made each word carry on for about three syllables.

"Hello," Vanessa responded. "I was admiring your lovely window decoration."

"You must be the lady from Chicago." Diane stuck out her right hand. "Welcome."

"Word travels fast around here," she said as they shook hands.

Diane patted her on the shoulder. "You'll get used to it. People really do mean it in a nice way."

"I'll try to remember that. Nice to meet you, Diane. I'm Vanessa Larkin." She pointed to the window display. "This really is absolutely eye-catching. I love the detail."

"Thanks. I love decorating the windows. Not just Christmas. Valentine's. Heck, I decorate for Flag Day. That's the benefit of owning your own shop."

"Well, you're certainly good at it."

"Thanks. I went to school in New York. Took a job doing windows in the city for a while. We did really elaborate stuff. I'm kind of competitive, so I really liked that."

"New York City? What brought you here?"

"I first came down to do a special project for the Porter's store window. It was a short-term project for a joint campaign they were doing with the company I was working for. My marriage was kind of a mess. My husband was a highly paid stockbroker who loved his job way more than he loved me. Well, I shouldn't really say that. He gave me lots of pretty stuff, but no time and that's all I wanted."

"I'm sorry."

"Don't be. We're both better off now. After being in this town, I knew where I wanted to be. This building went up for sale and I snatched it right up, and here I am. I figured he at least deserved a nod, so I named the store playfully after his real love. The stock market." Her laugh was light and unapologetic. "Get it? The Stalk Market? Now I'm livin' the dream. End of story."

I now officially know more about Diane than some people I've known for a number of years. How did that just happen? "And the ex?"

"He's still doing what he always did. Alone. No hard feelings. I visit when I go up there, but I'm always ready to come right back."

"It's nice that you figured out exactly what you wanted." Vanessa had no idea how someone made the leap from window dressings in bustling NYC to a tiny flower shop in Fraser Hills. She surely couldn't picture herself here. It had taken her a long time to even picture herself living out of the city in a neighborhood. "I was going to find some lunch. Do you have a recommendation?"

"You may as well go straight down to the end of the street to the Blue Bicycle Bistro. It's twice as far, but it's twice as good." She paused, pursing her lips. "Or maybe you just work up an appetite on the way, and it seems better because you're hungrier." She touched a finger to her lips. "I couldn't really say for certain, but it's my go-to. Best food in town."

"Then that's settled. Thanks. I'm going to head that way now. It was nice meeting you."

"You too. Stop back by one day. We can grab a cup of coffee, and share some city talk, and argue who has the best pizza— Chicago or New York City."

"I might take you up on that."

Vanessa walked by a pizza shop that smelled pretty tempting after the mention of it by Diane, but then could anyone really do pizza like Chicago? *Spoiled for life. Pass.*

Diane was right, it was a much longer walk to the end of Main Street than it appeared, but finally a long wooden building came into view. Fat, chunky wooden letters rose from the building rooftop, spelling out BLUE BICYCLE BISTRO. An old turquoise-blue ladies' bike perched atop the letters, with a shiny bell and streamers, along with a basket overflowing with bread, veggies, and fruits. Bright and whimsical, it looked like a fun place to eat.

An emphatic screech behind her caused her to nearly trip at the crosswalk. By the time she caught her balance, a giant theme-park-quality bird costume zipped by, flapping its huge furry wings and making the most awful squawk she'd ever heard.

The blue and gold falcon costume had to be every bit of seven feet tall. That daunting mascot ran around her, then crouched and flapped its wings.

"Squawk! Squawk! Falcons Rock!" the giant bird sounded off.

What the heck? She couldn't help but laugh. *Seriously?*

A blur of giggling girls yelling "Go Falcons!" nearly knocked her off of her feet as they charged up the block toward the mascot.

Vanessa watched them all hightail it down the street ahead of her. *Did I have that kind of energy when I was that age?*

Memories of her own cheerleading days flooded back. Crisp autumn days like this, and jumping up and down to stay warm while sneaking sips of hot chocolate between cheers.

It was perfect football weather. A HELP WANTED sign was taped to the front door of the diner next to a poster about tonight's game.

As soon as she opened the door, she was hit by an inviting mixture of aromas. Pots clanged beyond the dining area from the kitchen, but the place was cozy and inviting, with booths along the windows and blue wooden tables and chairs in the center. Seating assembled from reclaimed bike parts—leather bike seats mounted to poles on bicycle-wheel bases—made for a very interesting look at the counter, where bright blue pendant lights hung from old bicycle chains. She walked over to a booth next to the window and slid in.

A rapid tap-tap-tap on the glass startled her.

She yelped, then muttered under her breath. *That darn Falcon is going to give me a heart attack!* Shaking her finger in the big bird's direction, she said, "Stop that!"

It flapped and squawked, then swished its tail feathers at her.

She shook her head and focused on the menu printed on the placemat, while trying to avoid eye contact with that bird, which was still in her peripheral.

A loud snort came from behind her.

"People take football serious around here." The man's voice was deep, gravelly even. "You going to the game tonight?"

She twisted in her seat. A gray-haired man with a bushy

mustache sat there grinning at her. *Probably more of a soup strainer than a mustache.* "I might. They any good?"

"The team?" He nodded. "Excellent. That squawking mascot? A pain in the—"

"I agree!" She wondered how he'd have finished that comment had she not interrupted.

His twinkling blue eyes didn't match the gravelly edge in his voice. A slight dimple convinced her he wasn't dangerous.

"Buck," he said, followed by a head nod. "Welcome to town."

"It's that obvious?"

He shrugged. "You know what you know. It's a small town."

"Yes. I suppose everyone knows everyone around here."

"Even the folks we don't talk to. You should go to the game tonight. The whole town'll be there. It's a good time. Tradition round here."

"Maybe I will."

"Best chicken stew around."

"At the game? Or here?"

"At the game. You haven't visited this part of North Carolina before, have you?"

"Flown through Charlotte a few times. That's about it. Until this trip."

"Don't miss out on the chicken stew. They don't serve the good stuff at the Charlotte airport. Our chicken stew is something to write home about."

"Really."

"Oh yeah. If I do say so myself. It's my recipe, but a whole team of us make a batch of it that size. We make it in a huge cast-iron kettle so big it takes a boat oar to stir it. Don't worry, though. That oar is reserved for the chicken stew." He got up and tossed a few bills down on the table. "I'll see you there."

How was he so sure she'd go?

He ambled out with a slight limp on his left side. His worn blue jeans were starched and stacked atop dusty boots.

She scanned the menu for something light to hold her over until the ball game that she was apparently now going to.

"Hey there. You must be the lady from Chicago." The waitress raised an eyebrow. "I'm Lisa. Are you here to change things over at Porter's? Folks don't take kindly to changes around here. We like it the way it is." The pretty redhead eyed her, lifting her chin with a slight tilt to her smile. "What can I get you?"

"Something light. I thought I'd get a small salad, but those sweet potato fries sound so tempting."

"Best around. We make them fresh. Every single order." Lisa pursed her lips together. "We have our own secret seasoning. Everyone who comes through here raves about them."

"Then that's what I'll have. And an iced tea, please."

Lisa scribbled on her pad and then went into the kitchen, hollering the order to the back. Vanessa heard the clank of metal bowls and then the sizzle of food being dropped into the hot oil. A moment later the waitress brought a huge plastic cup of tea out and set it in front of her.

"Thank you."

"Your order will be up shortly. Sorry if I came off a little strong there earlier. We've seen too many of you corporate folks drop in here and try to disturb things over the years. They always think they know what's best—what'll make things better around here. They don't have a clue how things work."

"No offense taken." She sipped the tea, which was so sweet it made her back teeth ache.

"Good. I know you've come here to do a job, but all anyone

asks is for you people to get to know what this town has to offer. Hard workers. They're dedicated and Porter's is a huge part of the equation."

Heat spread to Vanesssa's neck and cheeks. *It's all business. It's not personal.* But something kept her from saying that out loud. Lisa looked like she was not someone she wanted to be on the wrong side of.

"Last goober that corporation sent here ended up getting himself locked inside a freezer. Who's really to say whether he made the mistake or someone helped him? Either way he left and never came back."

Maybe that was why Micky was so quick to try to shuffle off this account for the warehouse deal. He'd never live it down if the team back at corporate heard about the freezer scenario.

Vanessa tucked that little nugget in her back pocket for future tangles with Micky.

Lisa brought her order and placed it on the table along with the check. "Not rushing you, honey, but on football night people scramble around like they are gonna miss something. Let me know if you need anything else."

Vanessa tried one of the fries. Kind of sweet, kind of salty, and a little spicy all at the same time, they really were the best fries she'd ever had.

The bistro filled up quickly, and excitement about the big game raised the sound level threefold.

"How're those fries?" Lisa asked.

"Thank you for recommending them. You're right. They're amazing."

"Told you." Lisa refilled Vanessa's tea glass. "Can I get you anything else?"

"I think that will be all. Buck said I have to try the chicken stew over at the ball game, so I'm going to walk over there."

"You know Buck, huh?"

"Well, not really." Why had she even mentioned the old guy by name?

"He's in here every day." With a chuckle, Lisa patted the table. "It's a Southern thing. If you don't like the chicken stew, we're open late on football game nights."

"Thank you." Vanessa paid and then walked out to the curb. She hadn't been to a high school game in years, but tonight the air was bristling with a familiar excitement. People were moving, from all directions, up the hill toward the high school. The band played, and chants echoed, filling the night air. *Gimme an A. A!*

Even after more years than she cared to count, she remembered most of the cheers too. She fell in step with the rest of the people walking to the game. The band started playing "The Horse." Her old high school fight song. In her mind she could still bounce, jump, and kick like she was sixteen all over again. *I could probably still do that pom-pom routine.*

She replayed those moves in her mind as she shuffled along with the crowd. Even though she was in the middle of the crowd, it was as if she were on the outside looking in, because everyone else around her knew one another. A little eavesdropping went a long way. She'd quickly ascertained that the team the Fraser Hills Falcons were playing tonight was not only their biggest rival, but was undefeated.

Inside the gate, there were plenty of seats on the visitor side, but she couldn't bear to not root for the local team in blue and gold.

An arrow at the bottom of the bleachers pointed to the right. A white tent with CHICKEN STEW in faded red letters had a line snaking out of it that wrapped around almost to the goalpost.

She stepped into line. It took a while to get close enough to even see inside the tent. Men bantered with one another as they took turns stirring the pot. Buck hadn't been kidding. What they were using looked just like one of the oars on the johnboat her dad used to take out on the lake when she was a kid.

The black kettle sat above a cinder-block pit. Wood smoldered with cherry-red embers below. It smelled good, and holding a hot cup of soup would sure be nice to warm her up now that the sun had dipped behind the trees.

"Hey there, young lady," Buck called from next to that big black kettle of stew. "You got good taste."

Even having met him only once, she recognized that voice; it was unforgettable. "Hey, Buck. How could I miss out after your grand recommendation?"

"You couldn't." He held up a finger. "You wait right there."

It wasn't like she could go anywhere. She was hemmed up in the long line.

A moment later he was at her side, handing her a large Styrofoam cup of steaming chicken stew.

"You're not trying to make everyone mad at me, are you?"

Buck's eyebrows wiggled. He tapped the man in front of her on the shoulder. "You mad about me giving her some chicken stew?"

The man shook his head. "She's right pretty. Can't blame you." The guy laughed and smiled. "Hello. First-timer?"

"I am."

"Nobody'll be mad," the man said. "We're pretty proud of our chicken stew. Enjoy."

Buck shrugged. "See? On the house."

She called out a thank-you as he walked away.

Balancing her chicken-stew cup in one hand, she merged into the crowd climbing the bleachers on the home-team side. Not one for heights, she took a seat in the third row.

She twitched as three kids raced up to the top and then dipped under the railing and climbed down the side to the ground. That looked like an invitation to fall and break a bone if she'd ever seen one.

Her phone rang. She answered quickly to quiet the ring tone.

"How are you?"

Should have checked caller ID first. The last voice she'd expected to hear was Robert's.

Why is he calling? "Working. Fine."

"I thought once you cooled down, we could talk like adults. My offer is still open to come for the holidays."

Like adults? Seriously? "No thank you."

"You're going to just spend it alone?"

"I don't know, but that's for me to figure out."

"If you don't figure it out soon, you're going to die a lonely woman."

"And if that was supposed to make me run back into your arms, you're sadly mistaken. Merry Christmas, Robert." She ended the call and blocked his number.

Die alone? This is my choice.

*

She scooted to the center of the aluminum bench seat. She tugged the scarf from around her neck and folded it before sitting down, but the metal was still cold through her pants. She hugged the cup. The soup didn't look so special.

In fact, it appeared to be more like a really, really thin New England clam chowder than any kind of stew. At least it was warm. She lifted a spoonful to her mouth and blew on it.

Around her almost everyone else had a cup of the steaming stew in their hands too.

When she took the first swallow, she took back every negative thought. "This is so good," she said out loud to a woman coming up the stairs.

"Oh yeah. The best." The stranger lifted her cup as if to say *Cheers!* and continued on.

The band played back-to-back songs until the cheerleaders ran out onto the field carrying a huge banner. A drumroll filled the air.

"WE ARE THE FALCONS," the cheerleaders shouted.

A thunder of boys wearing blue and gold burst through the paper declaration of war against their opponents.

Vanessa bounced to her feet and cheered. The game started and everyone in the stands was participating. Enthusiastic waves of excitement were followed by monumental groans when the ref didn't call it as they saw it.

In between plays, the band played and the cheerleaders danced on the asphalt track below. The mascot did his part too. Vanessa chair-danced to the music—able to recognize almost every single song from her days as a cheerleader.

A broad-shouldered man with dark hair jogged up the stairs wearing jeans and a half-zip emerald-green sweater, with a jacket clutched in one hand. He joined the group of parents seated in front of her.

As he settled in the bleachers, his arm brushed her leg. "Sorry."

"No worries," she responded, realizing he looked like the

man with the horses. Were his eyes really as green as that sweater?

"Where do I know you from?" His smile was easy, his brows furrowing as he tried to remember. "You look familiar."

"Do you have horses?" she asked.

The guy sitting next to him laughed. "Does he have horses? Oh yeah, he has horses."

She ignored the comment. "I think I saw you on Main Street yesterday."

He clicked his fingers. "In front of Porter's. I remember now."

"That was me."

"I'm Mike." He extended his hand.

She shook his hand, but he didn't let go immediately.

"Passing through?" he asked. "Or do you have family here?"

"Kind of both. I'm spending the holidays with my cousin. She lives in Atlanta. She's meeting me here. I'm Vanessa."

"How'd you pick Fraser Hills?"

"Long story, but we're hoping for a picture-perfect white Christmas."

"We've had a white Christmas in this town the last ten years running. I think you're in luck."

"That's wonderful news."

"Are you going to talk to the pretty lady the whole game?" His buddy nudged him. "You could probably just sit back there."

He flushed. "Sorry." He turned in his seat farther from his nosy friend, then stage-whispered, "Nice to meet you." Then faced the field.

She placed her hand on his shoulder. "Nice meeting you too."

The Falcons ran the next play all the way to the end zone and the locals went crazy. The band played a victory song and fans were on their feet high-fiving. There were even a couple of belly-bumps as the guys grunted their approval.

She was on her feet too, but she never saw the elbow coming that slung her cup of chicken stew from her hand all down the front of her coat.

"No!" She twisted aside, but could only move so far with everyone on their feet around her. "Oh, my goodness" followed her gasp. She grabbed for her scarf and started dabbing at the mess.

Mike turned and his eyes went wide. "Did I? Did we just do that? Oh, no. I'm so sorry."

"It's fine. It was almost gone." Not quite true, but it seemed like the right thing to say. "Oh goodness." Now her hands were wet and sticky too.

"Great first impression," the guy next to him said.

"I'll go get you another—"

"No. Please don't. Not necessary," Vanessa said. "Really. It was delicious, but I had enough."

"I'm sure." He snorted. "You think that was good chicken stew, you should try mine. I'm known for the best chicken stew in this town. Your cup would have been empty, and you'd have been wishing for more."

"Are you bragging?" She raised an eyebrow and giggled.

His friend nodded. "His is the best."

"See?" Mike said. "Not bragging if it's true."

"Well, that's a little hard to believe, because this was pretty darn good." She held the now-empty cup in the air.

"Naw." He shook his head. "You just don't know any better, and I can prove it."

She swept a hand over her damp coat, hoping the milk

wouldn't sour before she could find a dry cleaner. "Prove what? That it'll taste better than what's on my coat?"

"Let me make you some *good* chicken stew. It's the least I can do. And I promise not to spill it on you."

Something in the way he looked at her with his playful green eyes held her for a half second too long, and before she could stop herself, she said, "You're on. Name the time and place."

The corner of his lip rose. "Right after the Christmas parade. Everyone goes. We can meet in front of the fire station around two forty-five?"

Am I actually considering this? "Okay. That sounds fun. I'll be there."

"Great." He quickly recomposed. "Wait. You're serious, right?"

"Yeah. Really." Only she had no idea why she was agreeing. Trying to look sure of herself, she took his phone from his shirt pocket and punched in her number, then hit dial. Her phone rang. "All set. Call me if anything changes."

"See you around."

She raised her hand over head in a backhand wave as she left. *What in the world did I just do?*

CHAPTER ELEVEN

Vanessa watched her step as she tromped down the bleachers. *What the heck was I thinking?* Reprimanding herself all the way down the stairs for agreeing to meet Mike, she almost ran straight into Buck.

Buck caught her elbow as she swung around the pole at the bottom of the bleachers.

"Where are you off to in such a hurry?" he asked.

She gestured to the front of her coat. "There was a little chicken-stew accident on that last touchdown."

"Ew. That's a mess. Told you we take our football seriously in this town."

"You did." She laughed. "I just didn't realize it was tackle in the stands too."

He tossed his head back with a hearty laugh. "I guess it kind of is. Glad you're being a good sport about it. Can I get you some paper towels or something?"

"No, I should say that I loved the chicken stew. However, I don't recommend it as a perfume."

A man stepped up, almost inserting himself between Vanessa and Buck.

"Talking to the enemy?" He was clearly talking to Buck, but looking squarely at Vanessa.

"Where are your manners, Vern?" Buck turned to Vanessa. "Don't mind Vern. He's forgotten his manners."

"It's no secret why she's in town," Vern said. "The meeting is right after the game. If there wasn't something going on there'd be no reason for a meeting. What're you about to announce, lady? Are we losing jobs? Right here at the holidays? How many?"

"Vern. Back up." Buck raised a finger in front of the man's face. "Don't get your skivvies in a bunch. You're all wound up without even hearing their intent."

"It's not good. It's never good when they send someone down from that big conglomerate."

The man's words chipped away at her good mood.

"I told you before: AGC promised nothing would change. Y'all are jumping to conclusions." Buck spoke with a confidence that shook Vanessa's.

The employee of Porter's raised his chin and narrowed his eyes. "What about last time?"

"Well, that guy is long gone and nothing has happened. Now, give this nice lady a proper welcome to our town." Buck didn't lift his gaze. "Go on."

Instead, the guy looked at Vanessa and shook his head. "I hope you do prove me wrong." He turned and stormed off.

She prayed Buck hadn't noticed her look of shock when he'd interjected. He meant well. She was sure of it, and AGC might have promised nothing would change, might have even meant it . . . at the time, but things were about to change and there was no stopping it. Her heart raced. She'd have to call the office and get the original documents sent over. Was there something in the agreement that she needed to know about?

"I'm sorry about that," Buck said. "Uncalled for. People lose their manners these days, and it's a doggone shame."

"Thanks, Buck." An acrid taste hit the back of her mouth. How could she talk to the employees with the agenda she had when clearly there was more to this story? She lifted her phone. "I need to run. I've got to return this call."

"Sure. See you later."

Vanessa held her breath until she was at the exit gate. Over her shoulder nearly a third of the people in those bleachers counted on Porter's for employment. Cheering and enjoying the brisk evening, unsuspecting of what she'd been asked to do here. But in a matter of weeks things would be very different.

The chicken stew stirred in her gut.

She'd sped up as her frustration grew, and, before she knew it, she was catching up to a group of people that had been way ahead of her.

One of the men in front of her said to a woman in the group, "You know it's never good when corporate comes around."

"It's Thanksgiving week. Maybe she's going to give out turkeys. Or Christmas bonuses. Wouldn't that be nice?"

"It would, but that isn't going to happen."

"Don't be so negative," the woman said. "You get what you expect, and you always expect the worst. They promised everything would be the same. Even Buck said it."

"I don't give a damn what Buck says. He doesn't know how ruthless those people can be, else—"

"Just stop." The woman held her hands to her ears. "I don't want to even talk about that again."

Someone at the far end of the group, closest to the street, said, "She's not like those other old farts they sent. She's nice. Not underhanded like they were."

It was Lilene proudly supporting her position. *If only she knew.*

As much as Vanessa wanted to continue to eavesdrop, she ducked into the alley to avoid being noticed, and dialed Edward's number. It went straight to voice mail.

Really? She typed him a text:

> **Vanessa:** Local concern that a promise made to Porter's is about to be broken. We need to talk.

She stood there waiting for her phone to ring back. Edward was always good about immediately returning calls, especially ones of this nature.

Time wasn't on her side. She raised the hood of her coat and tucked her chin as she headed to the elementary school, where she was supposed to be updating the employees shortly. Lilene was probably already there waiting on her.

Vanessa wasn't sure what that speech was going to be now. She knew what she'd been assigned to do, but if there'd been something in the contract that contradicted the plan, she sure didn't want to be the one to turn this town upside down for no reason. There'd be long-term dissatisfaction following a faux pas like that.

She stepped around the corner of the building and sent out a couple of emails—one to Micky, as much as she hated to do it—and another text to Edward.

A rousing cheer came from the direction of the football field. People would be pouring down the street soon. She still didn't have an answer, but she was running out of time fast.

Her mouth felt as thick as if she'd had sand for dinner.

If she'd stayed home tonight, she would have walked into an unsuspecting crowd and one hot mess.

What if Buck was right, and Edward had confused this contract with another? That had happened once. It was years ago, but still.

She took the alley street that ran parallel to Main, then turned left down two blocks to the elementary school. The side door was propped open. She went inside and climbed the stairs to the stage. A few people were already sitting in seats near the front.

Standing behind the curtain, she could hear the sizzle of energy as the room began to fill.

Why hadn't Edward responded? All she could do now was make no promises, and appeal to their sense of community to buy some time, and prevent a disaster.

Her project timeline might be slipping into the red already.

CHAPTER TWELVE

The last time Mike had followed a crowd into the elementary school lunchroom it had been for Misty's sixth-grade graduation. This time he was an uninvited guest. He followed the flow of Porter's employees from the football game into the building. He wasn't usually the nosy sort, but with Misty being so worried over the state of Porter's he couldn't help himself. He squeezed by a few guys still hyped up from the win tonight to ease into a spot out of the way in the corner.

Glancing around the room, he saw that he wasn't the only nonemployee who had crashed this party. Lisa from the Blue Bicycle Bistro, Diane from the flower shop, even Rusty from down at the mill.

In his mind, he envisioned them as dominoes lined up behind Porter's. If it fell, they all fell.

Someone placed a hand on his arm, startling him back to the business at hand.

"Hey, Dad. I didn't know you were coming. Come sit with us. We're up front."

He followed her gaze to the front row. There was no mistaking the back of his grandfather's head. That shock of silvery-gray hair was unmistakable. *Not today. Not in front of all these people.*

"I'm going to stay out of the way and observe from back here." *Not my business anymore* was what he wanted to say, but he kept it to himself. "I probably won't stay long."

She pushed her hair over her shoulder. "One of these days you two *have* to talk again."

"Not tonight," Mike said.

"Why not? It's almost Christmas, and it would be way more fun with the two of you . . . all of us together."

"He's a hardheaded old fool."

"Dad?" She cut her eyes.

There was a scolding tone in her voice, and he deserved it.

"I'm sorry." He wished he could take back the words. "This is between your great-grandpa and me. Our Christmas is going to be fine. The best ever."

She exaggerated a pout, which always melted his heart. "Promise?"

He cursed himself for making the comment about his grandfather. He was usually so good about keeping all that to himself, but it just went to show that he couldn't sweep it under the rug. It was still impacting her. "If there's one thing I can assure you of, it's that we will both love you . . . always."

"I know, Daddy."

A young woman from across the way waved a hand in the air toward his daughter.

Misty tiptoed, waving madly. "That's one of the girls from work. I'm going to go see her. Okay?"

"Of course." Wouldn't be long before she quit asking permission entirely. He was lucky at sixteen she did. They had a good father-daughter relationship and he prayed it would last forever.

Mike watched her dash to the other side of the auditorium to greet her friend. He tensed, preparing himself for that high-pitched squeal girls made when they got together. Always had been like nails on a chalkboard to him, but her smiling face made that easier. And there it was.

Why do they have to do that?

Misty was born wise, and ready to go. She'd kept him and Olivia on alert as a baby, never knowing what she'd be into next. She'd crawl out of her crib. Leave the house to go see the animals. The kid was fearless.

Losing Olivia was hard on them both. By the time Misty was fourteen she'd been champing at the bit to work. The day she turned sixteen, she already had a job lined up at Porter's on the retail side, like her mom had, and she loved it.

But she had his love of horses, and that had taught her discipline. The horses kept the two of them close. He thanked God for that every day.

It was hard not to watch as his grandfather sat in the front row talking to the people around him. He'd always been popular in this town. Even held the office of mayor when Mike was a teenager.

Mike moved out of view of his grandfather. The curtain on the stage fluttered. He saw the back of a woman looking down on the lit screen of her phone, tapping and swiping her fingers across the screen. He wondered about people like that. He had a smartphone only at his daughter's insistence. He'd have been happy with his old flip phone forever.

The woman turned, and Mike's knees gave. *Chicken stew? It can't be.* But it was the woman from the ball game. Vanessa.

Clearly there was more to Vanessa's story than she was sharing earlier. *Why didn't I put it together before?*

Misty had her mother's intuition. Her hunches were usually spot-on. He hoped Vanessa wasn't about to make all Misty's worries come true.

Knowing that Vanessa hadn't been entirely truthful niggled in his gut. That he'd let her capture his attention, even for a minute, bothered him even more.

He watched as she stood behind the burgundy velvetlike curtain. Lilene walked to the center of the stage.

She tapped the mic, sending out a loud thumpity-thump-thump followed by a squeal.

"Sorry, y'all," Lilene said. "Is that better?" Looking for a few head nods, she continued. "Good evening. Let's start with a big ol' congratulations to our Fraser Hills Falcons!"

The room came alive with applause, whoops, and whistles.

"That was one awesome game." The applause faded.

The tension was undeniable. Lilene repositioned the microphone. "We're here tonight to introduce you to Ms. Vanessa Larkin. She's from AGC headquarters, and she'll be staying in town for a few weeks. It was at her request that I scheduled this meeting."

Everyone in the room was stoic. Lilene attempted to soften the mood by offering a joking comment. "I know there's been a lot of speculation about why she's here. At least we're off to a better start with her than with the last guy. She's not sneaking around pretending to be someone she's not."

Mike nearly choked on that comment.

A thunderous groan rolled across the auditorium.

"Come on now." Lilene stuck two fingers in her mouth and let out a whistle. "Let's give her a warm Fraser Hills welcome."

The room quieted.

Vanessa walked out and stood next to Lilene, but the welcome was as icy as it was outside tonight.

"Thank you." Vanessa took the mic from the stand. "This town knows how to do football, and chicken stew. I haven't been to a game like that in years. It was a fun night. Congratulations."

Guys patted one another on the back.

"As Lilene said, I'm Vanessa Larkin with AGC out of the Chicago office. I don't have a lot to share with you at this point, but I did want to introduce myself and open the dialogue to keep things as transparent as possible."

She paused, and the room was so quiet it was as if everyone was holding their breath.

"I'm here because AGC has an opportunity to use some of the vacant warehouse space for growth in another area in our company. I'll need your help as we explore this. I know change isn't easy, but the one thing I can personally promise is that I'll be up front with you. I'll make every effort to convey information as we reach conclusions. Lilene will be setting up some meetings over the next week. Some of you may find that I'm reassigning you temporarily. There will be additional compensation for those tasks. Please give Lilene your complete cooperation."

A shout from the back broke the silence. "Let's cut to the chase. Are we losing our jobs?" The hum in the room fell to a hush again, but heads nodded and people leaned in expecting an answer. Slowly, an unintelligible mix of conversations began to rise.

Mike watched Vanessa onstage. She stood perfectly still except for one visible deep breath as the locals continued to mutter. Probably exchanging stories about the last layoff.

"I—" She lifted a hand in the air, trying to regain command of the room. "I understand your concerns."

The sound of doubt crossed the crowd like a crashing wave.

Even Mike doubted that this woman, dressed in her outfit that probably cost more than a month's salary, had any idea what it was like to count on others that there'd be a job tomorrow.

She took a step back, letting them have their moment. She moved the microphone from her right hand to her left, tapping her pants as if she were drying damp palms, and then rubbing her hand across her neck.

"Okay, so tonight, I'm not here to raise doubts or increase the rumor mill. I need your help. I wanted to offer a good-faith gesture by introducing myself and letting you know why I'm here. Yes, I'll be reviewing the profitability and forecasting of Porter's, but more important, evaluating the remaining footprint, and the buildings that aren't currently being used. It could mean new and additional opportunities for Fraser Hills. I look forward to meeting you and I will keep you updated. If there'll be any significant changes, I'll bring them to you in this forum so that we all stay on the same page."

"When will you know something?" another man yelled from the back. "We're all working double shifts to keep up with the orders. Business is good."

"Yeah, you could probably go home now," another man scoffed. "Things are fine the way they are. There's no such thing as good change."

"I can promise you that I'll work as quickly as possible. I appreciate your help and patience through the process. Lilene, put us down for a two-week touch-base. Same place, same time. Hopefully we'll be celebrating another good football night. Thank you."

Mike watched her step offstage on the high note, and head out the side door faster than a horse could canter. She hadn't even paused for one question. She'd handled the crowd like a seasoned cowboy herding wayward calves.

It was doubtful anyone else in the room even realized that she'd already made it out the door.

Smart lady.

CHAPTER THIRTEEN

When Vanessa stepped outside, the brisk air took her breath away. She pulled on her coat as she walked, lowering her head as she moved quickly around the corner toward the street. Luckily, a taxi was already parked there.

At least, it looked like a taxi, with the removable white glowing TAXI sign on top of the driver's side of the roof. Honestly, it looked more like a pizza-delivery car, but at this point she'd pay a hundred bucks to get back to the apartment.

She slid into the backseat of the black Toyota. "Are you Jimmy?"

"I am. Lilene asked me to be on standby tonight. Where to?"

Not *a* taxi. *The* taxi. One for the whole town. There were probably six taxis to the block at home. "Back to the apartment."

"I know where that is." He leaned forward, checking his mirrors, then slowly pulled away from the curb and drove down Main Street. From the backseat, she watched townsfolk walk out of the auditorium. No smiles. No joy. Some had their heads down, and some looked ready for a fight.

She checked her phone. Still no response from Edward. It wasn't like him to not respond at all. Anna had texted her, though.

Vanessa raised her phone in the air, checking for a better signal.

She texted Anna back. **Spotty connection. I'll call as soon as I get to the apartment.**

Vanessa had no idea what her driver's affiliation was with Porter's, but there was no sense in taking a risk by talking business in the car about things that no one else needed to know right now.

Jimmy pulled his car in front of the warehouse. "Will you need me to take you anywhere else tonight?"

"No, thank you."

He handed her a card. "Here's my number you can contact me directly. Lilene already has the payment handled."

"Great." She slung the car door shut and dialed Edward again as she ran inside. His phone went straight to voice mail again. This time she left him a detailed message, and asked for clarification on how to proceed.

She'd closed down companies before, but never when locals had such confidence that nothing would change. As if they'd been made promises. Usually, the locals knew it was coming and why. This seemed sketchy, and she didn't like that feeling at all. Knowing it had been Micky's account, and that he wasn't above that kind of deal, worried her most of all.

She walked into the apartment and hung her coat next to the door. She was too tired to deal with cleaning it tonight.

Kicking off her shoes, she lay across the couch and used the remote to turn on the gas log fireplace. One quick whoosh and the flames danced to life, flickering between the logs. She scooched from the couch to the floor, enjoying the soothing sound of the fire as she lay there thinking about the situation and thawing out.

She dialed Anna. "Hi, Anna. It's me."

"How'd it go tonight? It was your meeting with the employees, right?"

"I'm glad it's over. At least for now. Things have become complicated."

"How so?" Anna asked. "You handle this kind of business all the time."

"I know. I do. I have. It's different this time, though. Several of the people in town seem to think there was a promise that things wouldn't change. I don't know if it's hearsay, a handshake deal, or something that was in the contract, but my boss isn't returning my calls, and frankly, there's nothing in the papers I was given to prove or disprove it. Edward has always taken my calls in the past, but he's gone radio silent."

"I hope he's okay." That was Anna. Always caring and concerned for others.

"I hope he's not hiding something from me. You should have seen their faces, etched with worry, hoping I'd tell them everything was going to be all right. I couldn't lie to them."

"So, what did you tell them?"

"The truth. I mentioned reallocation of the unused warehouse space. I promised I'd work quickly to assess the site, and that I needed their help to make those decisions."

"Well. That's a promise you can keep, isn't it?"

Kind of. Bottom line was Edward wanted this cleared out

and ready for January first and the clock was ticking. "Yes, except I'm sure it's still going to result in a lot of unhappy people. Some of them will be able to transition into the warehouse positions that will come with the new business, but there are employees that have been with the company for over twenty years. They aren't young enough for the kind of physical labor required for those positions."

"That's not good. It's hard for older people to get work, no matter what all the equal-opportunity people want to say."

"I know. I can usually reskill and reallocate across projects, but there's a big difference between skills needed on this one."

"You'll find a way. You're always fair."

"I pride myself in that, but right now I feel like I may as well be green and stealing presents in this little Whoville town."

"You'll get it straightened out."

"I'm just the one executing the project. I didn't recommend shutting Porter's down. That was Edward. I honestly think they can do both from my first look at things . . ."

"But?"

"I've never felt so personally responsible before. I guess I haven't looked as closely at the people as I have here."

"Are you going to truly assess the site, and make recommendations? Or just do what your boss asked you to do?"

"Edward doesn't really like people challenging him on things. On quick jobs like this one, I usually fly in, sweep through all of the changes, and fly back with everything wrapped neatly in a bow."

"I'm sure you'll figure out the right thing to do. It's rather late. How long did that meeting run?"

Vanessa glanced at the clock on the wall. "Not long. I'd scheduled the meeting for five-thirty, but apparently this whole town goes to the football game. My assistant said I'd be facing an empty room unless we scheduled for after the game. So, she did. Have I told you all of this? It's crazy. By the time the game ended and everyone left the ball field to get to the elementary school for the meeting it was almost nine."

"I'd have been too tired to listen. But football is fun. I haven't been to a game in years. I loved watching you cheer when you were in high school. Cold nights in the stands, huddled up in scarves and blankets. Such great memories. Please tell me you at least went to the ball game and had a little fun."

"I did, as a matter of fact, and it was a lot more fun than I expected. I met some nice folks. And there's this one older man I keep bumping into. He said I had to try the chicken stew. They make so much of it they stir it with a boat oar!"

"Yeah, down here in Georgia we have something called chicken mull that's in a milk base. Must be like that. They do the same thing. Seems rather unsanitary, but I guess it's no different than stirring with a wooden spoon. A giant one."

"I really liked the chicken stew. Well, until one of the guys sitting in front of me at the ball game accidentally knocked me and it spilled down the front of my coat."

"I hope it wasn't hot."

"No. I'm fine. It had cooled down, and the guy who bumped into me was really nice about it. In fact, he asked me to go to the Christmas parade with him."

"I hope you said yes to the parade."

"I did. I'm not exactly sure why I did, but I'm looking forward to going."

"Good. You deserve some fun, and I can't wait to join you and share in it. You're already doing a good job of keeping your promise to balance some fun with the workload."

"I guess I am."

"Good. Keep it up. I can't wait to get there so we can have some fun together."

"It's going to be great. I need to have Lilene figure out where you can stay. They put me up in this little corporate apartment at one of the warehouses. It's fine for one person, but it's not that big, and it's kind of off the beaten track. I'll get her to find a place for us."

"Don't go to big trouble. I could sleep on the couch."

"No. If anyone is doing any couch sleeping it'll be me."

"I can find somewhere. I'm quite resourceful, you know."

A heavy emptiness hung over her. "I miss you, Anna."

"Well, it won't be as long as it has been."

"Thank goodness," Vanessa said. "It'll be great to see you."

"You get some rest. You can handle whatever this situation is. Everything will come together in good time."

Vanessa hung up and laid her phone aside feeling more confident about the task ahead. Anna had a way, as Mom always had, of making her believe anything was possible.

*

The next morning, rain blew sideways, making yesterday's pretty blue mountains nothing but a soaking gray blob. She'd already texted Jimmy, who was on his way.

Downstairs waiting, she checked messages until she heard his horn honk. When she opened the door, the wind caught it and dragged her outside, almost yanking her off her feet. She stutter-stepped to regain her footing, then slammed the door behind her and ran for the car.

"Thanks for coming. It's a mess out here," she said.

"At least it's not snow."

"I don't mind snow. I'm from Chicago. I can deal with snow."

He drove her to the office without another word. "Here we are," he said as he pulled in along the curb. "Have a good day."

"You too." Raindrops dropped, fat and rapid, on and around her as she made a dash for the front door of Porter's. She worked her key in the lock and let herself inside. It was quiet, but it still smelled of sugar and nuts and sweet confectionery and now she craved a pastry to go with the coffee she desperately needed.

Moving through the dim store, she made her way to the staircase that led to the offices. She wondered if running three shifts was an option for this space. She'd have to check into local ordinances. A third shift could give more opportunities to keep employees in their original roles if they didn't qualify for reskilling into warehouse positions. Plus, they could fulfill all the pending orders before the holidays and move all hands on deck to the transition date on New Year's.

She turned on the lights upstairs, and started the coffee. In her office, Lilene had set out the reports she'd requested exactly as Vanessa had asked. Lilene was proving to be very dependable. She spread the them out across her desk, then grabbed a cup of coffee and got down to work.

By the time she'd reviewed everything, she'd separated the employees into four lists.

Lilene marched into the room with that ever-present smile. "Good morning, early bird. Why didn't ya call and let me know you were coming in early? I'd have been happy to accompany you. Can I get you some more coffee?"

Vanessa flipped her wrist, checking the time. "Yes. I have time for one more before meeting the guys at the warehouse.

Thank you." She picked up the phone and called Chicago. "Kendra? How are things going?"

"Quiet. It's the day before Thanksgiving. Just about everyone is out of the office."

"I need a couple of incentive retirement packages, like the ones we did in Jersey last spring. Can you get them pulled together for me? Today would be great. I'd rather not push this until next week."

"Sure thing," Kendra said. "I saw Michael in the break room earlier. I'll grab him to sign off on them."

"Thanks. You're a lifesaver. As usual. I'll send you all the details."

"No problem."

"As soon as we get that done, you can take off."

"I'll be in on Friday. Anything to keep my sisters from dragging me Black Friday shopping."

"Whatever you decide. I have another question for you. I've been trying to reach Edward and he's not answering his phone. Any idea what's going on there?"

"I heard he flew out to Paris with Micky and Gary."

"If he'd put us on that project, he wouldn't have had to fly out to hold our hands to get the project done."

"You know that's right," Kendra said. "I don't know what he was thinking giving it to those guys."

"Can you please pull Micky's contracts with Porter's and send them to me? I'm looking for any addendums to the original contracts. Any promises to keep things status quo for a certain amount of time. That kind of stuff."

"Sure. Is something wrong?"

"Something isn't adding up."

"Coming from Micky's project? I'm not surprised. I'll look at them and get them right over."

"Thanks for everything. Have a nice Thanksgiving with your family, Kendra."

"Oh, I will. I hope you find a good way to celebrate Thanksgiving too," said Kendra.

Lilene's offer popped into Vanessa's mind, and as nice as it was, could she . . . should she do family dinner with the people she was evaluating? Mixing business and pleasure was never a good idea, but she hated to hurt Lilene's feelings too.

"Vanessa, I want you to know that I'm really grateful to be working for you. No matter if we get the projects in the cool cities or not, I wouldn't change my position to be working for any other person in this firm. I just wanted you to know that."

"Thank you, Kendra. I really appreciate all you do."

She hung up the phone thankful that it wouldn't be long before she'd be spending time with Anna over the holidays.

CHAPTER FOURTEEN

"I just put those last two meetings you asked me to set up on your calendar," Lilene said proudly from the door.

Vanessa straightened in her seat. It was the third time Lilene had startled her today. She just poked her head in the office and started talking like Vanessa had nothing else to do but wait for her next story.

Why couldn't she at least knock?

Pasting an appreciative smile on her face, she thanked Lilene. With the office closing early for the holiday, she'd been worried Lilene wouldn't get them scheduled before everyone left for the day.

Edna Barkley and Bill Campbell had more years of service than anyone else at Porter's. They'd probably cut their teeth on fruitcake, they'd started at such a young age. *Or chipped a tooth.* Vanessa giggled at her own terrible joke. Folks around here wouldn't have found it funny. They loved fruitcake. Wore it like a badge of honor.

"You're just going to love them," Lilene said from the door. "They are two of our longest-tenured employees. They know everything about the history of Porter's." Lilene clapped her hands, so excited for Vanessa to meet them.

A knot formed in Vanessa's stomach. *I'm doing the right thing.* "Thank you."

"Don't forget about Thanksgiving dinner tomorrow. I sent you the address in a little email earlier so you can just print it and tuck it into your pocket. I'm not going to ask if you're coming, you just be there. Edna is already here." Lilene stepped farther into the office, pulling the door closed a bit. "She's always early for everything," she whispered across the room. "Should I send her on in?"

"Sure." Vanessa took a long sip of her coffee.

Lilene walked Edna into the room. An attractive woman, she had hair as white as if she'd been caught under the powdered-sugar duster. Her rosy cheeks lifted a smidge when she smiled, as if recognizing an old friend in a crowd. Her sassy blue tortoiseshell eyeglasses matched her blazer.

"It's so nice to meet you, Ms. Larkin." Edna approached the desk.

Vanessa stood and came around her desk, extending a warm handshake.

"I'm a hugger." Edna had completely ignored Vanessa's extended hand.

Vanessa stiffened at her touch, closing her eyes as Edna spoke.

"Everyone is family around here. Welcome to our town. You've come at such a great time of the year."

Vanessa harrumphed under the squeeze of Edna's enthusiastic hug. "Thank you," she managed as she broke free and smoothed her shirt while escaping to the security of being behind her desk. "Have a seat."

Lilene still stood there, beaming.

"You can close the door on your way out," Vanessa said to Lilene.

"Oh. Yes. Right." Lilene scurried from the room.

"Thank you for your years of service, Edna. I was reviewing all of the personnel files and yours is quite impressive."

Edna glowed. "I love this company. Porter's is my whole life. I started on the factory floor, even improved the recipe a few times over the years to help make it easier to ship to our customers across the country. Now I oversee the quality of our products. My name, or someone on my team, signs off on every batch." With a snap, she'd tugged an ink pen from her blazer pocket. "Personally sign off on them." She squiggled her autograph in the air.

"That's important. I bet you have a stellar team."

"I do. I handpicked each one, and they are as dedicated as I am."

"Well, that is wonderful. To reward you for your efforts and long years of service and dedication to grow the brand and instill quality in the products . . ." Vanessa slid a stack of papers across the desk. ". . . I've put together a wonderful package for you. You've been entitled to receive retirement and pension benefits for quite a while."

"Well, yes . . . but . . ." Edna's face twisted as she reached toward the papers. "I love my job."

"It shows. Thank you so much. I've been able to provide you with extra compensation and a very nice bonus along with the package you're already eligible for. I'm so excited to be able to do this for you."

"Why?" Edna stared blankly across the desk. "Why would you want to do this for me?"

"We appreciate you." Vanessa smiled, trying to pull her into the good part of this news. It was a substantial bonus. She flipped over the first three pages and pointed to the bonus amount. "Right here."

Edna leaned in. "Wow. That's a lot of money."

"For years of dedication and service."

"This is very generous," Edna said. "I'm just doing my job, though. Like everyone else. We all love Porter's."

"I know. And now you can relax and enjoy the reward of all those years of effort."

"I see." Edna sat back in her chair. "Changes are coming," she said quietly.

"We'll be repurposing the footprint. Leveraging some of the unused space for warehousing, as I mentioned the other night. Were you able to join us?"

"Yes. I was there."

"Look, Edna, some jobs will change. You've been a huge part of Porter's success and I want to be sure you're well taken care of. Nothing is set. I'm just beginning the analysis and putting the plan together, but no matter what the eventual outcomes are, it's your turn to take advantage of what you've worked for all these years. I don't want you to lose any of that. I'm so delighted I was able to look after you a little with the extra compensation."

"I'm not that old, you know."

"Of course, but isn't that what makes this even better? You can use that bonus to do some of the things you've always wanted to do, and you're young enough to enjoy it. It also moves your salary into a different bucket, giving me a little extra room for others in this budget."

"I should be very grateful," Edna said as if talking to herself. "I'm grateful. Thankful, of course. It'll be interesting to see how things work out." She stood, then reached across the desk to shake Vanessa's hand.

No hugs this time, but Vanessa knew that most people didn't hear much after the first words in these types of conversations anyway. She was certain Edna would be delighted after a few days of sleeping in, and especially right here at the holidays. She could bake until her little heart was content.

"Thank you again." Vanessa came around the desk and gathered the papers for Edna. She tapped them straight and slid them into the envelope she'd already prepared with the contact information for corporate for specific questions about the package.

"You can have the rest of the day off, and I hope you truly enjoy every day going forward."

Edna nodded as Vanessa walked her out.

Bill sat in the chair across from Lilene's desk. He looked at Edna, then flinched and jerked his gaze toward Vanessa.

"You must be Bill, come on in."

He clambered to his feet and followed her into the office.

"Hi, Bill. Thank you for all you've done for Porter's. Some of these buildings are a little spread out. I was excited to see how much you've done across the entire site."

He flashed a wary glance. "Yes. I have. I've been here since before we had all these buildings. Since back when we only had one kitchen in the tiny corner store. We used to serve right out the window to people."

"I had no idea."

"Now that's the gift section of the retail store. It was a small five-person team when I started here."

"Amazing."

He shrugged.

"So, tell me about the warehouse buildings."

"Like what?"

Like pulling teeth, apparently. "I'm staying over at the corporate apartment. What is that building used for? Why is it not being used now? I don't know. What's the history there?"

Bill became a little more animated. "When Mr. Porter passed away, his son really began to grow the business. He built that warehouse. Part of it was used to store the boxes ready for shipment to retailers. One section was a garage for maintenance and repair of the vehicles they used to deliver everything across the region."

"You did your own distribution."

"Yes, for years. Then it became more affordable to outsource that part of the business. He was a smart businessman. People around here didn't always like his decisions, and he was kind of blunt about things. But in his defense, his smart thinking kept this town alive."

"What is that building used for now?"

"Just for you to stay in while you're in town, I guess. There's no hotel around here, so it works."

"Is everything else in working order?"

"Yeah. We make sure everything gets checked on a regular schedule. It can be bad to just leave a building sitting. I make sure she's taken care of. The HVAC systems are new. We upgraded all the wiring a few years ago."

"Why? I mean if the space isn't being used, why the new HVAC and electrical?"

"I'm not sure. I guess Mr. Porter was going to start something new, but then he sold to AGC instead."

"I see." She jotted down some notes. "How about the building directly behind us?"

"That's not really good for anything except a warehouse, and not up to code for food products anymore."

"But it would be usable warehouse space for nonperishables. Say, sporting equipment?"

"Definitely, if it was cleared out."

"How big is that one?"

"Oh, it's actually much bigger than where you're staying. The way it's laid out is deceiving. At one time there was talk of dividing it into three units. That could still be done."

"Great. Good. Well, you really do know your stuff about this company."

"There's old equipment stored in that building. I've been telling AGC that all of that surplus needs to be scrapped. There's a lot of money in that scrap metal. No one has listened, though."

"I'm sorry to hear that." It would have fallen on Micky, since this was his account to have kept up with the company. Even though some of the businesses got taken apart and consolidated with others, the bottom line was that they were supposed to do whatever it took to get the business on solid ground. "Can we work together to clear that old equipment out? It makes sense to do that."

"Sure. It won't take long. I know a guy. One call and I can have it taken care of. Just wasn't my call to make without corporate weighing in since they bought us out."

"I understand. Well, consider it a go. Can you make that call today?"

"I can. Won't happen until Monday. Holiday and all."

She turned to her computer and typed in the request. "Thank you."

Edna had seemed disappointed, making her stomach grind a little as she started to share the good news with Bill. *"Good" being relative.* "Bill, you've been an exemplary employee with Porter's. Well, you know that already, but we really appreciate it." She slid the stack of papers in front of him. "I'd appreciate it if you won't disclose the details of this, but in reviewing your . . ." The rest was kind of like reciting from memory.

Only Bill didn't look sad at all. A big toothy grin spread across his face. His scruffy mustache and beard bounced as he grinned. That was a grin . . . wasn't it?

She was still talking, trying to read the expression, when he burst out in a guffaw.

"Ah-ha-ha. You're paying me to retire, and the bonus is . . ." He flipped through the pages. "Enough to buy the boat of my dreams. And then some. I'll be dipped in mud!"

Is that a good thing?

"This just doesn't happen to people like me." His eyes glinted as he lifted them to meet hers. "Not in small towns like this. This is great. Thank you." He pushed a thick hand under his nose. "Look at me getting all misty. Joy. That's what that is. Pure joy. Thank you."

She let out a breath. Finally, someone that saw it the way she did. It was good news. An opportunity. *Isn't retirement what we all really work toward anyway?* "There's one more thing, and this isn't in the documents, but I'll have them drawn up after the holiday if you agree."

"What is it?" His brows knit together. "Should've known there was a catch."

"No. No catch. All of that is yours. This is completely separate."

"Yeah?" He leaned in.

"Yes. I think you could help me get a few things done quickly. If you'll help me evaluate all the warehouse space, I'll pay you a consulting fee on top of that package."

"I don't have to do it?"

"No. The deal is the deal, but I hope you'll help me. We have a sporting-goods company that needs warehouse space that will bring more jobs to the area. I need to make sure it will work."

"More jobs to the area?" He eyed her. "And make some jobs go away."

"I don't know. Corporate thinks it's an either-or, but I'm thinking we might be able to do both. Their priority is getting that sporting-goods warehouse ready to roll starting January first. We're in a time crunch. I need to prove doing both is still viable. Can I count on you to help me?" She wrote a number on a slip of paper. "I'll pay you this. Per hour. On top of what you're getting."

"You're really trying to see if the factory can remain the same?"

"It might not be exactly the same, but it's a possibility. Yes. There's way more opportunity, I think, in the other buildings for the project they want to bring here. Help me prove it's feasible. But it has to stay between us for now. I don't want to worry everyone."

He didn't respond.

"Look. I promised this town I'd evaluate things quickly. I won't ask you to stay quiet long."

He nodded. "Have you talked to Buck about this?"

"Umm. Well, I don't . . ." She stammered for words to answer the puzzling question. "Do you mean gray-haired Buck who was making the chicken stew last night at the game?"

"That's the one."

"No. Why would I? Did he use to work here too?"

"Not exactly." One brow curled up. "Never mind. Yeah, I'll help you. Let's make this happen. When do we get started?"

"Now. Sign the package. Or take it home and review it."

He leaned forward and scribbled his signature on it. "Done." He tapped the pen on the desk and dropped it.

"Great. How about we meet tomorrow morning at the warehouse? Eight o'clock? You'll be back before Thanksgiving dinner is served."

He shook his head. "Nope. Can't do that."

"I'm sure your wife would understand—"

"No. I hunt on Thanksgiving Day. It's tradition. Unless I get that ten-pointer tomorrow; then you'll see me on Friday. If not, it's going to have to be Monday. I promised my grandson we'd get that elusive buck this year. I don't break family promises."

Seriously? He's putting hunting before work? Does he realize he just got laid off?

She glanced down at the hefty consulting rate on the paper in front of her.

"Not for any amount of money." He stood and shoved his hands in his pockets, and stared at her. "We could walk over there now. I just got laid off. Got nothing to do for the better part of the day."

She scrambled to her feet. "All right then."

Two hours later she'd completed the inventory of equipment, tagged everything for salvage, assessed the property, and discussed roadblocks with Bill. She had everything she needed to get the plan together to transition that building for the January first deadline, and Bill had reassured her that there was enough space for a considerable expansion in the building where the corporate apartment was to cover growth.

"Bill, I wish you a very successful hunting adventure."

He shook her hand. "Thank you. I wish you luck too. I don't know what all this means, but I'm trusting you to take care of this town. You hear me?"

"Yes, sir." His grip was firm, and his eyes were kind, but serious. "I'm going to do my best." Accomplishment coursed through her.

His lips pushed together. "Best isn't good enough." He shook his head and did a half turn and waved a finger in front of his nose. "This is a special town full of hardworking people. Good people. Do right by them. I'm happy. Some folks in this town aren't going to see it the same way that I do, though."

"I promise," she said.

"People with good character keep their promises. My granddaddy told me that when I was a boy. I live by that. I believe you have good character, Ms. Larkin." He tapped his nose and walked away. "See you Monday."

She walked back to her office. She'd promised, and she never promised in business. She wasn't the only one making these decisions, but something about that man who wouldn't break a family promise to a kid had challenged her to dig deeper too. Especially since it seemed that broken promises might have been part of what had led to the situation at this site.

Fairly confident she had what she needed to prepare this place for a soft landing, she gathered her papers and her laptop.

She jostled her heavy tote on her shoulder and started the long walk to the diner. She didn't mind it really. At least it was a peaceful enough walk today without that giant falcon swooping after her squawking today. Most of the shops had already closed for the holiday.

A cherry-picker truck lifted an orange-vested worker into the air as two others shouted orders from below to install Christmas decorations on the lampposts down Main Street. While others relaxed at home thinking about the huge meal that would be consumed the next day, six-foot zigzag garland Christmas trees with golden stars on the top were hoisted one at a time and affixed to the utility poles, bringing a dazzling splash of color to the landscape.

It's beginning to look a lot like Christmas.

CHAPTER FIFTEEN

·×·

Vanessa noted the sign on the diner door. CLOSED ON THANKSGIVING.

She squeezed by a cluster of people hanging out by the door, apparently waiting on takeout orders. She took a seat already knowing that she'd order the chef's salad for tonight, and an extra one to go for tomorrow.

The waitress, Lisa, walked over, but rather than exhibiting her usually audacious attitude she handed Vanessa a menu. "I'll get you some water while you decide."

"Thank you," she said, but she doubted the waitress had heard her over all the commotion. She pushed the menu to the side, and checked her phone.

"Know what you want tonight?" She slid a glass of water onto the table. "The special is spaghetti."

"I'm going to have the chef's salad. Light Italian dressing. And I'll take a second one packed up to go."

Lisa finished writing on her tablet with a pounce of her pen to the paper, grabbed the menu, and walked away. The conversation was louder than it had been before, making Vanessa a little lonely. Thankfully, her phone rang.

"Anna? Perfect timing. I was just ordering dinner."

"I was hoping you'd be done for the day by now."

"Wrapped up early. You'd be proud."

"I'm glad you're finally starting to listen to my advice."

You'll never be truly satisfied by work until you are fulfilled by your personal life. "Uh-oh. Don't go getting motivated to dish out more advice. I can only accept so much life balance at a time."

"Now, isn't that the pot calling the kettle black? You're the one always forcing change on others. Isn't that in your job description?"

"Forcing"? That sounded harsh. "In a way. Yes. I suppose I am, but sometimes in a good way." Vanessa turned and looked over her shoulder. The booth behind her was empty, and the other people in the restaurant were busy in conversations among themselves.

"Well, don't go wasting the best days of your life doing it."

How am I even supposed to know I'm living my best days? Compared to what? Or who?

"Speaking of good," Anna said. "I have good news."

"I love good news."

"I found a place to stay in Fraser Hills. It's absolutely adorable, affordable, and roomy enough for two."

"That's great. I hadn't gotten around to asking Lilene to do that yet."

"You're too busy for all of that. I took care of it. It was quite easy. Do you want me to send you my itinerary?"

"Sure. I can have the driver here in town come get you at the airport."

"I've already got all that arranged too."

"You're making me feel unneeded,"Vanessa teased.

"Hardly. I'm simply lightening your load so we can spend more time together. Is everything going to plan out there?"

"It is. I had a great day today. Really made some good progress."

"I'm so glad to hear that, because I found a slew of fun things to do out in that area. I know you have to work, but we can make time for a few things too. There's plenty to pick from."

"Wonderful."

"I'm not going to keep you. I just wanted to let you know that I found a place to stay and I'll see you soon."

"I can't wait." As Vanessa hung up the phone, Lisa slid the large chef's salad in front of her, and placed a brown paper sack with the top folded over on the table as she slid herself right into the booth bench facing Vanessa. "Look. I know you might think that this is none of my business, but I just can't let it go without saying my piece."

The smile in her heart faded.

"I heard what you did to Bill and Edna today. That was wrong, and Edna is too much of a lady to say it for herself, but that woman loved that job. It was her whole life. What do you think she's going to do home alone all day?"

"I'm really not at liberty to discuss this with you."Vanessa kept her voice as friendly and calm as possible.

"I'm sure you're not, and even if you did respond, I probably wouldn't believe you anyway. I knew you were trouble when you came to town." She circled a finger in the air outlining

Vanessa's face. "You with your snow-white smile, perfectly streaked hair and fancy handbags. What do you know about life in North Carolina?"

"Location didn't factor into the decision. I did what I thought was best for two employees who had shown years of dedication to the company."

"If you think this was the good news, I sure hate to hear and see what the bad news brings!"

"Order up" came from the kitchen window, followed by the ring of a bell.

"Excuse me." Lisa stood, and went to the counter to retrieve the next orders.

Vanessa ran her napkin beneath her eye. It shouldn't have surprised her that the news had practically beat her here this evening, but she hadn't expected it to result in negative consequences. She took out the compact mirror from her purse and brushed at the mascara below. Movement in the reflection caught her attention.

She closed the compact and turned around to face him.

"Buck? I didn't hear you come in."

"Hello. I'm here every night for dinner."

"Every night?"

"Yep. Can't make this kind of food for what I pay here, and they know what I like." He leaned back and slung an arm up on the back of the bench seat. "You've had a day, huh?"

"You could say that. I thought it was a good day. I guess that's a matter of opinion. I had good intentions."

"You know what they say about good intentions. The path to h—"

"You know, I never really understood that phrase. Why is it that people want to turn good intentions into something bad?

Is it that hard to believe that people really want to do good in this world?"

"Right. I know. I've been caught by that over the years too. Here's the thing. Sometimes you're so focused on what you think is the best in a situation, that you don't see the collateral damage. The dominoes falling behind the scenes. Trust me. The older I get the more I realize how much I really don't know."

Before she could answer, he got up and came around to her table, taking the spot that Lisa had been sitting in. "All I'm saying is, just slow down. I'm sure you're on a crazy schedule, especially with the holidays thrown into the mix. But if you take your time, you might realize there are other things right here in front of you that could change everything." He pushed his hand through his hair. "You might be very pleasantly surprised what solutions you come up with once you get to know these people, and their talents. Talent doesn't run out just because you get a few gray hairs on your head."

She blanched. "Edna and Bill?"

He shrugged. "Just saying."

"I honestly think that the very attractive packages I gave them were far more than they'll get later. There's no guarantee what'll happen a year from now."

"They were. But right now, it's almost the holidays and you just took their jobs away."

"But not their money. They can celebrate and relax and enjoy the whole thing."

"Money isn't everything. In fact, it's the least of it. You're a smart lady. You've got to know that." He gave her a look that made her feel like a teenager being caught. She just wasn't sure what she'd done wrong. That was the problem with small towns. Everyone was in everyone else's business. She wished right now a few of them would mind their own.

She turned to see Buck walk out and Mike walk in. The two men paused for the briefest of moments. No hello. No conversation, just the tiniest pause that seemed uncomfortable.

A whoosh of cold air followed Mike inside.

Vanessa pushed her fork around her salad bowl. She wished now that she'd ordered both salads to go. She looked up to hail Lisa over to get another box, but Mike was standing there.

"So, you work for AGC." Mike cocked his head.

"I do."

"Why didn't you mention that before?"

"You didn't ask. We were having chicken stew and watching a football game."

He gazed almost right through her.

"Didn't quite tell the truth, though, did you? Visiting your cousin?"

"I wasn't trying to hide the fact I worked for AGC. Believe me, I am quite aware that half the town knows my every move."

"You avoided the layoff question last night. Then today you laid off two of the best employees. Good people who have put their life into that company."

"Those were not layoffs. I offered those two longtime employees very nice packages. There's no guarantee what would happen down the road. I promise you I did what I thought was best. I've seen situations where people with that many years of dedicated service get practically overlooked. This was something I had in my power, and budget, to do. They made out much better by taking those packages now, rather than waiting to see what the future holds."

"So, you think you did them a favor?"

"I've seen the graying workforce get caught in the restacking of talent when factories are updated, or roles are changed, and it's not always pretty. I'm not saying it's fair . . . it's just what happens."

"I'm sure you believe that company line too." He dug his hands into his pockets. "Did you really give them any choice?"

"Of course. There's always a choice. You can't make someone do something they don't want to do. I discussed the package with them. It was their choice entirely."

"I see." But his expression said otherwise.

"Believe me, they were compensated very well for their contributions." She pulled her lips together, sorry she'd let him bait her into a discussion about it. "I don't owe you an explanation." She picked up her bag and walked out of the diner. Her heart pounded as she walked down the street.

Adrenaline pushed her along. She didn't bother to call Jimmy for a ride, instead walking all the way back to the warehouse, and wearing a blister on the back of her left foot.

When she got inside the apartment, she took her shoes off and then put the salad in the refrigerator.

What was it about this town that had made her break every one of her own rules? She shouldn't have engaged with Mike. It would take a miracle to keep things moving smoothly if the gossip went wild.

First, no Paris. No fancy Christmas town and probably no bonus after the worst assignment ever. If folks around here dug their heels in, she'd never pull this off by the first of the year.

Her cheeks stung as her body adjusted to the warm room. She made a hot cup of tea, then pulled the quilt from the bed and wrapped up in it on the couch. Walking had been a stupid idea, but Mike had really gotten under her skin. With each sip of tea, she yearned for answers.

She was too embarrassed to call Anna and admit to the chaos she was creating already. Buck's comments hadn't helped either, but his words, honest and patient, kept haunting her. She didn't want to be the domino that disrupted life in this small town. There had to be an answer. Something that worked for everyone. Something she could be proud of.

CHAPTER SIXTEEN

U nlike last Thanksgiving, this year the weather was mild enough for Mike to walk over to Lilene's for Thanksgiving dinner. Ever since Olivia had passed, Lilene had insisted he and Misty spend the holiday with her family, and they'd done it ever since.

He carried a box containing his homemade deviled eggs, as had become tradition, and a bottle of wine he'd been given as a gift. This year Misty had gone skiing with her friends. It was lonely without her. Probably the first of many changes to come now that she was driving.

As he walked up to Lilene and Norman's house, Mike thought of when he'd been a kid and trick-or-treated the white Cape Cod with navy-blue shutters. The cool house on the block, they'd always given out the full-size candy bars. Norman was much older than Mike, but they'd become good friends over the last few years.

Mike knocked on the door, the scent of sage, turkey, and home cooking making his stomach growl.

Lilene opened the door wearing an apron with a stressed-out turkey on the front and TOO BLESSED TO BE STRESSED underneath it. She pulled him inside. "Hey Mike. I was afraid when Misty decided to go skiing with the other kids that you'd bail too."

"No way. Happy Thanksgiving." He gave her a quick hug. "You know me better than that. I wouldn't miss a home-cooked meal from you."

"You always say that, but I know you're really here for the desserts."

"Guilty as charged." He handed her the box. "Thanks for having me."

"And my dinner wouldn't be complete without your deviled eggs. What are we going to do when Henny, Penny, Oprah Henfrey, and all those celebrity chickens of yours get too old to lay eggs?"

"I hate to tell you this but we're on the third generation of some of those names."

"I thought they'd lived an awful long time." She took the box. "Ooh, this is heavy." She looked inside and pulled out the bottle of wine. "What is this?"

"You know I don't drink the stuff. It was a gift from when we did that big parade up north."

"Lucky me! Come on in. Norman's watching the ball game with the others. The rest of my family went over to the cemetery." She led him into the living room. "They're supposed to be back in about fifteen minutes. Then we'll eat."

"Sounds good." The dining room table was set and the buffet was already filled with covered dishes. Card tables filled the den, and there was one in between the couch and fireplace too. Each one was covered with a fall tablecloth and a playful cardboard-and-tissue-paper turkey as a centerpiece. At each place setting Lilene had gone the extra mile, crafting a special place card and treat as was her tradition, and with over twenty people expected to pile in this house for the holiday that was a big task.

He lifted one of the crafted turkey place cards made out of peanut butter cookies with a candy corn beak and a tail of almond slivers. "Is this edible, Lilene?"

"Yes! Aren't they adorable? I made one for you to take to Misty too. Peanut butter cookies, chocolate, candy corn ... what's not to love?"

"You never cease to amaze me. Where do you find the time?"

"Oh, it's fun." She swatted a dish towel in his direction. "I love making them even if I did have to go back to the store twice for more cookies because Norm kept getting into them."

"They're my favorite," Norman yelled from the other room.

"Everything is his favorite." She shook her head. "That man. He's a snacker. Don't ask him to share his snacks with you. Oh, no. He's very stingy, but he's plenty happy to steal mine."

"You were just playing with those cookies," Norman shouted in his own defense.

Mike stopped when he saw Vanessa sitting next to the hearth chatting with Lilene's mother.

He turned to Lilene. "You didn't tell me *she'd* be here," he said in a low whisper.

Lilene blanched. "Shh. She'll hear you. She's a guest in this house. I'd already invited her before ... before all that happened. It's Thanksgiving. Be nice."

He tried to hide the aggravation flooding over him.

"Come on." She dragged him into the living room. "Vanessa, you've met Mike, haven't you?"

She leapt to her feet, her mouth parting slightly in surprise. "Oh? Yes. Almost every day actually since I've been here." She lifted her hand and waved with a smile. "Hi, again."

"Hello."

Lilene must have noticed the tone in his voice, because she immediately spun around toward Vanessa. "Vanessa, can you help me with the wine?" She lifted the bottle like a carrot luring a donkey.

"Sure. I'd be happy to." Vanessa took the bottle of wine and looked at the label. "Goodness gracious. I know this wine. This is an amazing blend. It's won awards." She turned the bottle. "It's the 2014 too. Where did you find this?"

"Mike brought it."

"It was a gift," he said. "My hitch has been in their annual parade for over fifty years. They always give me some kind of extra gift to thank us." He was bragging, something he rarely did. Something he seemed to be inclined to do in front of her.

"Fifty years?" She seemed impressed. "So, your family has been doing the horse thing for a long time." She stepped closer.

Is she flirting with me? "A very long time."

Her eyes sparkled, but he wasn't sure what emotion they held.

She licked her lips, then broke their gaze to look down and focus on the wine. "Well, this is not easy to find."

The vein in his neck throbbed. He was still mad at her, but she sure had a way of getting him off kilter. Mom was in great spirits when he'd spoken to her this morning, but that didn't make what Vanessa had done right.

"Enjoy it," he said. "I'm not much of a drinker except for a champagne toast on New Year's, but Mom always taught me to be gracious no matter what . . ." He paused. *Why am I even telling her this? She doesn't care,* and he shouldn't care if she did or not. She wasn't even his type. Beautiful? Yes. But she didn't belong here in this town, or in this house for that matter. Not that he'd ever say that to Lilene.

"Yes, well that's good advice. Your mother is a smart lady." Vanessa nodded to Lilene.

"I'm surprised to hear you admit that," he snapped.

Vanessa looked confused.

He couldn't let it ride. "Laying her off the day before Thanksgiving? Really? Because jobs might change in the future? What does that even mean?"

She blinked. "Edna is your mother?"

He shrugged and turned his back on her, walking into the living room.

A little sound, almost painful, escaped from Vanessa's gaping mouth. She dashed into the kitchen still holding the wine bottle.

Miss Rose, Lilene's momma, gave him a was-that-really-necessary look.

Mike felt scolded, but only for a half second when Norman snickered from his recliner. "I didn't have anything to do with this."

But you knew, Mike mouthed. "You couldn't text me a warning?"

Norman lifted his hands in the air. "I've been married to Lilene a long time. I pick my battles with her. This one ain't mine." He leaned over and flipped the lid back on the cooler next to him, snagging a beer.

"Thanks a lot." Mike started to join him until he heard his name mentioned in the kitchen. He leaned in toward their voices.

"Mike was born and raised in this town," Lilene said. "He's such a great guy."

"I don't think he's my biggest fan right now."

"Well, I'm sure you had your reasons for what you did to poor Edna. I have to admit, I wasn't too happy when I realized what was going on either. Laying off the poor woman right at Thanksgiving?"

Mike admired Lilene's spunk. More so when she was using it against Vanessa on his behalf. He'd been on the other end of Lilene's lectures before. It wasn't always pleasant.

"It wasn't a layoff. They had a choice, and they accepted the offer. Edna and Bill both."

"You don't need to explain to me. I know you're just doing your job. The people in this town are close. Word travels fast, and sometimes it's not exactly as it happened. It's better if you have complete transparency."

"People knew before I got down the block."

"Sure, sometimes it's a pain to have everyone know your business, but at the end of the day you've got the support of the whole town. Let me help you with how to communicate around here."

"I'm not at liberty to discuss some things."

"I see. Well, you have to trust someone. You know, Mike was married to my very best friend's daughter. She worked at Porter's too. When she died this whole town felt the loss. Their daughter wasn't even in school yet. I'm sure Mike didn't want everyone rushing in to help while he was grieving, but he let them. Sometimes you just have to let things happen the way they are meant to."

"That's got to be hard. Raising a daughter by yourself."

"Mike would've done fine raising her on his own. They have a very special relationship, but folks around here like to be a part of the solution."

Is she going to tell my whole life history to that woman?

He wanted to walk in and put a stop to the conversation, but Lilene meant well. Everything she'd said was true, and he wasn't ashamed of it. He'd have never gotten through losing Olivia had they not rallied like they had. This village really did raise his girl, and he was grateful for the help.

"Be nice to him, Vanessa. I'm sorry it might be a little awkward for you. When I invited you both I had no idea that things were going to go all kaphlooey at the office."

"Will Edna be coming too?" Vanessa sounded worried.

Mike was half tempted to text his mom to tell her to come over right now. Instead, he pulled himself away from their private conversation and joined Norman, who had just hollered like a buck in rut as the Panthers fumbled again, leaving Washington in a really good position to pull out a win.

The doorbell rang and Lilene's family flooded into the small house. The men all hunkered around the television, and the women overflowed the kitchen, talking and cackling louder than his hens at feeding time.

Kids played on the floor in the living room, while a group of others went outside to throw a football.

Mike was thankful that the house had filled up, making it less awkward to be in the same space with Vanessa.

Vanessa walked out of the kitchen with a tray of piping-hot sausage balls. Carrying the tray, she introduced herself and distributed the tasty snacks. "We've got more in the kitchen. Take a couple," she'd say. Everyone in the room seemed captivated by the Chicago woman. That had been his first impression too, but he wouldn't fall for those misleading cues again—the sweet smile and the way she lowered her lashes when she spoke. She wasn't as nice as she looked.

She set the half-empty tray on the table behind the sofa. "Can you reach these, Norman?"

"Oh yeah. I've got my eye on them. Thanks."

She patted Norman on the shoulder as she walked by.

Mike got up and got a beer out of the cooler. He popped the top with a loud *schhhpt,* then took a couple of refreshing guzzles. Hopefully, the ale would take the edge off.

He'd been so busy watching Vanessa walk out of the room that he'd missed the final winning play of the game. Every other guy in the room was now on his feet cheering. He let out a whoop for good measure.

A few minutes later Lilene stepped out of the kitchen, stuck her fingers in her mouth, and gave one of her famous whistles.

As a kid, Mike had once believed Lilene could shatter glasses with the high-pitched whistle if she tried. Or maybe it had been his dad that had said it. He couldn't really remember. That was one skill he'd never perfected.

Lilene motioned her arms in a big air hug. "Y'all gather around. That ball game ended at just the right time, and thankfully our men will be in a very good mood all afternoon . . . unlike last year." She glared in Norman's direction. "You know what I'm talking about." Everyone laughed. "Dinner is ready. There are enough seats for everyone and a couple of extras so no one bellyaches about not being able to sit where they want. I think everyone has met my special guest, Vanessa. Welcome to our family gathering. We're so thankful to have you-all here."

"Thank you." Vanessa's cheeks slightly blushed.

Lilene tiptoed, looking around the room. "Uncle Sonny, will you bless the food?"

"Sure thing." He raised his hand in the air and stepped forward closer to the food.

Everyone got quiet and Uncle Sonny began the blessing as he did every year. Mike missed having Misty at his side. He'd have to get more used to that. Man, she was growing up fast. A tear tickled his lash. He ignored it, squeezing his eyes tighter as Uncle Sonny continued the blessing and a long list of things they all should be thankful for—the meal, health, family. Then forgiveness. "Especially when it's hard," Sonny said. "Forgiveness is a great way to cultivate a heart of thanksgiving."

Like one of those days when he was sitting in the pew when the preacher said something that felt like it had been directed toward him, a pang shot through him. *Forgiveness?* And here he was carrying around anger over his mom's retirement package.

I could be grateful that the forced retirement would make her slow down. I've been on her about that for over two years.

But somehow it seemed wrong for some stranger with no vested interest to force the situation. He lifted his head to look Vanessa's way. Everyone joined in an enthusiastic "amen."

He hung back, letting the others load up their plates first. Lilene always made enough to feed everyone three times over and still have leftovers, so there was no rush.

Vanessa's lively laugh carried in from the other room.

He waited, watching to see where she'd sit before picking a spot himself.

She sat to the right of Lilene.

He picked up a plate and started filling it, planning to go

back into the living room, where most of the guys were gorging themselves during the next football game.

"Mike," Norman called out before he got out of the room. "Saved you a seat in here, man."

He let his eyes close for a half second. *Just that far from getting away clean.* He turned with a smile. "Great." He took the seat at the table, and placed his napkin in his lap, trying to keep his gaze toward Norman and not across the way where Vanessa was sitting.

Lilene's mother placed her hand on Mike's arm. "I'm so sorry I won't get to see that sweet little girl of yours this year."

Mike nodded. "She's not so little anymore."

"Well, little girls are always their daddy's little girl. How old is she now?"

"Sixteen going on thirty-two."

"Ha! I had one just like that."

Lilene set her fork down. "I know you're not talking about me."

Norman rolled his eyes. "She's still a know-it-all."

"Norman! That was not nice. And on Thanksgiving." She shook her fork at him, and then blew him a kiss. "I can't help it if I'm always right."

"Sad thing is . . . she usually is right. I can't even debate it," he admitted.

"Wouldn't do you any good anyway," Miss Rose said to Norman. "How're those giant horses of yours doing, Mike?"

Mike buttered a hot yeast roll. "Great. We won the nationals and that really helped us bring in top dollar with the young horses we sold this year. It's been a very good year."

"Mike raises draft horses," Lilene said to Vanessa.

"Percherons," Mike added.

"They're beautiful," Vanessa responded. "The day I arrived I saw him riding through town. I almost couldn't believe my eyes."

Norman laughed. "Sometimes he's got eight horses at a time clomping down Main Street."

"Guilty." Mike jammed a forkful of stuffing into his mouth. He'd really rather not talk about himself today.

Miss Rose then directed her questions to Vanessa.

"I take it you're not all that familiar with horses. I used to love to ride." She swatted Mike playfully on the shoulder. "Not big horses like his, but I used to go trail riding with my friends right up the mountain line here. I had the prettiest bay horse. That was a long time ago."

"I've never ridden," Vanessa said. "I think I'm okay with that. I don't think I want to be on top of something that weighs as much as my car but has its own moods and opinions."

There was a murmur of agreement around the table, and somehow that made Mike feel a bit alienated, like they'd chosen to be on Vanessa's side instead of his. Even if they had no idea that he was harboring ill will toward her at the moment.

Finally, the conversation slowed as everyone got serious about the food.

Lilene's brother, Larry, put his fork down and turned to Vanessa. "While you're in town you should get Mike to show you around his barn. It's really amazing how he has things set up to handle everything with limited help."

"Don't be impressed. It's nothing really," Mike said. "It was out of necessity."

"But it's ingenious!" Larry said. "And wait until you get close up on those horses. They are so gentle, and he can answer any question you can think of about them."

"Well, I've lived with them my whole life."

"Seriously, you have to ask him to take you over there."

Vanessa pressed her lips together. "No. I couldn't. I'm really busy. I have a lot to get done before the first of the year."

"Yeah, she's a busy lady. She's been here less than a week and has already done a few layoffs." Mike swirled his fork in the air. "Even let my mom go, didn't you, Vanessa?"

"Well . . ."

"It's okay. I'm sure everyone has already heard anyway."

"I really don't want to ruin Lilene's lovely Thanksgiving gathering, Mike. I'm sorry you don't understand—"

"Oh, I understand."

The air in the room seemed to almost vibrate. Norm and Lilene both looked like they were afraid to interject, and then one by one everyone except Miss Rose left the table.

"You're not the least bit sorry, are you?" Mike said to Vanessa.

"I am," she said with the most beautiful smile he'd ever seen. "I'm sorry you're so upset. I really did what I thought in the long run was the best."

"For the company maybe. Not for my mom. AGC swooping in and stealing Porter's has been nothing but bad news from the beginning."

"Steal?"

"It was a family business. Generations of Porters and most of the other family names in this town have made a lifelong living there."

Vanessa calmly lifted the napkin from her lap and pushed her chair back. "Lilene, thank you for the invitation. This has been absolutely lovely, but under the circumstances I'd better leave."

"I can give you a ride," Lilene's niece said. "I'm getting ready to go over to my boyfriend's house."

"Thank you." Vanessa stood.

Mike looked her way. "You're just going to avoid me the whole time you're in town?" It had come out low, and regrettably a little snarky.

"Probably for the best," she said.

"Not easy in a small town. I guess that means you won't be joining me for the parade." He hadn't meant to say that out loud.

Lilene spoke, all heads turning in her direction. "He asked her to the parade? Oooh."

Norman sputtered.

Mike ignored the comments, and focused on Vanessa.

She picked up her plate, and for a split second Mike wasn't entirely sure she wasn't going to lob the scoop of mashed potatoes still on her plate right at his forehead. But she didn't. "I got caught up in the moment. I'm really too busy to go to a parade. I'm here to do a job."

"Clearly that's a priority over anything and any*one,* but I said I'd take you. So, I'll take you." He eyed her as if he planned to keep his enemies . . . namely her . . . closer.

Lilene's niece stepped next to Vanessa. "You ready?"

She lifted one finger, then glared at Mike. "We'll see about that. As I mentioned yesterday, there's always a choice. No one can make anyone do something they don't want to do."

CHAPTER SEVENTEEN

Vanessa slammed the door to her apartment behind her. She wished the echoing sound would erase the whole afternoon. She never let people get under her skin like that. Especially about work, but she had, and her stomach was tied in knots over this afternoon. She could picture Lilene and her extended family talking about the crazy lady that ruined Thanksgiving for years to come.

How can I apologize big enough for that mess?

She swept the basket of goodies Lilene had left from the kitchen counter and marched into the living room. Hugging it to her chest, she sat cross-legged on the couch scrounging for comfort food. When she'd snacked her way through half of the contents, she still didn't feel any better.

She opened the bottle of North Carolina wine from the basket. It smelled like grape juice, definitely not the vintage

Mike had brought, but that was fine by her. She poured a glass, then opened the loaf of homemade bread, sliced some cheese, and made a little buffet for herself.

"You are so sweet, Lilene. You must have baked for two days to put this together."

And to think I didn't appreciate the Thanksgiving invite in the first place. I thought I was doing something nice for you. Instead I ruined everyone's day.

She lifted her glass of wine in Lilene's honor. "Sorry."

The wine was even sweeter than it smelled. She dug through the basket some more.

Cheese straws. Fresh pears, individually wrapped in wax paper with a hang tag that said FROM OUR TREE. If a partridge flew out, she wouldn't be surprised. Another tin was filled with cookie bars drizzled in chocolate. She plucked one from the carefully arranged selection and popped it into her mouth.

She had no idea what it was. Rich, nutty, sweet, and a bit salty too.

She reached into the tin again and again while she turned from channel to channel trying to find something to watch on television, only the next time she reached into that tin, she hit the bottom.

I ate them all?

She pulled a blanket over herself, and then switched off the television.

Coming to this town the week of Thanksgiving was ridiculous. She should've stood her ground with Edward. Then again, she wouldn't have uncovered the discrepancies in the building use and profitability of Porter's yet.

Didn't really matter. What was done was done. She drifted off to sleep on the couch.

*

Friday morning, Vanessa woke disoriented. Never one to sleep on the couch, much less in her clothes, she put on her workout gear to get back on her schedule. Before she left for her run, she texted Jimmy to arrange for a ride to the office. Everyone except for the retail-store staff would be off today.

By the time she got to Porter's, the store was packed with active buyers leaving with large bags of holiday gifts. Vanessa used the front door, her mood lifting instantly from the smiles of the shoppers and the Christmas music coming from the speakers.

Upstairs the offices were empty. She hadn't noticed all the pictures hung in this hallway before. She stopped, looking at each one. The founder of Porter's, employees of the year. Edna and Bill among them. She took note of the others to see where they fell on the resource evaluation.

Thank goodness she didn't recognize any of the other names.

In her office, she reviewed all of the original milestones and goals. There was no reason she couldn't achieve every single one of them without disturbing Porter's at all. The only overlap would be if the sporting-goods company required meeting facilities, but they were not on the original plan. There was adequate office space for the day-to-day personnel at both warehouse buildings. If Edna wanted to turn down the retirement-package offer, she wouldn't recommend it, but her job could probably be carried a while longer.

She rubbed her hands together. "More than one way to get things done." Satisfied, she put her hands on her hips.

"Oh, sorry. I can wait out—"

"Bill? Hi."

"I heard you talking to someone. You on the phone?"

"No. I was talking to myself. I didn't expect to see you until after your big hunting weekend. Come in. Have a seat."

"Gladly. Got that big buck yesterday. Best Thanksgiving ever. You should have seen that kid's face. Man." He grabbed the phone from his shirt pocket. "Here." He swept and tapped, then handed his phone her way. "Would you look at that?"

A young boy in bright orange clothing stooped next to a deer with antlers as tall and wide as a tree.

"Been after that elusive buck for three years," Bill said. "He really grew over the summer. Enough rain for lots of food. Have to say it made me even happier for my grandson to get that fine buck than if I had done it myself."

She didn't really understand the attitude about killing Bambi's dad, but she kept her mouth shut, smiled, and returned the phone.

"And here you are." She was genuinely happy that he'd killed that buck yesterday, but for her own reasons.

"Yes, ma'am. As promised, and I have a team of four guys ready to take care of things. Honestly, I don't think it'll take but a few days. These guys are ready to work through the weekend to knock it out. I'm assuming they can clock in and out as usual?"

"Yes. Absolutely." She'd have paid them extra, but this worked out even better.

"We're going to start with scrapping that old equipment. It'll take most of the day, and then we'll clear everything else out."

"That works for me."

Bill slapped his hands on the arms of the chair, then rose to his feet. "I'll check in with you right here on Monday morning with the complete report."

She handed him her business card. "Call me if you hit any snags, or need anything."

He tucked the card into his pocket and walked out.

Today was treating her much better than yesterday.

She picked up her phone and dialed Edward's phone again. He still hadn't returned any of her calls, but he'd surely be back home for the holiday. She closed her eyes, hoping for an answer. On the third ring, a woman answered with a cheerful hello.

"Oh?" Vanessa pulled the phone from her ear wondering if she'd misdialed, but the display showed that she'd dialed Edward. "Hi. Happy Thanksgiving. I'm so sorry to call on the holiday weekend. This is Vanessa Larkin; I work for Edward. I was hoping I could catch him at home today. I've been leaving him messages all week, and no luck."

The woman laughed. "Glad it's not just me. I had the same problem. Hang on. I'll get him for you."

"Thank you so much."

"Hello?"

"Edward. I'm so sorry to bother you, but I need to discuss a couple things with you about the Porter's project."

"Is there a problem?"

"Not entirely bad ones, just things here onsite don't match up with the reports Micky prepared. Am I missing part of the story about Porter's, and the warehouse project? There's a ton of old equipment that needs to be scrapped. It's not on the inventory, it's taking up most of the space in one of the buildings. They've been waiting for approval from corporate to scrap that junk since we bought the place."

"So, scrap it. The mission is straightforward. Porter's isn't making money. We'll repurpose the buildings for the warehouse space. It's better than the town losing the business altogether. At least there'll be other jobs, and we'll increase our bottom line. What's the problem?"

"Porter's *is* making money, Edward. It's not huge, but the numbers that have been reported are against the square footage of the entire footprint. Porter's is only using a very small portion of all the properties owned in this portfolio. There is already vacant space once we get the rest of the scrap moved out. They've increased efficiencies since we bought them, the sales are steady, and—"

"But Micky was very clear that—"

"Sir, I'm not sure exactly what happened the last time Micky was in town, but more than a few people are saying they were flat-out promised things wouldn't change, and there's nothing in the contracts indicating changes coming. That clause was completely stricken."

"Not anything about changes not coming either, though, right?"

Did you really just say that? Was it an intentional gray area just to get them to sign?

"It's business, Vanessa. Take care of it as we discussed. Micky doesn't have any reason to misrepresent that account, and quite honestly even if they are *not* losing money, they aren't making enough for us to not move forward with this warehouse project."

"But we can do both. Easily."

"There are only so many people in that town."

"I took a look at the surrounding counties. With the right

compensation package, I believe we can pull plenty of good resources into the area. I can make it work."

"Vanessa. We have a schedule to meet. I promise we are going to treat everybody—I mean everybody—with dignity, fairness, and respect."

"But . . ."

"We can't take a chance on not being able to meet the workforce needs of the warehouse."

"You'll have both. You'll have the warehouse space you need in the timeline, but still maintain Porter's. I don't think it's fair to them to close. It's simply not necessary. That company is part of the fabric of this town."

"And if it changes, that town will survive. End of story."

Calling him on the holiday may have been a bad idea.

At this moment she wasn't getting the respect from Edward that she was used to. How could she convince complete strangers that he was in their corner . . . when clearly he didn't care? She took a steadying breath, but kept her mouth shut. There was no use arguing with him now.

"You know what," he said. "You do whatever you have to do to hand me over the thirty-thousand-square-foot facility for Outdoor Sports Pro as outlined in that contract. I really don't care what you do with anything else."

"Yes, sir." She disconnected the call, then closed her eyes and lifted her chin to the sky. Enough gray area in that statement that she could stealthily do the right thing and ask for forgiveness later.

I have a feeling this is going to be the worst Christmas ever. I'm just not sure if it's going to be bad for the town, or my career. Please help me come up with the right way to handle this.

A quiet tap at her office door broke her concentration. Expecting to see Lilene—not for anything business-related, but rather with some home-baked goodie or reminding her to "take a break!" with that big grin that was always on her face—she blinked twice before she put it all together. "Anna? What are you doing here?"

Vanessa clambered out from behind the desk to hug her cousin.

"I hope it's okay," Anna said. "I know you said you'd call, but I couldn't wait to see you. I was so excited."

"I can't believe you're here. This is a great surprise. How did you know where to find me?"

"I knew you'd be working. There are some things that anyone who knows you could guess. But we'll work on that while we're together." Anna wiggled her brows playfully. "Isn't this the cutest little town you've ever seen? How have I never heard a peep about it before?"

Lilene walked up behind Anna. "Best-kept secret. We don't want a bunch of city folk moving here. We saw what happened the next town over. New people built big ol' fancy houses, and then complained about the farm animals and the farm equipment—which were there long before those city biddies moved in. It was a huge fuss."

"I bet," Vanessa said.

"We like the town the way it is," Lilene said.

"I can see why. It's absolutely charming." Giving Lilene a nod of appreciation, Anna said, "I bumped into this nice lady downstairs. I was asking the gal at the register where the offices were and she swooped right in to help me."

Vanessa said, "Thank you, Lilene. What were you doing down there?"

"I had some goodies packed up for the staff that is working today. Just a friendly gesture from me, and I did do a little Black Friday shopping."

"You're really thoughtful." Vanessa admired the endless amount of energy Lilene put into her life in this small town.

"Mike said something yesterday about Vanessa meeting up with a cousin here over the holidays, but I thought he was mistaken. Then here I bump into you. What a small world!" Lilene pointed her thumb toward Vanessa. "So, you two are cousins. I'm glad you've got family here with you. This is a wonderful place to spend the holidays."

"And who is Mike?" Anna looked way too interested in that.

"Oh, that's a long story, and it didn't end happily. Don't ask."

Lilene said to Anna, "You just let me know if you want to do a little sightseeing. I know everyone in this town."

Anna's face lit up. "That sounds lovely."

"I'll let you two catch up," Lilene said, "but we have lots of holiday fun going on over the next couple of weeks. I'll make a list of the things you two won't want to miss."

"Thank you, Lilene."

Lilene walked out of the room.

"She's so nice, Vanessa," Anna said. "I can't believe how cute this town is. We're going to have so much fun."

"I'm glad you're here, but I've got my work cut out for me."

Anna didn't seem to understand the significance. "Nothing you can't handle. I know you."

"I hope so. I'll fill you in over dinner." She reached for her sweater. "It's freezing in this place. Come on. There's a great little diner here."

They walked down the street, stopping to enjoy the holiday décor in the shop windows. It was as if elves had spent all night, while the town was in a turkey coma, working to spruce up the place.

"It'll be so pretty at nighttime. I love those big artsy Christmas trees on the poles," Anna remarked.

When they got to the Blue Bicycle Bistro, the bicycle on the rooftop sign now had a Santa standing next to it.

"Seat yourself," Lisa called out.

"Thank you." Vanessa was happy to see that her usual booth was empty.

As they slid into the booth, Anna told Vanessa about her drive from Atlanta.

Lisa walked up to the table.

"We're going to both have the special," Vanessa announced. "And water?"

"Yes, with lemon please," Anna said, then leaned her elbows on the table and continued her story. "It was a beautiful day for a ride through the mountains. Next week's forecast looks a little iffy." She pressed her hands together, and grinned. "We might even see some snow here."

Vanessa had tired of snow a long time ago. Chicago promised white winters, and if you trudged through enough icy and snowy days you learned quickly how to dress in enough layers to stay warm, and still be stylish. Not that the latter made much difference around here. She forgot some folks pined for a peek of the white fluffy stuff over the holidays.

They ate over casual conversation, picking up right where they'd left off.

Vanessa placed her napkin on the table. "There hasn't been one meal that I haven't enjoyed here yet."

"Let's splurge on some dessert. Did you see those cakes in the case when we came in? That one looked like a banana cake with the vanilla wafers on the side."

"Works for me. Want to split a piece?"

"No, I do not. What I can't eat I'll take back for breakfast with my coffee in the morning." Anna slapped the menu closed again. "I'll have decaf tonight." She grabbed her purse and dug for her phone. "I'd better call the inn and let them know I'll be later than I'd planned, and get some directions. I tried to find it on my GPS, but it didn't come up."

Lisa came over and took the order while Anna spoke on the phone.

"Right now," Anna said, "I'm having dessert with my cousin on Main Street at the Blue Bicycle Bistro." She pulled an ink pen from the front pocket in her purse. "Route 29?" She shrugged toward Vanessa. "I don't think I came in on 29. I came in from the south. From Atlanta, up 85 and then west on 321."

Vanessa could only hear Anna's side of the conversation, but something seemed wrong.

"Yes, Georgia." She pulled her hand to her mouth. "No. North Carolina. Really? I'm so disappointed."

Vanessa tried to get Anna's attention to ask what was wrong, but Anna wasn't making eye contact.

Lisa brought the two pieces of cake and coffee over to the table.

"This looks amazing," Vanessa said to Lisa.

"Wait until you taste it. Let me warn you, once you try my cakes, you will crave them forever. You've been forewarned. I can't be held responsible."

"Oh great. I'll be two sizes bigger before I leave town if I'm not careful." Vanessa was still laughing with Lisa when Anna hung up the phone.

"All set?" she asked Anna.

"You won't believe this." Anna started doctoring her coffee. "I made an Airbnb reservation in this cute house that even had a Christmas tree set up already."

"How lucky was that?"

"Not quite as lucky as I'd hoped." She stabbed the banana cake like it was an unwelcome guest. "Apparently, it's in Fraser Hills, Vermont, not North Carolina. I can't believe I did that. I was so proud of myself for figuring that website out. It was a great deal too."

"Oh, no."

"They've been really nice about it. Refunded me and everything. I'm really sorry. I thought it looked like the perfect place for some fun and relaxation, and I know you already said there's no space for me at the little apartment they put you up in. Now look what a mess I've made."

"Don't be silly. Surely there's somewhere else in town."

Lisa grimaced. "Not really."

Anna shoveled a bite of cake into her mouth and moaned.

"Didn't I tell you? That cake is the best, isn't it? My great granny's old recipe. It's addictive," Lisa said.

Vanessa took a bite too. "I may eat this every day."

Lisa laughed and turned to Anna. "I already warned your friend here."

"We're cousins," Anna explained. "We're spending the holidays together for the first time in years, only my reservation got messed up. Do you know of any place to stay around here?"

"We're always booked up from Thanksgiving to New Year's. As far as I know, there's no room anywhere."

"I'm so sorry, Vanessa. I'll look for something in the next town."

"Don't be silly. We'll make it work." From over Vanessa's shoulder she heard, "I couldn't help but overhear you ladies."

It was Buck. Again. She turned around in the booth. "I didn't hear you come in."

"I'm stealthy like that." He smiled toward Anna and flipped his hand up in a wave. "Hi, ma'am."

"Oh, Buck. This is my cousin, Anna. She lives down in Georgia."

"Hello, Anna." Buck tilted his head, his gray hair brushing the top of his collar. "I've got a guesthouse no one is using. Your cousin is welcome to stay there."

"Nice to meet you." She thrust her hand in the air, giggling as she waved, then leapt from the table and practically skipped to his. "Oh gosh, Buck, thank you—"

By golly, she's flirting.

"Very nice to make your acquaintance, Anna. Where in Georgia you from? Beach, city, or mountains?"

"Outskirts of Atlanta."

"Ahh. Best of all worlds, I guess. Although I'm fond of the slower pace of smaller towns like this myself. The guesthouse is spacious. Two bedrooms, and room for a Christmas tree too. You could both stay there. It's just around the corner. You can even walk from Main Street when it's not too cold."

"I love this place already," Anna said.

"It's a good place to live." Buck's smile wiggled his mustache.

"It suits you," Anna said softly. "You look very happy."

In all Vanessa's years she'd never seen her cousin even talk about flirting. Before Vanessa had been born, Anna's fiancé had been killed in a car accident. She'd always said he'd been her first and only true love. Not once had she been known to go out on a date.

Vanessa turned around in her seat again, facing Buck. He *was* good-looking. "Are you sure you wouldn't mind letting Anna use the guesthouse? It *would* be fun to have a Christmas tree. I don't think we could very easily drag one up in the apartment they've put me in."

Buck's mustache poofed, a grin forming below it. "I heard they had you in the warehouse apartment."

"Nothing's a secret around here."

"Except that you have a beautiful cousin. Welcome to town, Anna."

Anna flushed, then cleared her throat, looking as if she was struggling to keep her cool. "Thank you."

"If you like, you two can follow me over once you get finished eating dinner."

"Well, then please join us, and let me at least spring for your dessert," said Anna.

"I never turn down dessert."

Chapter Eighteen

Anna and Vanessa followed Buck over to his house to check out the guesthouse.

Vanessa worried that it might be hard to graciously back out of the invitation if the place turned out to be less than desirable. She didn't need any more blemishes in this town while she was still working on the project.

Buck's blinker lit up, and then he turned down a tree-lined driveway that seemed to go on for about half a mile.

When the house finally came into view, Vanessa said, "Holy cow. I did not expect him to live in a house like this in this little town." Vanessa wondered how many bedrooms were in the sprawling home.

"This is a *very* nice home." Anna leaned forward over the steering wheel, taking it all in. "I can't wait to see the guesthouse."

Landscape up-lighting gave the house a warm glow against

the darkening evening sky. Through the double glass-front doors, hundreds of colored lights twinkled from a tall Christmas tree.

Buck's brake lights brightened as he stopped. He got out of his pickup and walked back to their car.

Anna lowered her window.

"The guesthouse is around back. Just follow me. I'll pull over to the right side, y'all can pull up around me and park in the spot right in front of the door. I'm going to turn on the back driveway lights over on that pole. I'll leave them on while you're staying. It's easier to see where you're going with them on."

"Thank you," Anna said.

Buck crossed the driveway to a pole with a birdhouse on it. With one quick touch, the asphalt driveway lit up like a runway. He gave them a thumbs-up as he walked back to his truck and led the way.

The driveway split in two directions.

When Buck pulled off to the right, Anna swung her car around him and parked in front of an adorable white house. She hopped out of the car. "This is the guesthouse? I love how it looks like a real carriage house."

"Used to be." He waved them to follow. "Come on. I'll give you the nickel tour."

Vanessa noted the old light fixtures, and the trendy barn-style doors.

"Welcome. I wasn't expecting anyone, so we'll have to uncover a few things, but I think you'll be comfortable here." Buck pulled out his keys and unlocked the door. The rooms lit up and the gas fireplace came on as he walked around flipping switches.

"You two can make yourselves at home. Vanessa, there's a second bedroom. You're more than welcome to stay here instead of over at the warehouse."

"We're going to have so much fun. Buck, this is perfect. It's so homey, and look at this kitchen."

Shimmering granite countertops, a Viking range with bright red knobs and double ovens, and an old farmhouse sink—this kitchen was big enough for a group of cooks to cook in at the same time. If this was the guesthouse kitchen, she couldn't imagine what the one in the house looked like.

Buck pulled sheets from the furniture revealing comfortably worn fine leather in rich deep reds, forest greens, and golds.

"There's a storage area at the back of the garage with Christmas decorations in it," Buck said. "Use whatever you'd like. Really, treat this place like your own while you're in town."

"We can't stay here for free. We'll pay you, and we'll hire a cleaning service when we leave to be sure it's back shipshape," Vanessa said.

"Oh yes, I insist," Anna said. "I'd planned to pay for that little place I'd rented anyway. You're doing us a huge favor. You saved the day."

His smile was humble, his cheeks reddening. "Well, I'm glad I could help out. I haven't saved any damsels in distress in way too long." He shuffled his feet, obviously a little uncomfortable. "This is on the house. Really. It'll be nice to know that it's being used."

Vanessa and Anna looked at each other, not arguing but knowing they'd make it right.

"The panel box is in the garage, but I don't expect you'll

have any problems," he went on. "The fireplace switch is here next the mantel. The heat is controlled there in the hall. I think that's all you need to get you through the night. Oh, let me make sure . . ." He walked into the kitchen and pulled out a drawer. "Yep, a whole bunch of those coffee pods."

"You're the best," Anna said. "Thank you so very much."

"Nah, just in the right place at the right time. I've been eavesdropping on your cousin all week. I'm glad I could do something to help rather than only dish out unsolicited advice, which by the way I'm kind of known for."

All three of them laughed at that.

"Can I help you with your luggage?" Buck asked.

Vanessa stepped between them. "No, I can help her. You've already been kind enough to get us all settled in. Thank you."

"Okay." He walked toward the door with Vanessa and Anna following him. "I guess I should mention there's pretty much nothing but coffee and condiments in here. I gave up grocery shopping when it became only me. I can eat down at the Blue Bicycle for just as cheap anyway, plus no cleanup and none of the waste. You'll have to stock the kitchen here, or maybe I'll see you over at the diner."

"No problem, we can do some shopping," Vanessa said, "but that does explain why I kept bumping into you down there. It's great food. I travel so much that I've learned to find a place with a nice varied menu and stick to it for the duration. So, I know how hard it is to cook for one."

They walked outside. Anna clicked the button on her key fob, sending the trunk lid up in the air. Vanessa stepped in front of her to get the bag. When she turned around, Buck and Anna were exchanging phone numbers.

It was kind of adorable, and weird all at the same time. She'd always known Anna as the fun cousin, but never so flirty or even the tiniest bit interested in anyone. This was a whole new side of her.

Vanessa wheeled Anna's bag into the house and wandered down the hall to check out the bedrooms.

Both were equally beautiful. One was painted a warm taupe with crisp white moldings. The bed was in front of old wooden whitewashed barn doors on what looked to be an authentic old iron rail. The bedspread was feminine, in a creamy tone-on-tone pattern with wispy skirted sides that swept the floor. Pillows in rich wine-colored velvet and cream, piled two and three deep, covered half the bed. It would probably take fifteen minutes to get them all moved off to call it a night. A ladder made of birch branches held an extra blanket.

Across the hall, the bedroom had floor-to-ceiling windows looking over the gardens in two directions. The raised ceiling made of whitewashed boards made it look as if you could dance on the ceiling if someone could just tip the room upside down. She pictured herself dancing on the whitewashed ceiling as the floor, the ceiling fan a pub table, holding a flute of the finest champagne and her skirt flowing around her ankles with each twirl.

An area rug covered most of the dark-stained wooden floors, probably original to the house.

She parked Anna's luggage in this room wondering what fantasies would dance in her cousin's head when she saw it.

"Oh, my word," Anna's voice echoed from the bathroom next door. "Did you see this tub?"

Vanessa went to see what all the fuss was about, but when

she walked into the bathroom she had to agree. "Oh, my goodness. This is gorgeous. I've always loved those freestanding tubs."

Anna lifted the top of a glass apothecary jar, scooped up rose petals, and sprinkled them back into the jar. "Seriously? These smell so good. Do you think we can put these in the tub?"

"Sometimes you just have to ask for forgiveness later. This is definitely one of those situations."

"Did you ever in a million years expect this?" Anna stood there shaking her head.

"No. Definitely not. I also wouldn't expect him to open up this part of his home to strangers."

"Not complete strangers," Anna reminded her. "I mean he said you two have been talking in the diner all week." She ran a finger across the dresser. "It's spick-and-span. Do you think they rent it out?"

"I don't know. I was under the impression the corporate apartment was the only place to stay for miles."

"Well, thank goodness he was sitting behind you," Anna said. "Why don't you take my car and go get some of your stuff so you can stay here tonight. I'll get unpacked and soak in that amazing tub."

"I'll do that."

"Here's the key to the car." She dug it out of her front pocket. "And this place."

"Seems like a nice start to our holiday."

"All we need is a Christmas tree."

Vanessa drove back over to the warehouse, noting the turns on the back of a gas receipt, since she had no idea what the address was. At least the crazy week was ending on a higher note.

Chapter Nineteen

Vanessa pulled into the parking area at the warehouse.
I'm really not going to miss staying here.

In front of the door, there was a cardboard box with big letters on the side that read THIS SIDE UP. As she got closer, she noticed the bright red envelope tucked into the top flap.

The box was heavy. Instead of taking it upstairs she took it over to the car and set it on the floorboard. It was probably leftovers from Lilene. That woman ran on thoughtfulness and kindness.

She let herself into the warehouse using the jiggly twist-lift approach Lilene had shown her, then ran up the stairs and grabbed pajamas and a change of clothes. Halfway to the door, she stopped and repacked all the rations Lilene had stocked for her to take over to the carriage house, too. They'd have plenty to snack on for a while until they had time to go to the grocery store.

She took two of the bags downstairs and put them in the passenger seat, then left the door open while she went back in to get the rest.

As she got closer to the car, she heard something behind her. She looked but couldn't see anything in the dark. Before she took a step, there it was again. A bark?

She walked over to the car.

A fluffy burst of gold scared the bags right out of her arms. She leapt back, letting out a yelp of her own.

"What are you doing in there?" It was a puppy. A little guy dancing around in the leather seat like he belonged. He opened his mouth in a wide yawn that sounded almost like a hello.

"You are the cutest thing." She collected everything that had fallen and put the bags in the car.

In response to the rustling bags, the puppy stepped back and barked, then pounced forward.

"Aren't you the little guardian dog? Where is your momma?"

He cocked his head to the side, then hopped down out of the car wagging his tail so hard his hiney lifted from the ground.

She reached down and picked him up.

He kissed her face.

"No," she reprimanded him for the assault, but really it wasn't so bad, until he licked right up her nose. "Eww. Okay, that's enough."

He took a mouthful of her hair and chomped.

She grabbed it back. "That is not for puppies."

He almost sounded like he was laughing as he panted with a "hh-hh-hh"; then he leapt from her arms and hightailed it across the gravel, his back feet kicking up like a burro's.

She stood there smiling. *Probably late for dinner.*

Vanessa got in the car, keeping a careful watch for her new

little friend as she left, but it seemed he was long gone. She turned up the radio on the ride back. No surprise, Anna had been listening to Christmas music on her drive. She wished she were a little more like her sometimes.

She pulled in front of the carriage house and carried everything inside. She was finishing putting away all the food and snacks that Lilene had gotten her when Anna walked out in a big fluffy robe.

"Did I die? Because seriously, this is heaven."

"I hope not, because we've got a lot of time to make up for." She hugged Anna. "It's so good to see you."

"You too. I forgot to ask you earlier, how was dinner last night? With your assistant's family?"

"It was lovely." She hesitated. "That's not entirely true. Well, I didn't actually stay very long."

"Why not?"

"It turned out that one of the guests was the son of the woman I gave a retirement package to. He wasn't appreciative. It was awkward."

She regretted not even getting the chance to get a sip of that wine.

"Oh, honey. I'm sorry. That's got to be hard."

"It is. Especially because I meant well. There were two outliers who have been eligible for full retirement for years. I gave them really nice incentive packages to ensure they'd get what they'd earned from Porter's, with a nice bonus. When things change, you just never know who or how people are going to be affected. As old as they are, it's not likely they'd get picked up for warehouse positions. I was trying to protect them."

"No good deed goes unpunished."

"That's what they say."

"Give them some time. They'll soften to the idea. I'm sure it just came as a shock."

"Bill took it great. He's already planning to buy the boat of his dreams with the extra money. Edna on the other hand looked upset at first, but seemed fine when she left. It was her son who came unglued. And about half of the town on her behalf."

"Well, look on the bright side. Today has been a much better day."

"It has. Oh!" Vanessa jogged over to the door. "I almost forgot." She ran outside and got the box out of the car.

"What do you have there?" Anna asked from the front door.

"I don't know. Lilene must have left it at the warehouse door for me. Probably leftovers or something yummy."

"This has already been the best Christmas I've had in years, and we've only been together a few hours."

Vanessa laughed, but she honestly knew exactly how Anna felt. She placed the box on the kitchen counter, then removed the envelope and ran her finger under the edge, and slid out the card. On the front, a pair of shiny black horses pulled a red open sleigh through snowy streets with a black dog running ahead of them.

"Isn't that a beautiful card," Anna remarked from over her shoulder. "It almost looks like this town, doesn't it?"

"It does. Probably is. Lilene is very in touch with every facet of the town. The woman should be the mayor." She opened the card and her head jerked back. "Oh?"

"What is it?"

"This isn't from Lilene." She closed the card and tucked it back into the envelope.

"What are you hiding from me?" Anna grabbed the card

and stepped out of reach. "Ohh." She raised her eyebrows, a wide grin spreading across her face. "This is from that chicken-stew man that asked you to the parade. Mike. How nice."

Vanessa plucked the card back from her. "It's a mess is what it is." She opened the box and lifted the Crock-Pot from it. "I'm not sure if we should even eat this. What if he's trying to poison me?"

"Vanessa. Don't be ridiculous. You said yourself everyone in this town is nice."

"Everyone but me. I gave his mother a package, encouraging her to take her retirement."

"It's not like you fired her."

"No! I gave her a very nice severance package, and a bonus along with her earned retirement. Trust me, it's better this way. There's no telling where she'd land when the warehouse comes in. A lot of things could change, and not everyone is going to be as focused on the employees as I am. I was honestly trying to protect the two oldest, most senior people working for the company while I could." She let out a sigh. The more she explained it the worse it sounded, even to herself. "Her son is overreacting. Totally unreasonable. He's making me out to be the most uncaring person in the world."

"I see. And this is the same unreasonable guy who left you this Crock-Pot of homemade soup?"

"It's stew actually." She folded her arms in front of her. "He's just trying to make me feel bad now."

Anna took a step back. "You don't really believe that, do you?"

"Maybe I do. I don't know. Great. Now you think I'm horrible too."

Anna didn't say a word; she simply took the Crock-Pot

over to the counter and plugged it in. "No. I don't, but I do think you're overthinking that man's intentions. The note says that he wants to meet you for the parade before it starts."

"He was very mad at me yesterday. This doesn't make sense." She sat on the couch and dropped her head into her hands. "I know better than to get involved with people in these situations. What was I thinking?"

"That you might have some fun?"

"All the time I have for fun will be well spent with you."

"Thank you, but I've been telling you that you need to get your priorities straight. I'm glad to be among them, but you're letting work become your everything. Vanessa, you're going to regret this down the road. Believe me. I know."

"What exactly do you mean by that? I always thought you were so happy with your carefree lifestyle."

Anna walked over and hugged her. "Everyone wishes they'd done something differently. The problem is the longer you avoid life, the harder it becomes to revisit those things in the future, no matter how badly you might want them."

Vanessa could see the pain in Anna's eyes. Had that always been there?

"Don't ask for details, just take into consideration the suggestions I've made. I only want the best for you. Your momma would want that too."

Blinking back tears that always came when she thought about Mom, she nodded. "I'm so grateful you've always been there for me."

"You're welcome. Now let's get some rest. It's been a long day," Anna said.

They turned off most of the lights and went to their rooms.

From between the crisp white sheets of the king-size bed, Vanessa said, "Good night, Anna. I love you."

"I love you too. This is the best Christmas gift you could ever give me."

Vanessa closed her eyes, thinking about what things she should be focusing on aside from work. Her mind was blank.

*

The next morning, Vanessa awoke after the best rest she'd had in a long time. It seemed to be very early, but when she checked her phone, she found that it was nearly eight. The heavy curtains had fooled her into thinking it was still dark out. Today was Saturday, thank goodness. She slipped her feet into slippers. The smell of fresh coffee hit her as soon as she stepped into the hallway.

"Good morning, Anna," she said, looking for her.

She made a cup of coffee and turned on the fireplace. Outside everything was white. A light snow had fallen overnight. She watched birds flutter through the nearly bare trees outside the windows.

Suddenly, Anna strutted past the window, her hands shoved deep into the pockets of her bright red coat. The door eased open, and Vanessa sat on the couch watching as Anna tiptoed through the entry hall, pulling her scarf from her neck.

"Happy snow day," Vanessa said.

"You scared the bejeebies out of me. But yes. It's wonderful. It snowed last night. It took everything I had not to wake you when I came out here for water and it was snowing and swirling at four. It was breathtaking."

"You should have."

"I won't lie. I did peek into your room, but you looked like you were sleeping so peacefully. Besides, there's more snow in the forecast."

"I hope there's a snowman in our future."

"We'll consider this a warm-up." Anna winked. "You know, for the real thing."

"Thanks for making the coffee before you left."

"My pleasure. I'm going to get a cup for myself right now." Anna's spoon clanked as she added cream and sugar. "What do you want for breakfast?"

"I don't know. I don't usually really eat much breakfast."

"Well, I do. And you should. It's good for your body. Why don't we have our coffee and then go over to the diner. It's close enough to walk."

"Sounds good to me."

"We'll need to dress warm. It's cold out there. I'm going to add a layer."

An hour later they were both dressed and walking out the door. A light snow swirled around them as they hitched their hoods up over their heads and made their way around the house toward the street.

A horn double-tooted behind them.

She and Anna both hopped over to the side of the driveway.

"Sorry." Anna waved as Buck pulled up next to them.

"Y'all sleep all right last night?"

"Very well. We can't thank you enough."

"Where y'all headed off to? Goin' for a walk?"

Anna stepped up to his window. "We're headed back over to the diner for some breakfast."

"Good!" His eyebrows arched wide over his eyes. "Jump in. I'll give you a ride. That's where I'm headed."

Anna ran around to the passenger side of the truck, so Vanessa followed her.

Anna slid into the middle of the seat and Vanessa tried to give her extra room by hugging close to the door handle, but her cousin didn't seem to even notice. She was leaned in asking Buck questions about the town and what activities would be going on that only the locals might know about.

They talked and Anna's laugh was more of a playful titter. "That sounds like so much fun."

"I'll take y'all if you want to go." Buck still had both hands on the wheel, but he didn't have either of his eyes on the road. "I know everyone in this town."

All one thousand nine hundred and eighty-seven of them, Vanessa mused to herself.

When they got to the Blue Bicycle Bistro, nearly every table was full. The snow hadn't kept anyone inside around here. Buck held the door for them, then sauntered over to his usual table.

Vanessa craned her neck looking for another one.

Buck swept his arm out by his booth. "Ladies."

"Why thank you." Anna scooched into the bench seat facing him.

Vanessa slid in beside her.

Lisa came over and brought three coffees with her. "Good morning. What's everyone having? Buck, today is biscuits and gravy for you, right?"

"Yes, ma'am."

"That sounds so good," Anna said. "Same for me."

"Ooh, yeah, I'm going to have to pass on that. Can I get an egg-white omelet, and the strawberry energy smoothie?"

"Sure thing. Be right back." Lisa stopped by two other tables on her way to the kitchen.

Buck lifted his mug up to that big mustache for a sip. "You know, you're lucky to have landed in Fraser Hills for Christmas. I've never spent the holidays in a better place than here."

"Have you spent a Christmas anywhere other than here? I assumed you've been here forever." Vanessa regretted letting that roll off her tongue.

"Yeah. I have, but my late wife loved to travel, and once the kids were grown Christmas was a great time to do it." He glanced over at Anna. "But this is home. It's where I grew up, and this is where I'm happiest."

"It's such a quaint town," Anna added. "I could see how you could be happy here. There's just such a good feeling here."

"Oh yeah. This place is the real deal."

"What did you do for a living, Buck?" Vanessa couldn't figure him out.

"Little bit of this. Little bit of that. You know, what really matters is what you make of it all. Don't get too big for your britches. Be humble and grateful and share what works with others."

Anna practically swooned at everything he said. "I hear what you're saying, Buck, but you know sometimes things are not so cut-and-dry." She glanced over at Vanessa.

Vanessa's stomach lurched.

"I mean sometimes business gets in the way of the right thing to do."

Buck swiveled his head toward Vanessa. "Well, hypothetically, if business were pushing me in a direction I didn't agree with, I'd have to really consider if I was doing the right thing. There's always a choice."

And hadn't she just touted those same words lately? Vanessa

almost choked on his advice. She recovered quickly, then set her coffee cup down.

He patted his hands on the table and leaned forward. "All I'm saying is, people in this town don't take to change very well. Their choice or not. It's not always clear what the good solution is until you really look into things deeper. Not just the surface level. Folks might hold a grudge, but not for long. Eventually, they'll even forget about those things. Don't let that keep you from doing the right thing."

She looked into his eyes. This was no lecture. The sincerity in his blue eyes comforted her. "Thank you, Buck." Her phone rang, moving across the table as it buzzed, breaking the moment. She picked it up and looked at the caller information. "I'm sorry. I've really got to take this." She pulled on her coat and went outside where she could hear, away from the busy bustling kitchen.

"Sally. How are you?" She tried to sound up, but in the pit of her stomach she feared it was bad news about the house being sold.

"Great. I have some news."

Sally didn't sound super-excited. Vanessa pressed her lips together, bracing herself.

Sally continued, "The price on your dream home just dropped twenty-seven thousand, five hundred dollars. I know it's still over the original budget, but this is a great deal. The seller is motivated to sell. Are you interested in making an offer?"

"I'm interested," Vanessa said, "but I really need to finish this project first. I'll be done by Christmas."

"Entirely your call. I personally wouldn't wait," Sally said.

"Put a bug in their ear that I'm interested."

A cold wind swirled around Vanessa. She pulled the collar up on her coat. As she turned her back on the chill, she saw Anna hanging on Buck's every last word. At the end of this trip was it possible that Anna could have a better option than picking up and moving in with Vanessa on the outskirts of Chicago?

CHAPTER TWENTY

When Vanessa walked back into the diner, seeing Anna nearly glow sitting there talking to Buck, she had to wonder if her hope that Anna might want to move in with her was just her own crazy fantasy.

"Sorry about that," Vanessa said.

"No worries." Anna scooched over to let Vanessa in. "Buck said he'd take me to buy a Christmas tree one day. Isn't that great?"

"That's very nice of you, Buck." Vanessa studied the gentleman.

"My pleasure," Buck said.

"I'm going to walk down to the office and work on a few things."

"I can take Anna back." Buck insisted on putting the meal on his tab, and then the three of them walked outside. The snow had been cleared from the sidewalks, but all of the grass still glistened white.

"You sure we can't talk you into coming with us?" Buck asked.

"No, thank you. I'll see you tonight, Anna."

She watched as they pulled out of the parking space in Buck's truck; then she turned and walked to Porter's. She wanted to observe the retail outlet and meet the manager and the rest of the staff.

She walked inside. Business was brisk. Misty, who had given her the card with the key to the apartment, was working the register again.

"Hello, Misty. Remember me?"

"I do." The young girl's eyes danced. "How are you enjoying your stay in Fraser Hills?"

"It's been very nice."

"I've always dreamed about how cool it would be stay in the city. New York City, maybe. Not live there, but, you know, visit for a while."

"Chicago is so much prettier than New York City. I've lived in both, but I prefer Chicago."

"I've never been to any big city. Do you travel lots of places for work?"

"Yes."

"That is the coolest thing ever."

Vanessa let her gush. Business travel looked like all fun and games from the outside. The truth was, Vanessa rarely got to enjoy the places she visited, usually stuck in office buildings or huge windowless run-down factories that had seen better days. "I'll tell you about it one day."

"I'd love that so much." Misty's eyes were wide in anticipation.

"I'll make you a deal. I'd like to understand how things are working here in the retail area, before I make any recommendations. Do you think you could walk me through the processes?"

"Sure."

"Great. I'll get Lilene to bring someone in to fill in for you."

"We actually have a couple of people extra working today. I think they can handle it without me. Should I punch out?"

"No. You'll get paid to do this. Who do I need to clear you leaving your shift with?"

Misty introduced her to the store manager, who knew exactly who Vanessa was and why she was there. "You do whatever you need to do, Ms. Larkin. We can handle things here today."

"Excellent. Thank you."

Vanessa and Misty turned and walked toward the front of the store. "Let's start at the beginning."

"Because profitability and customer satisfaction always start and ends with the voice of the customer," Misty said.

"Couldn't have said it better myself." Vanessa relaxed, enjoying this day already. "When we're done, we'll do dinner and not talk shop at all. You pick the place."

"Really?"

"Yes. I think it'll be fun."

With a gleaming smile, Misty looked as if she might actually lift off the ground from excitement.

"Let's get started." She motioned for Vanessa to follow her. "You know I have a lot of ideas for this place. Everyone here likes things just the way they are, but we're missing opportunities to make Porter's even better."

"Really?"

"Oh yeah."

For an hour, Misty walked and talked Vanessa through the store, barely taking a breath between ideas. From there, Misty showed Vanessa the new warehouse and shipping process.

"All of the cakes used to be baked in the building across the street, and then moved twice before getting stored or shipped out. I was able to streamline processes after convincing them we could increase production by relocating the factory line to a smaller space. Now the workers can shift to help out when there's a bottleneck, while also reducing the number of times each box is handled. We reduced the steps people had to make between stations by enough to pay for another employee. You should have seen the spaghetti chart I made to show the before-and-after improvements. It went from a whirlpool with an undertow to a lazy river."

"You did a spaghetti chart to prove your process?"

"For one. But that was definitely one of the most visually easy to understand. The bottom-line savings were pretty impressive. By shutting down those buildings and moving into this one, we were able to cut utility expenses in half."

"Very smart."

"A lot of people didn't like the idea at first. They couldn't understand why we'd consolidate while we have all these buildings. We moved all the warehousing of product, which used to go over there to where the corporate apartment is, to this area behind the store, which also puts some control around how much extra product we produce. We can throttle staffing and production to meet demand, but we don't over-produce, which resulted in a lot of waste in the past. When demand is high we're ready, when it's not we shift resources to other areas or encourage vacation time, which folks are usually happy to use."

"These are really good ideas," Vanessa remarked. "Very well thought out."

"Thank you. I've got project plans and some sketches for some other ideas too. Not that anyone will ever do anything with them."

"Never say never." This young lady was like a younger image of herself. "Do you mind if I ask how old you are?"

"You're going to think I'm too young for more responsibility, but I'm not. I grew up in this place. I'm a hard worker, and I have a work ethic like my dad's, and he's amazing."

"I promise I won't think that."

"Sixteen."

Vanessa felt as if her eyes popped with an "ahooga" horn like a cartoon character in amazement. "Sixteen? Seriously. You *are* amazing. I think we're about out of time for the day."

Misty looked at her watch. "Wow, this day has flown by. I've talked nonstop. I'm sorry." Her cheeks pinkened. "My dad is always saying that I was born talking and I haven't stopped yet."

"Not the worst problem to have. This has been so helpful. I'm really glad to have gotten to know you better too."

"Thank you. This place is so special to me. My mom used to work here. I'd sit at her feet behind the counter when I was little. As I got older, she'd let me help her stock shelves and stuff. She looked so beautiful in her Porter's apron. I really miss her."

"I'm sorry. I didn't know." She placed a hand on Misty's arm. "She'd be very proud of you. You're an amazing young lady."

Misty gulped for air, her eyes glistening. "Thank you. You don't know what that means to me. Thank you so much."

"Come here." Vanessa wrapped her arms around her shoulders. "It's okay."

Misty swiped at her tears. "Not very professional. I never do this. I promise."

"Don't be silly. I'm honored that you shared that with me." Vanessa faced Misty straight on and placed her hands on her shoulders. "Okay?"

"Yes. Thank you."

"All right then. We'll pick back up with the factory on Monday. I didn't mean to hog your whole Saturday."

"Are you kidding? This has been the best day." Her hands danced as she spoke. "What time on Monday?"

"Why don't you meet me at nine. I have a few things I need to do before we get to work, including clearing your schedule. You've been very helpful. You really do know how to bring this place into the twenty-first century." *It would be much less likely that people would balk at the changes if they'd been driven from the suggestions of one of their own. Much better than from me.*

"So, Misty, where would you like to go to dinner? My treat."

"Anywhere?"

"Well, not Chicago, or New York City, but anywhere within driving distance. Oh, wait. I don't have a car. Wait. I could borrow my cousin's. So yes, anywhere we can drive."

"I can drive us."

"Perfect. I don't know my way around anyway."

"There's this tearoom on the edge of town. It's only open on the weekends. I think you'd love it."

"That sounds delightful."

"Great."

Vanessa followed Misty through the parking lot, passing a compact car with a graduation tassel that she'd thought for sure would be hers, but ending up next to a huge Ford truck with dual rear wheels and running boards, which Vanessa quickly realized were necessary in order for her to hitch her hiney up into the passenger seat.

"This is a whopper of a truck. How'd you ever learn to drive this?"

Misty laughed, but her pride shone. "I've been driving this thing for years. Learned on the back of our property." She fired up the engine and shifted the truck into reverse, then turned around and headed to the outskirts of town.

She shifted gears like a pro. Most of the people Vanessa knew didn't even know how to drive a manual transmission. She had to pass driver's ed with both a manual and an automatic transmission, but that had been years ago. She wasn't sure she could still pull it off today, and even if she could it probably would not go well in a truck this size. She imagined a line of tumbling mailboxes in her wake if she were driving this truck tonight.

Misty was a lot like Vanessa in some ways, but the total opposite in others. Vanessa had been a tiara and pedicure kind of girl from the word go. Misty was clearly more athletic than Vanessa had ever been, but she had good business sense and she knew what she wanted. Vanessa liked her moxie.

As they wound through the curving roads, Vanessa thought about herself at sixteen. She'd been teased for being too frilly by the other girls. It might have been nice to be the girl in blue jeans and lace who drove a pickup truck—carefree and fearless. But she'd never been fearless. She avoided the conflict and cut all ties with anyone who'd given her a hard time.

Misty slowed and turned on her blinker in front of a big white farmhouse with twinkle lights in every tree on the property. When they pulled into the parking lot, she could see that the split rail fence had also been decorated with lighted garland and live wreaths with shiny red balls and bows.

"It's like a winter wonderland. This is going to be fun."

"I really hope you like it." Misty hopped out of the truck and slammed the driver's door.

Vanessa stepped on the running board and hung on to the pillar grab bar as she stretched to get her foot on the ground.

"Silent Night" poured through the speakers in the gardens as they walked along the path to the restaurant. The chilly air made her skin tingle. Inside, the old farmhouse had been decorated for the holidays too. Fires were flickering in all of the rooms, and a mixture of spicy and sweet filled the air. Poinsettias graced each double glass-panel door entryway, and smaller ones decorated each step of the grand stairway that led to the second level. Presumably the owner's quarters.

"Just two tonight?" The older woman with glasses hanging from a beaded silver chain around her neck lifted two menus. "Near the fireplace okay?"

"That would be wonderful," Misty jumped in. "If that's okay with you," she turned and said to Vanessa.

"That sounds perfect."

"It's my favorite table." The hostess gestured to a table set with lovely bone china with winter birds perched amid a wreath motif of pinecone, holly, and mistletoe and glistening shiny gold accents.

"I can see why." Vanessa took a seat and Misty sat down across from her. "Thank you very much."

A waitress came out from the back carrying a silver tea service, and set it on the side table next to theirs. "Today's flavor is Paris tea. May I pour?"

Vanessa flipped over her teacup and nodded.

Misty followed suit. "This is one of my favorite teas."

"Would you like to order off the dinner menu or do our popular North Carolina Tea Tray for two?" She leaned in. "I personally like the tea trays. It's more than enough and you get to try a lot of the things on the menu. Plus, we do some specifically North Carolinian things like pork barbecue on the savory level, and a smack-your-momma banana pudding in a fine pastry added to the desserts. Mm-hmm."

"Thank you for the recommendation. That sounds really good to me. Misty, what would you like to do?"

"The tea tray for sure."

"There will be no smacking mommas or anyone else, but we'll do the North Carolina Tea Tray." Vanessa handed her menu back with a smile. "I think we're all set, then."

"Good choice." The waitress collected the menus and went to the kitchen.

Vanessa said, "I know I said we weren't going to talk about work at all, but I have to say one more time how impressed I am with you. I have college graduates working for me that don't have the attention to detail and project-management skills that you display."

"Thank you. I do take some college classes. I qualified for

this Career and College Promise program we have. I don't know if it's just a North Carolina thing or not, but I really love taking the classes. I get high school credit and transferable college credits too. I'm concentrating on business and project-management-type courses."

"A's in all of them?"

"Yes, ma'am."

Vanessa lifted her teacup. "Here's to you, Misty."

Misty lifted her cup and tapped it to Vanessa's. "Thank you." She sipped her tea. "Have you ever been to Paris? Like the tea?"

"Yes. I have, but I'll be honest: I didn't get to experience it like a tourist. I'd love to go back."

"What's stopping you?"

"From going to Paris on vacation?" She lifted her teacup and saucer to take a sip, and to buy a moment to collect her thoughts before she answered. "I can't say that I know why. I've got tons of vacation time saved up. I work all the time. I guess . . . I just haven't . . . made the time."

The waitress came to the table carrying a lovely three-tiered tray filled with delectables.

Vanessa sat wondering at the fact that she never extended any of her work trips to see the sights. She was always so eager to start the next project that it never occurred to her to stay on.

Thankfully the waitress pulled her from her reflection. "If you haven't been to tea before, you start at the bottom for the first course of savories and tea sandwiches, then move to the scones. Our jams are all made in-house. Then, to top it all off—dessert."

Misty clapped her hands together silently. "Thank you for letting me pick this place."

"You earned it." She lifted a small sandwich and took a bite. "This one is good. It's like a really spicy pimento cheese."

"That's my favorite." Misty took the other. "Yes. Just like I remember it."

"So, tell me about school. Clearly you're an honor roll student."

"I am. I like the studies and everything, but I'd really rather be at work."

"Why is that?"

She shrugged. "I don't know. I'm not very popular. I don't do a lot of the things the popular girls do. It's fine. I don't care."

"I know how you feel. I used to be the same way. I was even younger than you when I started Vanessa's Fine Vintage Frills."

"A business?"

"Yep. When I was in junior high school, I dreamed of being a fashion designer. All the kids teased me, but they all came to me for fashion advice. I guess it was the price to have friends. I wasn't confident enough to say anything when they picked on me."

"What did you make?"

"I'd go to swap meets and sales with my cousin, then I'd alter and embellish the clothing or handbags and sell them. It was a pretty good little business."

"That is so cool. I have zero fashion sense. I'm the least girly girl in our school. I get picked on for the opposite."

"I'm sorry. No matter what the reason, it's unkind. I still remember the nicknames and jokes they made. I'm doing so much better than those girls now, but those words still sting."

"I do know what you mean."

"I wish I had some good advice for you, but honestly I didn't handle it well. I don't know what someone should do in that situation, but I will say this. If you need fashion advice, consider me on speed dial for you." Vanessa took another sip of her tea.

"Thank you. I might have to take you up on that."

"I'd love it," Vanessa said. "You know what else I loved. I went to the football game last week. Your team is good."

"They always are. I love the football games too. I was there that night." She nibbled on another sandwich quietly. "I got asked to the winter dance this year."

"Really? Is it your first formal dance?"

"It is."

"You must be so excited."

"I'm not sure. I ordered a dress, but it hasn't come in yet, and I'm worried how my dad is going to act when my date shows up. Dad has always said I couldn't date until I was thirty. He's kind of protective. In a good way, though."

Vanessa laughed. "Misty, every father says that. Don't worry. You'll survive it. I did, and my dad scared my first date so bad the poor guy could barely speak for the first hour we were at the dance. I was mortified."

"Oh my gosh."

"I still remember it like yesterday. His name was Brad. But it turned out fine. I think most dads act that way. Must be in their DNA or something. Don't worry, you're going to have a great time. Tell me all about your dress."

"I don't know how to describe it. It's kind of a deep blue color. Dark, but bright at the same time."

"A jewel tone."

"I guess." She shrugged. "It's kind of simple, but it looked pretty online."

The rest of the night was mostly talking about the food.

Who liked what best, until they both tossed their napkins on their plates and admitted defeat.

"I can't eat one more bite," Misty said.

"Me either. This was such a treat."

The waitress came over and with a playful tinge in her voice said, "What, you can't finish?"

"No way. Thank you for suggesting this. We've really enjoyed it."

Misty nodded her head the whole time Vanessa spoke. "It was fabulous."

Vanessa handed the waitress her corporate card.

Misty placed her hands on the edge of the table. "Tonight was better than I'd even hoped. You made my whole year."

Vanessa loved her enthusiasm. "I tell you what. If we can implement those changes together in a super quick time frame, we will come back to celebrate that too."

Misty sat back in her chair. "Really. You're taking me . . . my ideas . . . seriously under consideration?"

"I am. They are sound, and well thought out. If you have data to back them, we'd be crazy not to put them into action. It's all the work I'd have had to do to make a plan, only you have the benefit of having worked in the environment. We're going to sit down Monday with your plan and documents. We'll tighten them up, and get down to work."

"Oh my gosh. I can barely breathe right now." Misty fanned her face. "I've dreamed of this, but I never thought it would happen."

"I promise you this. Whether we'd ever met, you are going to do great things. Don't ever doubt that."

CHAPTER TWENTY-ONE

Sunday morning, Vanessa woke up before the sun came up, beating Anna to the kitchen to make coffee. She sipped a cup of coffee thinking about the parade this evening. Her first impression of Mike had been good. He was handsome and nice. If they'd met anywhere else, when she wasn't shutting down a company, maybe things would've played out differently for them.

Staring into the fireplace, she argued with herself. The odds of meeting Mike, or anyone, somewhere other than a jobsite were slim to none. She never did anything but work. The problem was she didn't know how to rearrange her priorities and balance out her life.

Work was what kept her going. Anytime she slowed down she couldn't stop thinking about the work she should be doing.

She tucked her bare feet underneath her, resisting the urge to go check on the status of things.

"Good morning." Anna pulled the belt of her fluffy robe around her as she came down the hall. "I love the smell of coffee in the morning."

"Me too." Vanessa jumped from her chair and made a cup for Anna, meeting her in the kitchen doorway with it. "Here you go."

"Big day with the parade this afternoon. Buck said the tree lighting is at six at the hospital. I bet it'll be beautiful."

"We can do both."

"We? You'll be doing the parade with Mike."

"It's not a one-on-one date. Everyone in town will be attending that parade. Including you." She scrunched her lips. "All I care about is spending time with you."

"You should meet Mike for the parade without me. Just let go and enjoy all this town has to offer. We can do something tomorrow."

"You need to come to the parade. It'll be fun. Besides, I have to work tomorrow."

"Actually, I was going to talk to you about that. Buck offered to take me to get a tree tomorrow. A live tree. We're going to cut it down ourselves." Anna gulped down the rest of her first cup of coffee. "Are you ready for more too? I'm a two-cup-a-morning gal."

"What? When did that happen? You don't just drop a headline like that and then offer to serve coffee." Vanessa was stymied a bit, but also excited about this for Anna. "I want details."

"As soon as I get us more coffee." She disappeared into the kitchen, then came back in and sat on the couch next to Vanessa. "I went for a little walk yesterday. I met the nicest lady at the bakery. I think she was a friend of the owner of the place. She and I got to talking, and she recommended the best cupcake. Oh gosh. You missed out, but we'll go back together and get one. Anyway, while I was there, Buck came in. I'd asked the shop owner about where we could buy a tree, and she was telling me where the local tree lots are. Buck overheard and insisted he take us to his friend's tree farm. We're going to pick out, and cut down, our own tree."

"That's going to be fun." Vanessa rubbed her hands together at the thought of all that sticky sap getting on her hands. "I bet fresh-cut pine trees are sappy. I bet you're as sticky as duct tape."

Anna ticktocked a finger in the air. "I'm going to let that big strong man carry it! Chivalry is not dead, my dear."

"Since when?"

"Sometimes you just have to remind men what they need to do. Trust me, it's not hard, and I think they kind of like all that door opening and pampering when given the chance."

"Clearly I've been doing this all wrong. I need a date coach."

"Careful what you wish for, Vanessa. I do grant wishes."

Anna always had been like a fairy godmother. "I was joking about the date coach. I'm not ready for all that, but I'm glad you have plans you're so excited about. I don't feel nearly as bad about working now."

"I never want you to feel bad about working. I just wish you had better work and life balance. You do what you have to do tomorrow. Don't you worry about me, but promise me we'll make a plan to attend some of the festivities together too."

"Deal. We can get them on my calendar and I can work around them."

"We'd better get dressed," Anna said, jumping to her feet.

"The parade isn't until this afternoon. They are calling for snow, though. I wonder if they'll still have it if it snows."

"Oh, Edna said the parade is rain or shine."

"Edna?"

"Yes. The lady I met at the bakery. Weren't you listening?"

"You never mentioned her name. Edna Barkley?"

"Well, she never mentioned her surname. I don't know."

"Older woman, about your height with white hair and rosy round cheeks? Glasses?"

"That sounds like her. Isn't she great?"

Tightness at the back of Vanessa's neck caused her to raise her shoulders and take in a breath. "That's the woman I gave the retirement package to that everyone in town is so upset about."

"Oh?" Anna pulled her lips into a tight line. "She seemed to be on top of the world."

"In a small town I guess we're bound to run into people." Vanessa wished Anna hadn't run into Edna, though. No telling what they talked about, and the last thing Vanessa wanted to do was raise any more emotion in this town than necessary.

"Anyway," Anna said. "It'll be fine. She's a delight and Buck seemed to be very tight with her. Church service is in an hour. We better get dressed."

I'm pretty comfortable right here. "I haven't gone to church in a long time."

"All the more reason for us to go while we're here together."

"I really try to keep my distance from the people impacted by the changes I bring to their community. It makes things easier," Vanessa explained.

"Come on. It's the holiday season, and have you seen the

church? It's so inviting. It's begging for us to attend today."
Anna put her hands together. "Please do this for me."

"How can I say no to that?"

"You can't."

*

At the tiny white church on the hill, there wasn't going
to be any chance of fading into the crowd. A few people
waved at Anna, and she was cheerfully reciprocating as if
she'd known them her whole life.

"I love this town," Anna remarked as she waved to another
lady across the way.

Vanessa slid into the second-to-last pew, and Anna scooted
in next to her. Her body temperature rose in response to the
narrowed gazes from the people around her. One woman
even grabbed her child's hand and pulled her closer, as if
Vanessa were some kind of outlaw. How did Anna not notice
the reverberation of resentment surrounding them?

Anna sat there beaming.

The preacher came out and welcomed everyone, making
the announcements for the upcoming events and church-
related gatherings, including a game night.

"Now, that sounds fun." Anna nudged her.

Then he announced the details for the Christmas cantata and
encouraged everyone to come and bring someone new along.

Anna nudged her again. *We should come,* she mouthed.

Vanessa relaxed as the preacher began the service and all
hearts and minds clung to his words. By the time they'd sung
and made it through the service, she found herself smiling at
the others rather than worrying about how they felt about her.

When they walked out Buck approached them. Edna was in his wake.

"You made it," Buck said to Anna.

Anna made a beeline for them. "I didn't see you come in."

"We always sit on the other side in the back row together. Kind of our spot."

"Hello, Ms. Larkin," Edna said, extending her hand. "It's nice to see you here."

A baked-potato-size lump formed in Vanessa's throat. "Thank you. It was a lovely service."

"We both enjoyed it," Anna chimed in. "Will we see you at the parade later?"

"No one misses the parade," Edna assured them.

Buck nodded. "She's right."

"We'll see you there." Anna grabbed Vanessa's hand. "I love this place."

Vanessa squeezed her hand, and the two of them walked over to Anna's car.

Anna followed the other cars out of the parking lot and then made the turn on Buck's road. "Everything is so close. It takes me longer than this just to get out of my neighborhood to go somewhere back home."

Inside, they each had a bowl of Mike's chicken stew, then went about getting ready for the afternoon festivities.

*

At 2:40 P.M., Vanessa and Anna stood in front of the fire station, dressed in layers and their wool coats along with the earmuffs Anna had brought for the two of them. Vanessa's hands were so sweaty she wondered if they'd ice over in the frigid air.

Dark nimbostratus clouds hung low, looking weighty enough to really drop a load of snow.

"Do you smell that?" she asked Anna.

"It smells fresh." Anna took in another lungful. "Nice."

"That's the smell of snow." Vanessa loved how the world got quite before a big snowstorm.

"You came," a man's voice said behind her. Mike walked up looking very sharp in a heavy black wool collared shirt, and a deep red wool vest with antiqued silver buttons. FRASER HILLS PERCHERONS was embroidered on the left chest with bright green holly with shiny red berries circling it like a wreath.

"Wouldn't miss it," Vanessa answered, but truth be told if Anna hadn't been in town she never would have shown up. But here she was. "Thank you for the chicken stew." She reached back for Anna's coat and tugged her closer. "Meet my cousin, Anna."

"Nice to meet you, ma'am." He touched the brim of his black cowboy hat. It was clean, but had a well-worn look to it.

"Thank you, it's nice to meet you too," Anna said. "And I've got to tell you, that chicken stew you sent over was delicious. Thank you."

"You're welcome." He focused in on Vanessa. "What did you think?"

She'd been contemplating how to answer that all afternoon. "It's hard to compare the two so far apart. I didn't get any spilled on me this time, that was a plus." She let out a sigh. "If I'm completely honest, yours was better."

"Told you." He looked proud.

"So you did."

"Okay, so here's what we're going to do for the parade." He slapped his hands together and rubbed them, crouching a little as he spoke. "Y'all are going to get comfortable right up here on the parade line. Me and a couple of my buddies are going to carry some chairs out here in a minute."

"We don't need chairs. We can stand," she argued.

"Chivalry," Anna whispered to Vanessa. "Let him do it." She lifted her chin. "Thank you, Mike. Chairs would be lovely. Right, Vanessa?"

Vanessa smiled. "Thank you. Yes. Very thoughtful."

"It's a long parade, and you'll stay warmer in the chairs because they block the wind from your backside," Mike said. "I'm telling you, it's the only way to go. You won't be the only ones sitting."

Vanessa and Anna looked at each other and shrugged. "Okay."

"I'm in the parade, so about—"

"You're in it?" Vanessa's eyes widened with realization. "Are you riding that horse and carriage—wait, wagon, I meant horse and *wagon,* like that first day I was in town?"

"If you thought that wagon was special, hold on to your earmuffs."

Is he making fun of my earmuffs?

"So, midway through the parade I've got to run to the other end and get ready. Y'all stay here after the end of the parade, and I'll meet back up with you. Okay?"

"Got it," Anna chimed in.

"Good." Mike jogged off toward the fire station.

Anna had a sly look on her face. Rather than let her engage on whatever she was about to say about Mike, Vanessa said to her, "You're going to be amazed when you see his horses. I'd never seen anything so big and powerful. It's quite impressive."

A moment later Mike and three other guys were back with

chairs on each shoulder. They lined them up to the left of the fire truck doors on the road two rows deep, staggered so everyone would be able to see. "Ladies." Mike led them to the two end chairs on the second row. "Warmest spot to be unless you planned to watch from a window."

They sat down, mildly amused by all the effort.

"Where did he go now?" Vanessa turned in her seat.

"There are so many people here. There must be people from nearby towns here for this too." Anna pointed out a man across the way in camouflage coveralls and a camouflage hat, standing next to two kids in full snowsuits. "Everyone is bundled up for the weather."

In the distance music from a marching band filled the air.

The crowd pulled in closer. A few whistles followed by hoots and hollers started the excitement. Everyone turned their attention to the parade route.

Kids wearing light-up Christmas-bulb necklaces waved and jumped up and down in anticipation of the floats. NICE LIST pennants waved in the air. Suddenly, Vanessa felt seven years old again.

Mike walked over carrying three cups of steaming hot chocolate with whipped cream and a cherry on top. "This helps keep you warm too."

Vanessa looked into his smiling eyes. "Thank you. You've thought of everything."

"I'm a real process guy. Can't help myself."

What's not to like about that? But she hadn't said it out loud, because she was still hung up in his gaze and that smile. "I didn't know that about you." Vanessa blinked, weighing the rocking-chair emotions that took over when Mike was around.

"There's a lot you don't know about me."

Anna beamed. "That's the fun part about meeting new people." She bobbed her head from side to side, then clapped wildly. "I can see the band."

"Joy to the World" got louder by the step, and almost like the wave at a baseball game, kids raised their hands into the air trying to catch candy being thrown by men in elf costumes riding four-wheelers.

Anna squeezed Vanessa's wrist. "This is so fun!"

The band moved with precision, lifting and twisting their instruments as they marched closer. In front of the band, a man dressed in a nutcracker suit carrying a candy-cane baton lifted the red and white stick up and down in the air, adding in a happy kick every now and again. The shock of silvery-gray hair shone in contrast to the tall black furry hat.

Vanessa recognized him immediately. "Look!" She pointed him out to Anna.

"Lordy goodness!" Anna stood. "That's Buck!"

Mike remained seated. "He's been doing that for as long as I can remember. He was mayor when he first took on that role."

"Isn't that fun." Anna clapped and raised her hands in the air, shouting, "Merry Christmas."

After the last note of "Joy to the World," the drum corps tapped out a rhythm, then began playing "Jingle Bells." The whole town sang along, including Vanessa and Mike.

"Fun, right?" he asked.

She nodded as she sang.

Next, a loud tractor putted down the parade route, pulling a trailer filled with decorated Christmas trees. She could smell the fresh pine from her chair. 4-H kids walked by, leading their goats and sheep with champion banners across their backs, followed by a pickup truck pulling a flatbed trailer with streamers hanging from the sides and three men wearing cowboy hats sitting on bales of straw, singing and playing "The Christmas Song" on guitar.

"I love this song," Mike said.

She snuck a peek at Mike as he watched them sing. She admired how relaxed he was.

The Fraser Falcons Marching Band came next, with flag team and baton twirlers, doing a jiggy version of "Jingle Bells."

"Okay, I'm going to head on down. Y'all are okay?" He made a thumbs-up.

"Yes."

"See you right here. Don't leave."

"We won't," Vanessa said.

"I promise I won't let her," Anna said.

"Thank you, ma'am."

"I like his manners," Anna said as he jogged away.

"Yes. That's nice, isn't it." She watched him far too long, because somehow she hadn't even noticed that the band had completely passed by and that crazy falcon mascot was right in front of her flapping its wings and wiggling its hind feathers again. *Squawk!*

She let out a sigh as Lilene stooped down next to her. "I thought that was you. Hey."

"Hi. This is an awesome parade."

"I know. Are you enjoying it, Anna?"

"I am."

Lilene commentated the parade, filling in the backstory as a group of horseback riders carrying flags from a ranch nearby passed them, and four-wheelers full of dogs dressed up like

Santa's elves zoomed by. "Those are all rescue dogs up for adoption. Aren't they cute?"

"They are."

Everyone around her was smiling. Holiday spirit overflowed as they enjoyed the annual festivities. Guilt rushed over her about all the changes coming to this town for these people. People with families.

Sleigh bells rang, but not like the ones the band had used earlier. This jinglejangle was powerful and strong. The varying tones and pleasing tempo made her smile.

Everyone clapped and cheered enthusiastically. She and Anna stood to get a better view.

Two huge black horses clip-clopped, their huge feet lifting high with each step, and four more followed behind them, two by two. The nostrils on their black velvety noses flared, vapor puffing in white clouds as they trotted forward.

Lilene stood and cheered. "We're so lucky to have these horses right here in our town."

Six horses in all, just like she'd seen that first day in town, but rather than a simple wagon they pulled a shiny one big enough to carry a Christmas tree and Santa in the back with room to spare. This wagon had fancy gold accents and pretty lights. Santa ho-ho-ho'd as he waved and tossed favors.

All eyes except hers were on Santa. She was focused on the man sitting in the front of the wagon in the black shirt, red vest, and cowboy hat. Mike. Next to him, someone wearing a taupe Western hat held the reins. Between their feet, a black Labrador retriever had its paws on the rail, enjoying the ride.

FRASER HILLS PERCHERON HITCH sparkled in shimmering gold letters down the side of the high-gloss black wagon with red-and-gold wagon wheels. SPONSORED BY had been painted in script above the Porter's logo on the front corner. *I didn't notice a sponsorship. I'll have to look into that.*

Lilene pointed to the very back horse in the hitch, closest to them. "That horse is almost twenty-five years old. He's won blue ribbons and trophies galore. He's well known in the horse world for his good genetics. He's even been in magazines. He's the closest thing this town has to a local hero." She put her fingers in her mouth and whistled.

Mike offered a lazy smile that parted his lips.

Her heart tumbled, betraying the resistance she'd been trying to hold.

The hitch suddenly stopped. He turned and said something to the person driving the team; then he stood and stepped to the edge of the cart and extended his hand toward Vanessa.

The dog leapt from the wagon and danced alongside one of the handlers standing next to the horses.

Mike hooked his finger in her direction.

She raised her hand to her heart. "Me? There?" Her brows pulled together as she turned to Anna for support. "I can't get up there."

He nodded, encouraging her. At that moment big fluffy snowflakes began to fall around her.

Floats began to bottleneck behind the wagon.

Anna pushed her toward Lilene, who hurried her to the street. "Go!"

Chapter Twenty-two

The rest of the crowd seemed to fall away as Vanessa raised her foot to the step with her hand in his.

"Is there room?"

"Sure." He pulled her up. His strength was notable. His hands were warm. In a mere second she was sitting next to him on the velvet bench seat.

He stretched his arm behind her and said, "Wave."

She couldn't contain her nervous giggle as she tried to spot Anna in the crowd again. "This is definitely a tight squeeze."

"It's warmer that way." He laughed. "More fun too."

"It's high," she said, a nervous titter to her voice.

"I've got you," he said, putting his arm around her.

She could barely move. The firmness of his muscular arm steadied her as the carriage lurched forward and continued down the parade route in the falling snow. Snowflakes collected on the horses' coats in front of her.

"This is amazing," she said, looking at all of the decorative leather and shiny bells on each horse.

The horses were being managed with small moves and flicks of the wrist holding the bundle of long reins. Four men dressed in all black with red Santa hats and bandannas walked alongside the hitch.

Vanessa's insides spun. The impact of their dinner-plate-size hooves vibrated through the wagon.

Smiling faces huddled together along the parade route, people waving and hoping for a surprise from Santa.

Kids tried to catch snowflakes on their tongues with so much delight that tears tickled her eyelashes. The hitch slowed to a walk up the next block, then turned down the alley behind the fire department.

Anna stood surrounded by firemen as they pulled to a stop. Mike helped Vanessa to the ground.

"You looked so great up there. Both of you. You too," Anna yelled to the driver, now seated alone. "We've got hot chocolate for everyone." One of the firemen handed out sparkly red paper cups to everyone.

"Thank you for joining me," Mike said to Vanessa. "Now, admit it. This town is special."

"It is. You're right." She meant it too, but that didn't mean business wasn't still going to happen, and she was trying to make it the softest landing possible. "And there's still a Christmas tree lighting to attend."

His eyes pleaded with her.

"Help us." He took her hands into his. "Just help us. And I'm really sorry about getting so angry about Mom. You're right. She's perfectly happy with that package."

A wave of relief flowed over Vanessa.

Anna walked up behind Mike. "I can't believe how big these horses are. I've ridden horses but these make the ones I rode look like Chihuahuas. These are like the Clydesdales, right?"

"No. Not at all, except they are both draft horses. Percherons originated in France, taking their name from the former Perche province."

The driver of the hitch wagon climbed down and walked over to them. "One more reason to go back to Paris, right, Vanessa?"

"Misty?" Vanessa's mouth dropped wide. "Anna, this is who I've been talking about." She swung back around to Misty. "Is there nothing you can't do? This is crazy! Why didn't you tell me?"

She shrugged. "Kids at school kind of tease me about it. I didn't want you to think less of me. Especially after you liked my ideas."

"No way. You blow me away! I loved that ride. I can't believe you can do that. I was impressed you could drive a stick shift. But this . . ."

"Yeah. You were. I didn't know you knew my dad."

"I . . . ?" Vanessa blushed.

Anna lifted her hand to her face as she laughed. "Mike's your dad?"

Misty nodded.

Vanessa finally put all the pieces together. "I had no idea he was your father." She turned to Mike. "This is your daughter who went skiing on Thanksgiving?"

"That was me," Misty said as Mike nodded.

The snow fell in smaller flakes now, but they were covering everything at an incredible rate.

"My, this *is* a small town." Vanessa had herself braided right into everything in this town. Something she'd never meant to do.

"Small towns," Mike said. "Whole different animal."

"Dad, Vanessa is helping me implement some of the improvements I'd suggested at Porter's."

He looked at Vanessa. "Really?" Lifting his chin. "You're not just leading her—"

"No. Not at all. I'm serious."

He shook her hand. "Well, thank you. I jumped to some wrong conclusions about you."

Thank goodness.

Anna rushed to Vanessa's side. "Hey, buses are taking people over to the tree lighting. We need to go if we don't want to miss it." Anna shoulder-bumped Vanessa. "And you," she said to Mike. "You seem to be pretty perfect. Handsome, knows how to admit when he's wrong, and you do make a mean chicken stew."

Mike pushed his hat back on his head an inch, grinning. His eyes locked with Vanessa's. "I like your cousin. She's one smart lady."

"You'd like anyone on your side," Vanessa teased, but she still wasn't sure he wasn't just throwing himself at her to get his way for the town.

"Thank you, Mike. We had the best parade seats around," Anna said. "And the boys took good care of me."

Mike did a half turn, his back to Anna, but thumbing that way. "*She* likes me."

He was cute all right, but she'd never admit that to him. Vanessa gave him a flirty grin, then turned away. "Come on, Anna, we're going to miss that tree lighting if we let this guy go on and on all night." She lifted her hand in the air, calling out over her shoulder, "Thank you, Mike. We had a great time."

One by one, school buses filled up and took folks over to the hospital for the tree lighting, then circled back around to get another load of passengers. It wasn't all that far, thank goodness, else those five buses would have taken forever and they would be lighting the tree at midnight.

Still excited from the parade, people chatted and laughed, sharing goodies they'd purchased earlier. Some families had laid out blankets on the ground and sat down around the huge tree that stood tall in front of the hospital building.

Colored glass and metal, the architecture looked sorely out of place in the small town. New too. From here she noticed that each room of the hospital's second and third floors had a single candle in the window. Some patients stood at their windows peering down on the activities.

After the second round of buses unloaded, teens wearing white choir robes carried wooden trays filled with beeswax candles with red ribbons wrapped around the bottom of each one toward the crowd.

"Here you go." A young lady plucked two tapered candles from the tray and handed them to Vanessa and Anna. "The paper keeps the wax from dripping on you. You can light yours from mine."

"This is so neat. I've never done this," said Anna.

"Merry Christmas," the young woman said as she moved through the crowd handing out more candles.

As the minutes passed, more and more candles were lit, bringing a joy to the crowd.

The moan of brass instruments was followed by the rest of

the band in an instrumental version of "Have Yourself a Merry Little Christmas." Everyone hushed and moved in closer to the Christmas tree. The choir circled the tree, holding their candles in the air, and began singing along with the orchestra.

A single guitar plucked a few notes of "Silent Night," and then everyone joined in and sang along, followed by "It Came Upon a Midnight Clear."

Then a special trumpeting sound, not so different from one announcing that a bride was going to walk down the aisle, sounded, and everyone began singing "O Christmas Tree." At the end of the first chorus, the lights on the tree lit up. Bright red, green, blue, gold, and white brightened the hospital lawn, and everyone collectively gave a gasp, then picked up with the next verses of the song.

Everyone cheered, then began blowing out their candles and making their way to the buses to go back to Main Street.

Anna pointed toward one of the windows above. "Look."

"There must be six kids in that window." Vanessa wondered what was wrong that kept those children inside tonight. It was easy to forget the heavy sorrows of the world when you were concentrating on the big picture.

"In several windows." Anna waved. Some waved back. Anna clutched her heart. "I am so glad we came here."

Vanessa took Anna's hand. "Me too."

CHAPTER TWENTY-THREE

M onday morning, Vanessa got to the office before seven. When she sat down, she had a weird feeling that things on her desk had been moved. She looked around, unsure whether she was imagining it or not, but there didn't seem to be anything missing.

She took her laptop from her bag and placed it on the desk. When she opened her email there was one from Robert.

She groaned, unable, or maybe more like unwilling, to deal with him right now. She had to admit that, with Anna here, she understood his tie to being with family over the holidays. And even more so from being around all of this here in Fraser Hills.

Anna had been so excited about going with Buck to cut down her own Christmas tree, she said she hadn't slept a wink all night. Not in a complaining way, but with exuberance that superseded all the happiness she remembered with Anna. Real happiness.

Vanessa was glad she'd taken the time to set the expectation with Anna that she would be working late and would be staying at the corporate apartment tonight to get as much done as possible so they'd have time to do something fun on Tuesday.

Misty showed up at 9:00 sharp with her computer and a three-ring binder of reports.

"Knock-knock," Misty said from the doorway. "Are you ready for me?"

"I am. Come on in."

"Lilene said she'd adjusted my schedule."

"She has. So, let's get started."

Vanessa moved over to the table next to the window so she and Misty could review the plans together. She listened quietly as Misty shared every project and the supporting documents with her, further ensuring the discussion points they'd gone over last night.

They uploaded the project plan into Vanessa's system and then Vanessa walked through her thought process and the changes she'd make and where additional details needed to be fleshed out.

"Everything should be time-framed, and dependent milestones should always be connected. If some of those earlier steps get dropped you can end up with an eleventh-hour failure, and you never want that."

"I see. So like right here." Misty pointed to one of the steps that was required to get started.

"Exactly. So, let me show you how to mark those dependent steps." She made examples out of the first few, then backed up the file. "You try it."

Misty took over as Vanessa looked on.

"You've got it," Vanessa said. "The other thing I see in new project managers is they overcomplicate things. That's where really talking to the people who know and live the process is so important. Simple solutions are often the best."

For the next two hours they talked through potential failure points and what checkpoints needed to be put in place to ensure they were on time and on budget.

At one o'clock, Lilene poked her head inside the door. "I hate to bother you two, but I brought a homemade turkey pot pie for lunch. Y'all haven't moved from this office all morning. Can I bring you some lunch? I think you'll like it."

Misty said, "Oh you'll love it. Lilene makes the best turkey pot pie around."

"Then make it two. Thanks, Lilene."

"My pleasure, ladies."

They continued working and Lilene brought them lunch. Rather than stop, they kept right on working. While Misty worked on refining the retail and factory plan, Vanessa worked on the plan to completely empty the other warehouses and begin prepping them for Outdoor Sports Pro to take over the first of the year.

She picked up her phone and dialed Bill. "Hey. It's Vanessa. Can you provide me with an update on how things went over the weekend, and see if we have any unexpected hurdles to clear on the project?"

"No, ma'am. The guys are making quick work of this. All of the scrap equipment is gone. We've got a few guys blowing out the dirt and cobwebs, general cleanup, and a couple repainting some areas that were in bad shape. We had the paint. We were going to paint earlier this year and then it got pushed as not a priority. Anyway, that'll be done. I'm doing an inspection now to see if there are any building repairs that need attention."

"Good job. Were those offices part of the repainting plan?"

"Sure are."

"Good. They were a mess. I think we can get rid of those old desks too."

"Buddy down the street has a shop where he repurposes old furniture and stuff and turns it into other things. Rather than dump it, do you mind if we give it to him?"

"Of course not. I'm adding that to the plan right now."

"He's going to be your biggest fan."

"I could use a few of those right now."

"You're gonna be okay," Bill said. "Anything else, boss lady?"

"No, thank you. Call me if anything pops up that I need to allocate time for."

"You got it."

The line went dead, and she put her phone on the table. At this rate she could be out of here by Christmas. She and Anna could fly somewhere else to finish celebrating. *Maybe Paris?*

"How are you doing over there, Misty?"

"Great. I like this tool. It makes things so much easier. I found a few other things that needed to be simplified and one that there was no way to know when it was complete. I think I have that fixed."

"Go ahead and find a stopping point, and print out what you have and we'll go over it together."

The printer chugged out a copy of the project plan as Vanessa walked over to the window to look outside. The town looked pretty all covered in white.

"I've got the reports." Misty sat back down at the table.

Vanessa joined her and they went through each line, double-checking resource and capacity along with timelines.

"This looks really good." Vanessa tapped the pile of pages back into one neat stack. "Why don't you call it a day?"

"You sure? I don't mind staying longer."

"I'm sure." The last thing she needed to do was lay her own bad habits on Misty. Maybe she could help her have life balance from the beginning of her career, because it sure felt near impossible to do it once you were already in the unbalanced side of the equation.

Lilene's and Misty's voices carried down the hall as they left together.

She reviewed all of the entries and made sure there were no overlapping steps between the two projects she had going here. The warehouse prep, and the upgrades and reduction of footprint for Porter's. From her calculation, the changes would result in more than a 30 percent lift in revenue with the smaller number of employees. The rest of the employees would be the ones that would be re-skilled to the warehouse team at Outdoor Sports Pro.

She texted Anna to let her know she was still going to work late tonight, but she'd see her tomorrow.

At nine o'clock the retail store closed and the holiday music that had played all day suddenly fell quiet. Silence whispered in her ears.

Vanessa stood and stretched. Her body cracked and popped with each movement. With her hands clasped behind her back, she slowly leaned forward, thankful she'd taken the time to learn yoga last year after dealing with backaches that no amount of pain reliever soothed. A few stretches each morning had changed her life, but tonight she needed a double dose.

She gathered her things to leave. She locked the front door of Porter's behind her and began to walk toward the corporate apartment. The exercise would do her good.

A horn tooted twice from across the street.

She recognized Jimmy's car and walked over. "Did Lilene call you? I'm sorry, I had no idea—"

"No, ma'am. I didn't have anything else to do and it's cold out. I thought I'd just hang out here and wait to see if you needed a ride. Did some studying." He lifted a hefty college book. "I'm trying to finally finish my degree."

"That's not easy when you're working full-time too."

"You're telling me, but I can do it." He looked pleased with himself. "Hop in."

She climbed into the backseat, and Jimmy pulled away from the curb. The tires slid a little beneath them when they turned.

He dropped her off at the door, and then pulled away.

As she fumbled with the key in the dark, something shuffled behind her. *Please don't let it be a skunk.*

She fumbled with her phone to get the light on the lock so she could hurry inside, but as she did, something bumped against her leg.

Her breath caught. She stood as still as the wind right before disaster strikes. With her eyes squeezed shut, another prod hit her about midcalf. She inhaled, but the air was fine.

She slowly tilted forward to look down.

Still half expecting a skunk, she let out one long breath as she realized it was nothing but that little puppy again.

Sitting with his chin straight up in the air, he lifted one paw and pushed on her leg.

"What are you doing?"

He cowered and backed up a few steps with his tail between his legs.

"It's okay. Come here."

He flopped to his belly, putting his chin on the ground with eyes squinted closed.

She opened the door to the warehouse, then leaned down and scooped that little puddle of a pup into her arms. "What are you doing here? Where'd you come from?"

He commenced a serious flurry of kisses, his soft little paws patting her face as he did.

"What is all that for? Do you want to come upstairs with me?"

He answered with a high-pitched yelp, then licked her ear. His sharp little nails grazed her neck.

"You are just a baby. Don't scratch me, buddy."

He laid his head on her shoulder.

"Do you want to come in with me? You do seem quite content, but someone has to be looking for you."

Vanessa stepped outside. "Here doggy, dog. Are you missing a puppy?" She whistled a couple of times, but didn't hear even a skitter.

She walked inside and locked the door behind her.

The puppy didn't squirm as she climbed the stairs to the corporate apartment. "Hopefully, you won't pee on the floor. At least it's for the most part hardwood flooring, and there are a ton of paper towels stored in that closet. Welcome to my house."

She put him on the ground.

He sat there looking more like a stuffed animal than a dog, the way he was sitting on his butt with his paws forward.

"Let me find something for you to eat. You've got to be hungry." She opened the cabinets. "Let's see. How about saltines?"

She took a couple out of the sleeve and sat on the floor in front of him. He jumped up and spun in a circle. "Here you go." She broke one of the crackers into a few bite-size morsels, and held them out in her flat hand.

He gobbled them as if they were steak.

"You make those look pretty tasty." She got the jar of peanut butter out of the cabinet and fixed a couple of peanut butter crackers for herself. He climbed into her lap trying to get her cracker. "Hang on." She scooped some peanut butter onto her finger. The puppy lapped it up. "Oh, you really like that."

Long after he stopped licking the peanut butter from her finger, he licked the air with his sticky tongue, his tail going a mile a minute.

"Now that our bellies are full, we can relax." She filled a bowl with water and put it on the floor for him, then turned on the television and sprawled out on the couch.

Just as she'd kind of hoped, the puppy ran back across the room, coming to a sliding stop by her on the slippery hardwood floor, then tried to climb up on her.

"You're still a little too small for that." She reached down and gave him a lift of the butt. He walked on top of her, then licked her chin before wrapping himself into a tight little ball right in front of her stomach.

"Oh my gosh. Now I really want a house so I can have a puppy. You are the sweetest thing."

She stroked her fingers along his shiny coat. "We'll find your family tomorrow."

With the puppy asleep on the couch, she had to slip out from behind him to go get some work done. At the desk by the window, she saw that the snowy skies had finally cleared up enough that there were stars out tonight.

She worked quietly, happy with her progress.

The puppy had slept nearly an hour before he woke up and yapped for attention.

"I thought you might sleep all night. I bet you want to go outside." She put her shoes back on and grabbed a jacket. "Come on." She patted her leg and he ran right over to her. He bravely ran for the staircase, taking one step at a time. His fat belly skimmed the stair tread as he stretched to the next one.

She passed him and waited for him at the bottom, encouraging him along the way.

Two steps from the bottom he went rolling tail over nose to the bottom.

"Oh no." She raced to the bottom of the stairs.

He sat there looking around.

She could almost picture the tweety birds circling his head after that fall. "Are you okay, little guy?"

She opened the door and he walked outside, yawned, and then sat down. Vanessa walked out toward the tree line and whistled, wondering if the mother wasn't bedded down in the thick woods with a whole litter of these little guys, but there were no barks. No whimpers from pups.

Vanessa lifted the puppy into her arms. "Look at all those stars. Isn't it beautiful?"

He seemed to look to make his own decision, then squirmed. She placed him on the ground, and he ran off to the grass and did his business, then ran back over to the door.

"I guess that means you're staying the night."

She opened the door and he started bounding up the stairs, but he was dangerously wobbly. She picked him up and carried him the rest of the way.

Back in the apartment he was full of energy, jumping and

playing, but his teeth were like little needles. "Okay, I need you to play with something besides my hands. I definitely do not have enough bandages for all these bites."

She'd packed a pair of casual socks in her bag in case her feet got wet in the snow. She pulled them out. They were pretty expensive to turn into a puppy toy, but they'd been in her bag forever and she'd never worn them, so what was the waste in that? She tied the heavy woolen socks together, then swung them in front of her.

The puppy leapt into the air like a crocodile after a bird. She played tug-of-war, and that little puppy was strong. He was going to win this game.

He barked, the socks still in his mouth.

She wrestled them away and threw them across the room.

He went flying after them, then stalked them and pounced on them. Fearless. Barking again, he stomped his feet as if daring the socks to attack.

Vanessa couldn't resist grabbing them and throwing them again.

"Maybe I'll become a little fearless in Fraser Hills too. What do you think, little guy?"

He crawled into her lap and started licking her face again.

She screamed playfully. "You're a suck-up. But adorable." She put the sock in his mouth and scooted him off. "I need to get some more work done." She fluffed a towel on the floor next to her feet. "Why don't you play or settle in there?"

He sat down at her feet and cocked his head.

How could anyone deny puppy eyes?

Without a whimper, he crawled onto the towel and curled up with his chin on her feet.

Chapter Twenty-four

The next morning that little puppy was lying face-to-face with Vanessa when she opened her eyes. She backed up with a start, and the puppy woke up ready to play. "Oh my gosh, what am I supposed to do with you today?"

She pulled on her robe and shoes and took the puppy outside. It was freezing and the snow held a shiny glaze on top now. "Go on." Vapor formed billows of white with each word. He made quick work of it, and then ran inside and up the stairs ahead of her. "Well, you're doing stairs a lot better today."

Once she got dressed, she found the puppy lying on her shoes by the door. Her heart skipped. "You better not have chewed on those."

Eyebrows rose on his face.

She grabbed the shoes; thankfully, they were still intact. She'd heard horror stories of women with dogs that ate one of each pair of her good shoes.

"I'm sorry I doubted you. You're going to need real puppy food, but until then Lilene left me some oatmeal. Does that sound good?" She did her best to get the water hot, but not too hot, in the microwave and mix everything together. "One for me and one for you."

They ate and then he disappeared into the bedroom for a moment and then came racing back in dragging her curling iron behind him. "No, sir. Drop it."

He stopped, staring at her for a long moment with the white cord hanging from his mouth like a long mustache. Then, he dropped it and came running to her.

"Good boy."

She gave him praise, then went and put the curling iron back on the counter where he couldn't reach it.

"I'm going to have to call you something if you're going to be hanging around a little while. What should we call you?"

He barked.

"How about . . . Henry."

He pulled his chin back.

"You don't seem to like that one. How about Porter?"

He jumped up and started running around. "Come here, Porter."

He ran in front of her, then raised his hiney in the air and barked. "I think you like that." She picked him up and held him to her face. "Do you like that name?"

He put his chin on her shoulder.

"Porter it is." She was pretty certain that even in a town the size of Fraser Hills a puppy and sanitation for baked goods was not a good mix. She couldn't very well walk into the office with a puppy in her arms.

She texted Jimmy to see if he could take her to the office.

Jimmy: Right around the corner. Be there in five.

"How lucky is that? We'll get there before anyone else. You can stay under my desk." She shuffled through the cabinets in the kitchen until she found a large paper bag. She tucked the towel and the sock into the bag, then wrapped Porter up in her coat and went downstairs.

Jimmy never noticed the puppy, and she was able to get into the building and upstairs before anyone else arrived.

"We're here," she said to Porter. "How do you like your home for the day? Someone around here has to know who you belong to. But if they don't . . . you could stay with me. I'm getting ready to buy a house with a yard and it needs a cute puppy like you."

She worked while the puppy slept and played in intervals.

"Good morning," Lilene said as she walked into Vanessa's office. "I brought homemade eggnog. You do like eggnog, right?"

"I love it. Can't say I've ever had homemade, though."

"Nothing like it."

Porter woke up and barked. Vanessa flushed.

"What was that?"

"I had a visitor last night."

She took a step backward. "And he's under your desk?"

"He is." She scooted her chair back and grabbed Porter and sat him on the blotter on her desk. "Meet Porter."

"Ohhhhh. Isn't he adorable? Is this one of Mike's puppies?"

"Mike?" Just how much coincidence was there going to be on this job? "Are you serious?"

"I think he's the only one that raises Labs around here. He's awfully cute. Rein, that's his female, the one that was on the wagon that night. She had a litter a month or two ago."

"I don't know. He came out of the woods next to the corporate apartment."

"Oh. Yeah. Must be one of Rein's pups. Mike's farm backs right up to the other warehouse. Y'all are practically neighbors."

"He never mentioned that."

"No secret really. His horses are usually right out there in that pasture. Then again, it's a big pasture. I guess if you're not looking for them you might not see them."

She remembered the horses running in the field while she was jogging last week. This town seemed to get smaller every day.

"I'll give Mike a call, and let him know I have the puppy." She should be relieved to know who the owner was, but part of her wasn't really ready to let go of the little guy.

"You have his number?"

She nodded. "I do."

"Okay, let me know if you need anything."

Vanessa had almost finished aligning every resource from the current Porter's staffing records to the new warehouse project or to their current position in Porter's until they adjusted the processes when Misty walked in an hour later.

"Hi, Vanessa. I brought the old mail-order catalogs that Porter's used to use, along with the mockups and social media plan for an online platform to revive that but on a more current level."

"Great. Come on in."

Porter scooted out from under the front of the desk and ran to Misty.

"Oh my gosh. How did you get here?" Misty looked confused, but she lifted the puppy in the air, then tucked him under her arm. "I'm so sorry. He runs away all the time. He doesn't know he's a dog."

"He showed up at the apartment. I didn't know what to do with him. He's so sweet."

"He is. We call him Scooter. When he was born, he was so little, and all of the other puppies bullied him. They wouldn't let him eat. He was so weak. He just scooted around on his belly. It was so sad. Even Rein, she's his mom, had pretty much pushed him out of the litter." Misty cuddled Scooter. "We really didn't think he was going to make it for a while there, but I started bottle-feeding him and working his legs and he got up on his feet one day and he's gotten stronger and stronger."

"I loved having him for the night."

"You can come over and visit him anytime you want."

"Really?"

"Sure. You can take him for a walk, or for the night. He obviously likes you."

"I've never owned my own dog before."

"Never?"

"Nope. My dad didn't like dogs and then I started working and I guess I forgot how badly I'd wanted one all those years."

"I can't imagine being without a dog in my life. I better take him home real quick." She lifted his paw and waved in her direction. "Say goodbye, Scooter. I'm going to get you back home. I won't be long. I promise."

"Bye, Scooter." Vanessa watched them walk out of her office. If she bought that house back in Chicago, maybe they'd let her buy the puppy and take him to Chicago with her. *I'd still call him Porter.*

CHAPTER TWENTY-FIVE

Parked behind the stables, the Fraser Hills Percherons' semi rig and trailer stretched over fifty feet along the loading-paddock fence. Mike finished winching the show wagon into the back, and locked down the straps to keep it from moving during the trip. He brushed the sweat from his brow and walked down the ramp to close the doors and secure the latches.

It was an all-day affair getting ready to leave.

In a few hours, the guys would arrive to help load the horses and start the trip to Pennsylvania for the annual Christmas parade appearance. The parades were one of Mike's favorite parts of the business, and he was lucky to have a team of men that had been with him for over eight years to help make it all happen. They worked together with barely a word. Quick and precise down to every buckle and bell that went on each horse.

He knew he couldn't do this without the generous gift of

time and muscle his friends gave him. He was so thankful for them.

He went inside and packed his suitcase, then had some lunch. As he was putting his plate in the dishwasher, he heard Randy's truck pass the house toward the barn.

Mike checked his watch. The morning had flown by. He carried his suitcase out of the house to put it in the trailer. Randy was already moving hay into the front storage area when he got there.

Mike walked around to the side of the trailer and opened the doors there to get ready to load the horses. Inside, the equipment boxes had already been rolled on and secured for the long ride.

Mike heard Scooter bark. That puppy was like Houdini. Impossible to restrain.

He tromped down the ramp to see what Scooter was into now.

"Look who I found." Misty walked toward him down the stable alley with Scooter in her arms. "He must have crossed the pasture last night. He was at the front door of the warehouse when Vanessa got home. She took him in."

"He's venturing too far away. He's going to get himself eaten by a coyote, or hit by a car."

Misty rubbed the pup's head. "Vanessa loved him. She's never had a dog. Can you believe that?"

"Her dad could have had allergies. I'm sure he had his reasons."

"She said he didn't like dogs, so even though she'd always wanted one, she never had one."

"That's too bad," Mike said. "They bring a lot of joy to our lives." He gave Scooter the stink eye. "Most of the time."

"They sure do, and I've taken some of that for granted," she said. "Thanks for being such a great dad."

"You make the job easy."

"I love you, Dad." Scooter jumped from her arms and ran into the stables with his feet kicking at an angle behind him until he stopped in front of Big Ben's stall, raised his nose, and barked. Ben hung his huge head over the door and blew a puff of air in a snort.

Scooter yipped and pushed his paws into the air as if he were telling the horse a story. Half the size of the Percheron's head, Scooter didn't seem to notice the size difference.

"Can you believe that dog?" Mike marched into the barn and grabbed the puppy before he scurried away.

Big Ben raised his head with a bounce, his mane tossing.

"You've got to stay with your family," Mike scolded him, then put him in the stall where Rein was feeding the other puppies. "You're a dog. Figure it out."

"I think he thinks he's related to Big Ben." Misty gave the horse a pat on his soft muzzle.

Big Ben nickered.

A hello came from the barn doorway. "Anyone here?"

The silhouette of the woman walking through the shadowy barn with the sun behind her looked like an angel for a moment.

"Hey." Mike stepped into the alley, trying to make out who was here.

"Dad, it's Vanessa." Misty ran past him to greet her. "Hi. Are you missing Scooter already?"

"As silly as it sounds. Yes, kind of." She lifted the brightly colored socks in front of her. "He loved playing with these so much last night. I thought maybe I'd leave them with you."

"That's so sweet," Misty said. "Look, Dad."

"I see." He tugged on his ball cap. "How are you?"

"I'm good." An awkward silence lasted a beat too long. "This place is amazing. And that tractor trailer out there. Wow. It's bigger than a moving truck."

"Not really. It's about the same size. I know because it was one before we had it converted for the horses."

"Wow," Vanessa said. "Oh!" She stepped back as Big Ben pushed his head forward over the stall door again. "I don't know how you get used to being around them. They are so big."

"I grew up around them," Misty said.

"Don't you get worried that one will get hurt riding around in that big trailer?"

Mike shook his head. "No. We're careful. Believe me, that trailer was built for their comfort. Enhanced air-cushioned suspension and thick rubber flooring. Plus, we have cameras in the trailer so we can watch the horses during transport."

"Of course you do."

"We just put Scooter back in with his mom, and all the other puppies." Misty motioned her to come and see them.

Vanessa walked over. "Aww. They are so cute, and so much bigger than Por-Scooter."

"Poor Scooter is a pain in the butt," Mike said. "He keeps getting out. I don't want to kennel him, but I might have to just for his safety."

"He'd hate that," Vanessa said.

"So would I," said Misty. "I'll try to work with him more. His obedience training starts in two weeks. That will help too."

"You obedience-train all those puppies?"

"We do," Mike said. "We'll train them all and from the best

we'll choose one to keep and train with Rein. She's getting older, and we need to start preparing her replacement to ride with the hitch."

"You'll sell the rest?" Vanessa looked interested.

"Yes. We've had a couple go on to be assistance dogs for veterans."

"That's wonderful." Vanessa took a step over to the next stall. "I can't get over how big the horses are. Look at those feet."

"They need big feet to carry all that weight." He pointed to the horseshoe hanging on the wall next to the stall. It was painted high-gloss black, and a shiny brass plate with the name GUS engraved on it had been tacked at its center. "These guys wear shoes the size of a dinner plate and about five pounds each."

"Is that a real horseshoe?"

"It is. An old one."

"Five pounds? I thought my hiking boots were heavy."

"Sometimes they are heavier. In principle, the heavier the weight on the end of the leg, the farther it will swing. That inspires that high stepping everyone loves so much."

"In people sizes, I guess we're basically talking Sasquatch . . . in cement boots."

"I never really thought about it that way, but yes. Sort of." He pushed his hands into his pockets. "You got some time? I'll show you around."

"Sure. You coming too, Misty?"

"Yeah. Hang on." A moment later Misty fell into step with them, with Scooter at her heels.

"And that . . ." Mike pointed to the puppy. ". . . is a big part of why that little guy always wants to get away from the others. You're spoiling him."

"But he's so cute," Misty and Vanessa said in unison.

"You've decorated the barn." Vanessa twirled around, taking in the pine wreaths with the peppermint-striped bows hanging from the stall doors at this end. A Christmas tree reached to the full height of the barn in the middle. "That tree has to be every bit of twenty feet tall."

"We have an open house every year. Cookies and punch. Nothing real fancy. A few of the guys bring guitars. They'll play Christmas carols around the firepit. Kids will roast marshmallows and hot dogs. It's a really nice gathering. You should plan to come. And bring your cousin, of course."

"That sounds like fun."

"It will be even more fun if you come." He wished he could take it back as soon as he'd said it. He knew better than to be so forward. She probably thought he was full of himself.

"Is it this weekend?"

"No, I'm heading out tonight. We have an annual parade run up north. The party is the following week."

"Then, yeah. Count me in. I wouldn't miss it."

"I'll pick you up."

"I can walk over."

"I'd rather pick you up."

"Do you always get your way?"

"I've been alone a long time. I usually give myself my way. It works."

She laughed. "Okay. This isn't a date . . . is it?"

Mike looked around. Misty was over by the Christmas tree trying to keep Scooter from dragging the garland to the ground. *Am I really going to say this?* He swallowed hard, and sucked in a breath. "Do you want it to be?"

She pressed her lips together. "I'm not opposed to that."

"I'd like that a lot." He let out a breath, and pushed his

hands into his pockets. "I haven't done this in a long time." A horn honked out back. "I've got to run. The guys are here and we need to get these horses loaded so we can stop at the feed mill before they close and get on the road."

"Sure. Yeah. Do you mind if I watch you load the horses? I'll stay out of the way."

"Not at all. There's a bench over there." He pointed toward a long plank with wagon wheels on each end. "Block your calendar for next weekend. I'll touch base when I get back in town." He couldn't contain his smile.

"Perfect. Thank you." Her chest heaved, and then she smiled. "I'm looking forward to this. Have a good trip."

"Yeah, thanks." He walked outside, then turned to watch her walk away.

Chapter Twenty-six

V anessa sat on the bench, setting her purse down next to her, which really seemed ridiculous. *Why didn't I just leave it in the car?* At least behind the barn the building blocked the cool winter breeze, making the sun almost warm against her cheeks.

Everyone moved with purpose, getting the horses ready to load.

She pulled her foot up underneath her on the bench. It was a little intimidating watching the big horses get led by the small lead lines. There was no way they could manhandle the huge animals if one decided to go wild. It would be like a rubber raft trying to pull a cruise ship.

"Get over here," Misty yelled. "You are not going."

The pup put his nose in the air and sat down next to the horse trailer.

It appeared to be a standoff to Vanessa.

Misty picked up the puppy, then raised her hand and petted the nose of the horse waiting for his turn to load onto the trailer. Misty looked so tiny next to that horse. "You're last to load, Big Ben. You know that."

Big Ben leaned forward and sniffed at the pup.

The puppy lifted a paw to his nose, in a *hey buddy, I'm gonna miss you while you're away* expression. Vanessa slid her phone from her purse and took a picture. It was amazing to see animals large and small interact like that.

The horses' coats shone like high-gloss lacquer, their muscles rippling like an iron machine but graceful and fluid as they stepped up the ramp into the vast trailer one by one. They were even more beautiful now, up close.

Mike oversaw the whole thing, jumping in where needed and encouraging the horses. She liked how he thanked and acknowledged the skill of the people working for him. Misty was right in the middle of it all. Completely unafraid, and as skilled as the big guys at handling the giant horses.

Big Ben and Scooter were standing over by the water trough. From here it looked as if Scooter could be swept into the horse's nose with one big breath. Part of her wanted to run over and rescue him. The other was just as pleased to sit and watch the dynamics between them.

They finally loaded Big Ben. Scooter stood at the bottom of the ramp.

Misty came around the corner of the trailer. "Well, they're about loaded." She stood next to Vanessa.

"Do you usually go with him to the parades?"

"Sometimes, but not this year. I have too much going on with school. I'm sitting this one out."

"You're going to be home by yourself?"

"Yeah. No problem."

"You're welcome to come with me. I'm going to help Anna decorate our Christmas tree."

"Thank you, but I'm staying home because I have school-work. I need to focus on that."

Vanessa laid a hand on her shoulder. "You call me if you change your mind or need anything."

"Thank you, but I'm sure I'll be fine."

Vanessa almost asked if she could take Scooter with her for the night, then decided against it. Besides, she didn't know that Buck would appreciate her bringing an untrained puppy into his guesthouse, and he was being so generous.

"Okay, well, have a good night," Vanessa said. "Tell your dad I said good luck with the parade."

With a slow smile, Misty said, "I definitely will pass that along."

Vanessa drove Anna's car back over to Buck's house. The new Christmas tree filled the whole space in front of the double windows on the carriage house; white lights twinkled in a flashing sequence. "It looks so pretty." She wished she'd thought to pick up a wreath today.

When she walked inside, the aroma of fresh pine hung in the air. The fire crackled and a plate of brightly decorated cookies had been set out on the coffee table near the tree.

Vanessa heard laughter from the kitchen.

"Hello?"

Anna came running out of the kitchen, almost like she'd been caught doing something. "Vanessa. I'm so glad you're here. Did you see our tree? It's gorgeous."

"It is." She ran her fingers over the soft, thick needles. "It smells so good."

"You should've been there." Anna swung around toward

Buck, who was sipping from a mug, leaning casually against the doorway. "Right, Buck?"

"Yes, ma'am. It was quite a day. I haven't had that much fun in a long time. Your cousin here insisted on getting her hands dirty too."

Anna held up her fingers, barely able to pull them apart from the sap. "So sticky. I know you warned me. It was a labor of love, though. Thank goodness, Buck was there to help decide which tree was the perfect one, because apparently I don't have much sense of scale when looking at trees in the great outdoors."

Anna looked at the ceiling-scraping tree.

"This was the one I said was too little."

Vanessa let out a hearty laugh. "Oh goodness. You'd have had to decorate a tree any bigger than this outside."

"That's what he said."

Buck pushed a hand through his hair. "Yeah, they don't look nearly as big against the mountainside. I've got years of experience."

"What's all this stuff," Vanessa asked, pointing to the two large stacks of boxes.

"I wasn't sure what y'all would want to decorate with, so I brought a bunch of stuff up. When you're done decorating, I'll move the boxes out of here."

Vanessa lifted the top from one of the boxes and pulled out a heavy bag of pearl garland. "This will be pretty."

"Oh, I really like that. Isn't it fancy?"

"Look." Vanessa raised a shiny ball with a flocked design on it. "I can't believe it. You never see these anymore. This is exactly like what we had on our tree growing up."

"There's all kinds of stuff in those boxes. Different themes, and colors. My late wife . . . she loved Christmas."

"Thank you for letting us use this. Are you sure you're okay with it?"

"Absolutely." He wagged a finger in Anna and Vanessa's direction. "Smiles like that. They're priceless."

"Thank you, Buck," Anna said. "Oh, Vanessa, you won't believe how we got the tree back to the truck."

"Please don't tell me you carried it."

"Heavens, no. It has to weigh a ton. Buck even had someone come help us get it into the house, but they had this sleigh—well, it looked like a sleigh, but it had wheels and this big old mule pulled it with us on the sleigh too."

"That sounds fun."

"It was, and Buck's a great singer." Anna glanced his way with a smile that pushed a dimple in her chin. "He sang 'O Christmas Tree' all the way back."

"I might've been caught up in the moment." His cheeks flushed. "It was nice."

"It sure was," Anna said. "I want to get a tree exactly like this every year. . . ." She appeared flustered, as if she hadn't meant to say that out loud. Switching her attention back to Vanessa: "What did you do all day while we were cutting down the Christmas tree?"

"I went over and watched them load up the horses to go to a parade up in Pennsylvania. They are even bigger up close. Fraser Hills Percherons," she mentioned to Buck. "You know them? Well, of course you do. Small town and all."

"I do."

"Look at this." Vanessa ran over to Anna with her phone.

"This little puppy showed up at the corporate apartment last night. Isn't he adorable?"

Anna looked, then grabbed the phone. "Oh my gosh, I bet he still has puppy breath."

"He does. It reminded me of your dog, Sam."

"I loved that dog so much."

"I never really understood how people thought of pets as family. I guess because I'd never had one of my own, but I totally get it now. That pup stole my heart last night. If I didn't live in a condo, I'd have kept him for myself."

"I wouldn't let that stop you," Anna said. "They bring so much to your life."

"That's true," said Buck.

"And look at this." Vanessa brought up the picture of Big Ben and Scooter together. "It's like they were having a discussion. He's the cutest thing."

"I'm so surprised to hear you gush over that puppy." Anna started laughing and pulled closer to Buck. "She used to go crazy if my dog, Sam, licked her. You'd have thought we were forcing poison on her." She could barely catch her breath as she laughed at the memory. "She'd have a complete hissy fit."

Vanessa laughed. "I know. She's not exaggerating. I did lose it. That was so stupid, Anna. You must've thought I was a nutcase. Last night, that little guy was licking my face like I was covered in peanut butter. That little tongue of his even went right up my nose, but I didn't mind one bit. I was a little sad when Lilene knew exactly where the puppy had come from when I brought him into the office with me."

"You took him to work?"

"I couldn't leave that sweet little face at home all day alone. He's so precious."

Buck put his arm around Anna and gave her a squeeze. "Thanks for a lovely day, fine lady. You two have a joyful night together decorating that tree. If you need help with the angel on top, Anna knows how to reach me."

He gave them a wink as he walked out the door.

Anna and Vanessa stood there in silence watching him all the way back to the main house.

"He likes you," Vanessa said.

"Do *not* get my hopes up."

"I'm not. I'm serious. Did you see the way he listens to you? The way he smiles when he's looking your way?"

"Vanessa, we had the best day. I mean, truly the best day of my life. It was perfect from beginning to end."

She took Anna's hands into her own. "I'm so glad."

"He gave me this ornament for the tree too." She walked to the side of the tree facing the front door, right at eye height, for her anyway, and cupped the single ornament in her hand. "Isn't it beautiful?"

The thick wooden ornament had been sanded to a furniture-quality finish. In the shape of the carriage on the Porter's logo, FRASER HILLS, NC was etched across the wagon in what looked like gold leaf.

"That is beautiful. I didn't see anything like this over in the store."

She shrugged. "I don't know where he got it, but I like it. It's the thought that counts."

Anna and Vanessa sat on the floor among all the boxes of ornaments trying to decide which ones to use on the tree. Finally, they'd decided to use the pretty pearl garland, a collection of Lenox ornaments, and red balls and bows.

Anna hung ornaments while Vanessa tied bows made from

a spool of velvety ribbon. Mom had taught her to make bows when she was little. They were forever making them for weddings, church, even school. She was a little out of practice, and it took her a couple of goes to get it. Finally, she lifted one in the air. "What do you think?"

Anna nodded. "As beautiful as the ones your mom made."

Vanessa held the perfect bow. She wished she could spend just one more Christmas with her mother. She blinked back a tear that threatened to fall, concentrating on the ornaments.

They decorated for over an hour before they were finally satisfied.

"It looks so pretty."

"I love it." Vanessa stepped back, taking it all in. "I haven't put up a tree the last few years."

"Then you were missing out. Doesn't it make you feel . . . I don't even know how to describe it. Young? Hopeful? In awe, I guess."

"It does."

Anna cocked her head. "Is that your phone ringing?"

Vanessa rummaged through the piles of paper and box stuffing for her phone. "It sounds like it. Where is it?" She finally put her hand on the phone. "It's a local number. Hello?"

"Hey, Vanessa. I'm sorry to bother you. It's Misty."

Vanessa flashed a look of concern in Anna's direction. "Misty. Is everything okay?"

"Yes, well I'm not hurt or anything, it's just I went to lock up the barn and Scooter is missing again. I was kind of hoping he'd showed up back at the apartment."

"Oh, gosh. I'm not there. How about you stay where you are and keep looking around, and I'll zip by the apartment and then swing over with the puppy, or to help you look. Sound good?"

"I can drive over there," she said.

"No. Really I don't mind. Anna just tossed me her car keys. I'm headed out the door now." Vanessa tucked her phone in her purse and grabbed her coat. "Misty is home by herself, and the puppy is missing. Do you want to ride along?"

"No. You run on. I'm going to do a few tweaks here and then jump in the tub for a nice long soak. Take your time."

"I hope he's okay." She ran out and drove straight over to the warehouse. Unfortunately, there was no puppy waiting for her there. She checked around the building, and called for him, but the night was quiet.

She'd hoped the puppy would be at the warehouse waiting on her, as if somehow he'd chosen her to be his forever home. And just as quickly, she knew it was a crazy idea. She was never even home to take care of a puppy. It wouldn't be fair to saddle Anna with one, even if she did agree to move to Chicago, which seemed iffy given how much she'd complained about the Chicago winters. But the priority was finding that pup.

She drove over to check on Misty, who came out the front door as soon as Vanessa pulled up.

She stepped out of the car, holding her arms open. "I'm sorry. He wasn't there."

Misty's shoulders slumped. "I hope he didn't get himself eaten by a coyote or an owl or something. Dad was just talking about that."

"No! Don't even say that. Oh, my goodness. That would be awful. Now, let's think some positive thoughts."

Misty sniffled, nodding her head. "Yeah. Let's find him."

"Okay, so where could he have gone. Have you checked

inside the house? Maybe he's curled up somewhere sleeping while we're panicking trying to find him."

"I don't think he would've gotten inside. Dad's pretty funny about that, but we can look."

They scoured the house. At one point, Vanessa had screamed success, but it had turned out to be a light golden brown beanie in the laundry basket.

Misty deflated. "Dad said I should kennel him. I wish I had now."

"Let's go back out to the barn," Vanessa said. "You said yourself he thinks he's a horse. Let's double-check all the stalls."

"Okay, maybe he's bunking with one of the other horses since Big Ben and Jake are gone. They seem to be his favorites. He absolutely loves being around the horses."

"Well, that's okay. Maybe that's who he's supposed to be. Like a natural horse-herding dog or something."

Misty laughed. "Maybe." She whistled and called for Scooter.

Vanessa walked down the alleyway of the stable in the opposite direction peeking into each stall, but there was no sign of Scooter.

I should have stowed him away at the apartment. At least then he'd be okay.

"I think he's gone." Misty leaned against one of the stalls. "I can't believe I let that happen."

"Misty, it's not your fault. You know that."

"I was supposed to take care of him. I've been nursing him back to health all this time."

"And he's doing great. It's not your fault he has a wild streak."

"No telling where he could've gotten off to."

"The good news is most everyone knows you're the only

people raising Lab puppies. It took two seconds for me to find the owner, someone else will too."

"I guess."

Seeing her so defeated left a heavy ache in Vanessa's stomach. "Let's go inside. It's cold out here."

Misty trudged toward the house. She wasn't in much of a hurry, but that actually kind of worked in Vanessa's favor, because she really had no idea what to suggest.

When they walked inside, the telephone was ringing.

"I bet someone found him," Vanessa said.

"Make yourself at home." Misty ran for the phone, her boots sliding across the shiny wooden floors, to answer it. "Hello?" She dropped the phone to her chin. "It's my dad."

She slipped off her boots and walked into the other room while explaining to him what was going on.

Vanessa took her shoes off and left them at the door, then grabbed some paper towels to clean up the mud they'd tracked in.

When Misty came back, she was carrying hot chocolate. "Here. Sorry I brought you out in the cold to search for Scooter."

"Don't be silly. I'm glad you called. I'm happy to help. I grew kind of attached to him during our slumber party. He's so cute. Probably too smart for his own good, but cute."

They sat in big leather chairs in the living room. This room looked as if it didn't get a lot of use—that, or these two were phenomenal housekeepers. The furniture was big and sturdy. The end tables were rustic and heavy. Across one whole wall there were trophies and ribbons behind glass built-ins.

"Wow. That is a lot of ribbons."

"Not just ours. The horses won most of those before I was even born."

"It's a very nice legacy to be a part of."

"Yeah. My family is the best."

"Do you have some markers and paper or cardboard?"

"Sure." She got up and opened the middle drawer of a desk in the study. "What are you going to do?"

"Let's make a couple posters to hang up, and a flyer. In the morning we'll zip by the office and make copies of the flyer, and hand them out all over town before we get our day started."

"You're going to help me do that?"

"Yes. Yes, I am." Her eyes shot wide. "And, I've got this." She scrolled through her phone and showed Misty a picture she'd taken last night. "It'll be perfect. I'll print some four-by-sixes of this to put on the posters."

"You really think he's okay?"

She didn't want to give her false hope. She considered the situation a moment. "You know, I really do. It's Christmas. He's probably snuggled up somewhere, or in someone else's house doing a sleepover to see what kind of treats he can get out of them." She quickly wrote out "LOST" across the top of the page. "And we'll get him a collar tomorrow too. My treat."

They made the flyer template and Misty seemed much more relaxed about the situation. "Would you like to come stay with me tonight? My cousin Anna is there too, but I don't mind if you'd rather not be alone."

"The apartment is tight quarters even for one."

"Oh, we're not staying there. I was just using it last night to do some late-night work. There's room. Come stay."

"No, thank you. I'm fine, but I can pick you up in the morning so we can make the copies at the office. Is that okay?"

"That would be great."

"Where are you staying?"

"It's a long story, but when my cousin got to town, we were trying to straighten out her Airbnb reservation, with something nearby."

"There's not a lot of places to stay around here."

"Exactly. But there's this older gentleman I kept bumping into over at the Blue Bicycle Bistro. He overheard us and offered us his guesthouse."

"You're staying at the carriage house? Off Porter House Road?"

"Yes. Back there around the curve. Do you know Buck?"

"I do." She kind of smiled, but with a lift of her brow. "He's the best. Does my dad know you're staying over there?"

Vanessa shrugged. "I guess not. No, probably not. I'm sure he wouldn't have any problem with you staying with us for the night. I'd be happy to call him."

"No. Don't do that." She smiled brightly. "No need to do that. I'm just fine here. I'll be there in the morning to pick you up. Does seven work?"

"That'll be great." Vanessa started to walk away, but Misty called after her.

"Buck's awesome. Just as awesome as my dad."

Vanessa's heart tugged. Yes. They did have some good men in this town. "He was so kind to let us use that place. It's amazing. He even helped Anna cut down a live Christmas tree. We had just finished decorating it when you called."

"That sounds just like him."

"I'm going to run over to the warehouse one more time and make sure Scooter's not there before I head back." She waved goodbye as she got in her car. "I know we're going to find him."

"I'm feeling better about things too," said Misty.

CHAPTER TWENTY-SEVEN

The next morning Anna and Vanessa were sitting in front of the fire, enjoying the beautiful Christmas tree and sipping hot chocolate, when Misty walked by the windows toward the front door.

Vanessa jumped up from her chair to get the door. "Come on inside."

"I hope you don't mind that I'm early." She unwrapped the red scarf from her neck.

"I thought for sure I'd hear your truck come up."

"I parked over by the side entrance of the main house. I figured I should at least stop in and say hello to Buck if I was going to be here."

"You're such a sweet young lady." Vanessa motioned toward her cousin. "You remember Anna. Can I get you some hot chocolate, or are you ready to go?"

"How about hot chocolate to go?"

"I'm way ahead of you," said Anna. "I saw a thermos in the kitchen. Give me two minutes I'll have y'all all set up." She looked like an elf in her bright red-and-green pajamas, walking through the Christmassy room.

"Let me know if I can be of help." Vanessa turned her attention back to Misty. "Where should we start?"

"I thought we'd make the copies at the office and then start out near the warehouse and work our way back."

"Sounds good to me."

"I brought some bright poster board and packing tape," Misty said. "I figured we could tape the flyers to the poster board. We can hang a couple along the school bus route. Then I'll hand the flyers out along Main Street and let everyone know. Word of mouth is faster than anything around here."

"Easy enough."

"I just hope it works."

Anna came in with an old-school vintage plaid thermos. The tall one with the cup attached to the top. "Here you go, girls. Good luck."

"Thank you." Vanessa put on her coat and Anna tossed a knitted scarf her way.

Vanessa caught the toffee-brown scarf in midair. "Where'd this come from?"

"Just a little something I worked on while watching television the other night."

"I love the leather button accents," Vanessa said.

Anna beamed. "I knew you would."

"You made this?" Misty reached over and ran her hands across the stitching. "This is beautiful. It's so soft, and not too frilly-looking."

"That's a simple checkerboard pattern. I'll make you one. I

brought yarn with me. I can't stand to not have anything to do with my hands. I have red, black, a pretty cocoa color, and—"

"Red! Really? You'll make me one too?"

"Absolutely. I'll work on it today." She leaned in sweetly. "It'll give me an excuse to take a lazy day in front of the fire."

"Merry Christmas to me."

"I'll make you a deal," Anna said. "When you find that puppy, I'll make him a bright red sweater so he can't hide so easy!"

"That's seriously a good idea."

Vanessa agreed. "We're off! Love you, Anna."

"Love you too. Good luck." Anna stood waving from the front porch.

Vanessa followed Misty around the corner to her truck. Misty hopped right in, while Vanessa fumbled with the running board to get a good solid step, then grabbed the handle and pulled herself up and buckled in.

After a quick stop at the office, Misty was on her way to get the word out.

"Are you sure you don't need my help putting up the posters or anything?"

"I'm sure," Misty said. "Thanks for helping me, though. I really appreciate it."

"You're welcome. Keep me posted."

Misty rushed out the door and Vanessa stood there holding her hand to her heart. "Here's hoping you find that little guy."

*

At the end of the day, Misty knocked on Vanessa's door. "I'm headed out. No calls on the puppy."

"I'm so sorry."

"I wanted to thank you for your help. I mean, that has nothing to do with work. I really shouldn't have burdened you with it. It wasn't very professional of me."

"You didn't burden me. I was glad to help. I love that little guy too. He and I bonded during his visit."

"I can give you a ride back to the carriage house if you're ready to leave. Just thought I'd offer."

She glanced across her desk. She still had some things she wanted to work on, but most of it could be done from the house, and the fireplace did sound inviting. "That would be great. I'll ride with you to check for Scooter again if you want to take me the long way home."

"Sounds good. We'll stop at my house first, then the warehouse and over to Buck's."

"Before we go, I need Lilene to schedule something for me. I'll meet you downstairs."

Vanessa gathered her things, then stopped at Lilene's desk, where she sat singing along with a Christmas song on the radio as she checked time cards. "Lilene, I need you to schedule a meeting for tomorrow night."

She laid down her pencil. "For everyone?" Her nostrils flared as she sucked in a slow breath and leaned back, a deep crease forming over her brow. "Is this from the call earlier today with corporate?"

"It is, but it's not bad news. I just need to update everyone."

She let out the breath. "I'll call and schedule the elementary school. What time, six?"

"Let's make it immediately following shift, so about five fifteen." Vanessa started to walk off. "You know, let's not do that. Instead, have everyone gather here at Porter's."

"Where will they sit?"

"They'll stand. It won't take long."

"What about customers?"

"They'll be mostly locals anyway. No secrets. Let's keep it low-key. It's winter. It'll be a little cozy, but I think the holiday decorations will be nice, and if I speak from the third or fourth stairstep I'll be able to see everyone just fine. Could you buy some of those cookies you had in the red tin in my basket?"

"The Retrops?"

"I don't know. They were in ornament shapes and drizzled in chocolate."

"I made those."

"You did? Why do you call them Retrops?"

"'Porter' spelled backwards. I use the not-quite-right Porter's cakes that they are going to throw away. Usually they are just a little too done on top. I add a few little things to it, roll them out, rebake them, and decorate them. I named them Retrops because I start backwards with a fresh finished product to make a new one."

"I cannot believe those are made from fruitcake."

"Not just any fruitcake. Our fruitcake. Yeah. Just for fun, ya know. Everybody loves them."

"Including me. Okay, well I can't ask you to make three hundred cookies for tomorrow night. How about—"

"No. I can do it. I've been baking all weekend anyway. I can just do more tonight." She grinned wide, and clapped her hands together. "I'm so glad you liked them."

"Well, great then." Vanessa joined Misty at the front door and they drove over to the farm to check for the puppy, but there was still no sign of him. Zack hadn't seen him since they loaded the trailer yesterday either. Misty pulled around the barn to the house driveway to leave, but as they passed the front of the house, she stomped her foot on the brake. The truck lurched to a stop.

"Oh my gosh. Look!" Misty pointed toward the front porch at something golden. She bailed out, running to the door calling for the puppy with the enthusiasm of a teenager.

Vanessa relaxed a little. *Thank goodness.*

But near the porch, Misty slowed to a stop and then walked the rest of the way.

Vanessa leaned forward in her seat trying to see what was going on, unsure whether to run and help or sit and wait. Then Misty stooped down and scooped something up, but it didn't look like Scooter.

As Misty got closer, she could see it was simply a big yellow padded shipping envelope.

"I'm sorry," Vanessa said as Misty climbed into the truck and laid the package on the console.

"It was just my dress for the dance," Misty said.

"Well, that's good news." Vanessa picked up the package. "Let's open it."

"It can wait." Misty shrugged, and Vanessa wasn't sure whether the mood was from being worried about Scooter or being shy about the dress.

"I want to see it."

"You do?" She'd pulled away from the house, heading to the warehouse to check for Scooter.

"Yes. I was Vanessa's Fine Vintage Frills, remember. Of course I want to see it."

"Okay. I guess. If you're sure." Misty turned at the end of the street.

"We can open it when we get to the carriage house. I know Anna would love to see your dress too. It'll be fun. Just the girls."

269

"Really?"

"Do you know how many years it's been since I went to a dance?"

Misty giggled.

"Yeah. Don't guess that. Let's just say it was a long time, but, Misty, being all dressed up is like becoming a different person. I still remember my first dance. It was like I'd become beautiful all of a sudden, and brave; this is going to sound stupid, but it made me feel better about myself."

"A dress?"

"It's the dress. It's the formality of it. The corsage. The decorations. The music." A tickle at her nose made her take a breath. "It's the most magical thing."

"You make it sound wonderful."

"It is. I'm so excited for you. Is he nice?"

"Who?"

"The boy you're going with?"

"Luke? Super nice. He's really active in school programs and all. He makes me laugh."

"The best kind," Vanessa said.

Misty's phone rang. "Excuse me. If it's Dad and I don't answer he'll get worried." She pulled off the road and took her phone from her purse. "Hello?"

Vanessa sat quietly as Misty spoke until she realized the conversation was good news about Scooter. She clasped her hands. So glad to know he was okay.

"He's fine." Misty's eyes sparkled as she put her phone down. "He's all the way over in the next town. It's like a thirty-minute drive."

"How did he get that far?"

"The only thing I can figure is that he must've gotten on the trailer or in Dad's truck when they were loading up, and then gotten left behind when they stopped at the feed store to stock up. Dad's good friends with the guy who owns the place."

"Let's go get him."

"They are going to keep him tonight since they live up the mountain. It's already snowing up there and the roads get iffy quick." She smiled wide, then put the truck in gear and pulled back onto the road. "They'll take really good care of Scooter. They're the ones who told me what to try to get him healthy. I trust them."

"I'm so glad he's in good hands."

"Me too. I have to admit, I really thought he was gone for good."

"He's not. You can breathe easier now." It was hard to believe the young lady sitting next to her was only sixteen. *I suppose losing your mother at a young age forces a certain amount of quick growing up.* "Better to trust things will be okay than worry about the worst-case scenario. Worrying will give you gray hair." She pointed to hers.

Misty laughed. "You must never worry, then. You don't have any gray hair."

"I have the secret weapon."

"Not worrying?"

"No. A magnificent hairdresser."

"We don't have a fancy shop like that around here."

"Here's a piece of advice one of my managers told me early on. It's what I always go back to. Not just in work, but anytime I get worried. He said, 'Decide what's more important to you: the dream that's your desired outcome, or your fear.'"

"The dream," Misty said. "Always."

"Right, and as long as you stay focused on the dream, you'll see opportunities. But if you let the fear take over, all you'll ever see is obstacles."

"Like we did with making the posters for Scooter. We saw an opportunity to get the word out."

"Exactly."

"Thanks for sharing that. Dad texted earlier. They'll probably roll in around eleven tonight. I'm going to go home and get some rest. It'll be busy at the farm getting the horses and gear unpacked."

"I guess you can't leave the horses on the trailer all night, can you."

"Travel is tough on them, we'll want to get them unloaded immediately and give them some time to move around, stretch and rehydrate. They can lose like five percent of their weight on a ride that long." She snapped her fingers in the air. "Just like that."

"They always look so relaxed when you see them on the trailers."

"Think about standing in the back of my truck for the ride home. You'd be shifting your weight to stay upright with every turn and repositioning at every bounce. It's a workout."

"I'm glad this is my stop," Vanessa said with a laugh. "Go home. Good luck unloading tonight. I'll be in slumberland by the time you get started." Vanessa grabbed the door handle and got out of the truck. "Good night."

*

The next afternoon, Vanessa sat at her desk munching on one of Lilene's Retrops as she went through her notes for the meeting tonight. Lilene had gone down to the retail store to manage getting set up for the meeting. Cookies were layered on raised cake plates on the display tables, and small plates and napkins were put out too.

The shift ended and the noise level rose as more and more of the factory workers made their way into the store.

She walked downstairs to check on things. People were talking among themselves and enjoying Lilene's cookies. It was apparent Lilene had included an "it's not bad news" whisper along with the meeting invite, because the vibe tonight was completely different than in the elementary school cafeteria that first night, which was what she'd hoped for.

She spotted Buck and Anna standing at the counter talking to Misty. She waved in their direction and worked her way over toward them. Anna waved and Buck gave her an encouraging smile.

It took Vanessa a few minutes to get across the store, stopping to say hello to the guys who had helped Bill get the warehouse in shape. "Thanks for your help." She shook hands. "Good to see you." She was being met with smiles rather than fear and speculation this time.

Bill grabbed her hand and gave it a firm shake. "You should stick around and run this shop. I'd consult for you any day of the week."

The compliment meant a lot to her. Bill had gotten his start at this company. She teased, "Unless it's a hunting day, and there's a big buck on the loose, right?"

"I might even sacrifice one of those days for you, Vanessa. I respect your style."

"Thank you, Bill. You're a huge part of this success."

Moving closer to Anna, she thought, *This is definitely a different room to talk with tonight.*

She paused as she stepped away.

Talk *with*?

A tiny shock of realization sizzled inside her.

Talk *with* rather than *to* the people. It sounded like a subtle change, but was it? She swiveled, taking in the faces around her. The room seemed to silence, although she could still see the people talking. She could name one, two, three . . . more than twenty-five of the people standing nearby. It'd be easier to count who she didn't recognize.

Hardworking people who genuinely cared about one another and this town.

As she turned, Buck caught her arm.

"Are you okay?" He put his other arm on the top of her shoulder. "You look unsteady."

"No. I'm not. I was just . . ." She patted his hand. "I'm fine. Really. I was coming over to say hello and got sidetracked along the way. Let me make this announcement. I'll be right back."

She walked over to the stairs and climbed to the fourth step and looked around. The crowd seemed like a hive of energetic bees below. She clapped her hands in an attempt to regain control. One second later there was that loud whistle of Lilene's and the room quieted to a hush.

"I'm going to have to learn that whistle." Nervous laughter broke the tension as Vanessa regained control.

"Merry Christmas. I hope you're all feeling the holiday spirit after the great parade this weekend." She started clapping and folks joined in.

"Thank you for gathering again on short notice. I promised to bring you updates as soon as I had them, so that's what we're doing here tonight. Before I go through the changes, I want to share a couple of personal observations."

"Here comes the bad-news sandwich," someone groaned from somewhere among the display cases.

Buck's unmistakable voice boomed. "Hush up, Tinker. Let the lady speak. You're always stirring up stuff that doesn't need stirring."

"Sorry."

Vanessa never had seen who had made the comment. "Thank you, Buck. I admit I was in line for an assignment in Paris this holiday and I was not happy about being sent to Fraser Hills, North Carolina, but I've had the great pleasure to get to know many of you in the past couple of weeks as we've evaluated the footprint and business activities. Thank you for being such a good team."

Nods and a few whispers spread across the floor.

"Initial plans included confirmation of warehouse space. As you know, we've had a team heads-down on clearing out the facility on the next block in preparation for that. The team has made quick work of it and we've been able to recoup some of the money for repairs by scrapping old equipment, or in some cases donating it to be repurposed for other things in the county. I want to thank Bill Campbell for his leadership on this effort."

People cheered. No one seemed to even remember how mad they'd been with her for giving him that package not that long ago.

"Great job. Really it was a team effort. We have a few more requirements that have come through and my goal is to have that warehouse up and running, ready to begin receiving inventory by the first of the year." She raised her hand as people grumbled. "I know. It's super fast. Racks and equipment will be coming soon. I have a detailed plan to get us done by December eighteenth. It's aggressive, but I want you all to have the time you deserve with your families over the holiday. It'll mean all hands on deck, but it also includes some changes to Porter's. Before you jump to conclusions, these are positive changes, many of them proposed by one of your own." She waved to Misty. "Misty, join me up here."

Buck's mouth fell open.

Misty looked as if she'd frozen to her spot.

"Come on, Misty."

She ran toward the stairs and stood next to Vanessa with her cheeks a bright red.

"Misty brought me several ideas to help move the needle on Porter's. We'll be doing some really great things, including a new online store and ramping up production goals for 2020."

For the next twenty minutes she fielded every question about the upcoming changes, and let Misty respond to some of the Porter's-specific ones, which she handled with ease and confidence.

"Thank you, everyone, for your support and dedication to our future here in your beautiful town, and thank you for making me feel such a welcome part of it. Our task is to have everything done prior to my meeting back in Chicago on December eighteenth. Everyone who works the entire time will get paid days off through the holiday for the extra time and dedication. And I'll be back in town taking some time off too, with my cousin here for our first Fraser Hills Christmas." She scanned the room for any remaining raised hands or uncertain expressions. "If there are no more questions, that's it for tonight. I'll bring us together when we have more news. Thank you."

Everyone filed out of the store. Surprisingly, even with the crowd the store wasn't disheveled, but the store employees did a quick walk-through to straighten up before they closed for the night.

Vanessa was the last one out. Buck and Anna sat in his truck in front of the store waiting on her.

She stopped at the double front doors. As she slipped the old key into the shiny brass lock, through the watery glass it looked like a dream. *And to all a good night.*

She dropped the key into her coat pocket and got into the back of Buck's car.

"That's good what you did in there." Buck's eyes met hers in the rearview mirror.

"Thank you. This old guy gave me some good advice. Not that I'd asked for any." She laughed. "But I've been trying to put it to good use."

"I'd hoped you would."

He grinned, nodding as he pulled away from the curb.

"Can I tell her?" Anna looked about ready to explode. Had she been a hiding a secret?

Vanessa leaned forward in the seat. "Tell me what?"

"Misty is my great-granddaughter." Buck lifted his gaze from the road to the rearview mirror again. "Did you have any idea?"

"None." Misty had never mentioned it, and there'd been a clear chance when Vanessa had talked about Buck and the carriage house.

"Nope. She's a smart kid. Came out of the womb that way. Confident. Determined. Strong. I'm very proud of her. I'd do anything to be sure that child has all the opportunities she deserves. Thank you for recognizing that in her."

"Don't thank me. It was certainly not done as any kind of

favor to you, though you've been terrific. I liked what she'd planned. It was a good solid plan, and she had the data to back it."

"I think it's going to be a pretty good year around here next year." Buck lifted his hand from the wheel and dropped it to Anna's leg. "I'm gonna see more of you next year too, won't I?"

"If I have anything to say about it."

Vanessa probably should have put her hand over her mouth to hide her cheesy grin. *How sweet is that?*

There was no way she was going to break that little cloud of happiness by asking Buck whether he was Mike's grandfather or Misty's great-grandfather on her mother's side. In a town of people who knew everything about everyone, she was clearly the outsider, because she was always at least one detail behind.

CHAPTER TWENTY-EIGHT

From the morning after the meeting, everyone who worked at Porter's and several who offered to pitch in during their personal off-season worked hard to make everything on that project plan happen.

Morning red-yellow-green meetings were held with task owners to make sure everyone was on schedule, and a SWAT team was put together to take on any roadblocks or obstacles they bumped into, which ended up being few.

Vanessa attributed it not to her experience, but to the full-disclosure approach. The plan was posted so that every single employee, no matter their level, could see it. In some cases, people stepped up to help on things they hadn't been tapped for, and that had ended up being an unexpected boost, cutting several hours from the bottom line.

The calendar that took up the entire whiteboard on the wall next to Vanessa's desk was a flurry of scribbles in all different colors. From back here it almost looked like a Monet, or a Kandinsky—a masterpiece of color.

She picked up a green marker and walked over to today's date. December 18.

Exactly one week before Christmas Day. That block held a colorful drawing of a Christmas tree with a bright yellow star on top. It wasn't artistic at all, just a squiggly green line for the tree, but someone had put it there overnight a week ago. Like a Secret Santa present.

She raised the marker, and rather than x-ing out today as she had every day since the third, she drew a big check mark, then dropped the pen into the tray below.

She made one last sweep of the office. If it weren't for Anna she could've left and never come back. Except for her handwriting on the wall, literally, there was no personal sign of her ever being here.

Her hands tingled. There was no way she could just walk out of Porter's today, close the door, and never say goodbye to the people she'd met here. She was used to being disconnected—never looking back on the places she'd been. The emotional tug made her a little dizzy.

She took one last look down Main Street from the office window, then gathered her things and went down to the parking lot, where Anna's car sat packed and ready to roll for the Greensboro airport.

The local weatherman had been calling for snow for three days, but the first flakes had started to fall when she stepped outside. Dry flakes blew around like Styrofoam packing debris, skittering along the walkway around her. She got into Anna's car and started the engine, patiently letting it warm up as she'd promised.

She eased out of the parking spot and headed out of town. The roads were clear, and there was very little traffic. Singing to Christmas carols at the top of her lungs, she couldn't wait to get today's meeting in Chicago over with so she could do some shopping and catch the last flight back.

Our tree is beautiful, but it needs some presents underneath it.

As she drove out of town, the snow started falling faster. She double-checked her GPS to be sure she was still on the right route, because she hadn't seen a sign in a while.

The snow was coming down harder, but thankfully the roads weren't bad, and the heat in Anna's car was keeping her toasty warm.

The radio station became fuzzy with static. A few twists of the knob didn't find anything but more of the same, so she switched it off.

The steady squish-swish-thrump of the wipers made a rum-pumpum-pum melody. On top of the world for nailing this project in record time, she was anxious to tie it up in a nice neat bow, then get back and relax with Anna until the new year rang in. Jetting off somewhere tropical to watch the ball drop in short sleeves with her bonus money sounded pretty good right now.

The heavier snow produced a fluffy layer across the median and trees. Every once in a while, the snow would swirl into a bunch, making everything seem as white as if she were in the clouds.

She clutched the wheel as a gust pushed against the car, sending her heart on a Tilt-A-Whirl for a moment there, but she'd stayed the course.

Nothing to see here.

Alone with her thoughts as she was, the beauty of the

winter wonderland forming right in front of her made her feel like a speck in the vast beauty of nature. The pines stood tall, and the white pellets seemed to define the space between the hefty bark pieces like a puzzle snow line.

She forged ahead, silently appreciating the time she'd had in Fraser Hills, and Anna. All the others too. She'd continue to mentor Misty from Chicago. Misty could take the reins at Porter's someday if she wanted to. Meeting that young lady had elevated Vanessa's own awareness. Her immediate response had been to coach Misty to balance things. *Talk about "Do as I say, not as I do."* She was horrible at it, and Anna had tried to tell her a million times.

She thought of how Anna had looked at Buck. Anna looked ten years younger this morning.

Then her phone sounded and about scared her out of her lane.

Bear right at the next exit.

She slowed and got into the right lane, happy to finally get off the highway. The snowflakes were getting bigger and falling softer.

She followed the signs to the airport, and valeted the car. There was no line at security, so it seemed overkill to be in the TSA PreCheck line, but the habit had led her there. Her bags made the scan and she still had time for a cup of coffee before they began boarding.

The coffee shop boasted a holiday special: an insulated travel mug filled with Ho Ho Mocha Gingerbread Latte. "I'll have the special, please."

A few minutes later she was walking through the only gift shop on this concourse. Mostly necessities, but in the back corner they had a cute assortment of locally crafted holiday items for last-minute shopping travelers. Velvety wine-colored stockings trimmed in gold satin cording. One style had a gold vine and stylized poinsettia blooms, and the other a partridge in a scrolling pear tree.

She'd totally forgotten about the stockings she'd had embroidered before she left Chicago. She picked up a few little stocking stuffers, then checked out. Pleased with her purchase, she headed to the gate.

She walked over, but no one was lined up at the gate yet. The airline counter attendant made an announcement:

"Passengers in the gate area waiting on Flight 3333 to Chicago, this flight is being delayed due to a mechanical problem. I'll provide you an update as soon as I have one. At this time, we are showing a delay of forty-five minutes. Please—"

Passengers grumbled.

Vanessa glanced down at her watch. One delay would make it tight for her to make the meeting. Any longer than that, and she'd miss it entirely.

"Hi, Kendra," she said into her phone. "My flight is delayed. Can you check Edward's calendar and see if we can switch my meeting with him to later in the day?"

"Actually, I was getting ready to call you. He just rescheduled. He's got you down for Monday afternoon at four now."

Four o'clock? "That was a long drive in the snow for no reason. You know that Monday meeting will get pushed."

"We both know it. The good news is he'll feel bad for pushing you off today, and he won't even know you didn't make it back in for the meeting. Go treat yourself to a spa day or something."

"There's no sense flying in over the weekend. I'll come in on Monday."

"I thought you'd be jumping at the chance to come back. Isn't that little town driving you crazy?"

"No. I'm actually enjoying it down here."

"I've seen the reports coming in. Your assistant there is on point. Don't you think about replacing me."

"Actually, those aren't being done by my assistant Lilene. I pulled up another resource to handle them. She's good, isn't she?"

"Yeah, I haven't had to reformat or tweak a single report this time. I've been basically filing my nails here, and taking very long lunches to get my shopping done."

"Thanks for holding down the fort. You know I appreciate you managing the workflow to the big guys."

"I do," Kendra said. "Well, if I don't talk to you again before the holiday, I hope you and your cousin have a merry Christmas."

"We will. It's going to be wonderful. You're not going to believe this, but we even put up a tree." Vanessa could picture the look of disbelief on Kendra's face, and darn if the sarcasm and doubt didn't show in her sassy response.

"Is it a picture you put on your phone home screen?"

Vanessa knew Kendra so well. "No. We have a real honest-to-goodness live Christmas tree. Sap and everything."

"Sounds messy." Kendra tsked. "Count me out."

"It is messy." Anna had the DustBuster out vacuuming those needles up again this morning. "But it smells so good."

"You're not going country on me, are you?"

"Me? Never. I'm a city girl. What would I do there?"

"I have no idea. Cut down trees maybe? I'm just checking. I'd hate to have to break in a new boss."

"You're safe. I better head on back so I can get there before nightfall. Those country roads are dark."

"I'll reschedule your flight for Monday morning. You can always cancel it if you want to. Might as well do it on the phone at this point. He's marked 'out of office' all next week already."

"Thanks for the update." Vanessa ended the call and headed out of the airport terminal to cash out with the valet. She stepped up to the red, white, and blue sign. "Larkin. I literally just dropped off my car. Shortest valet in history." She handed the tag over to the older woman wearing a Santa hat.

She clicked around on her keyboard, then reached behind her on the wall. "They haven't even moved you yet. You're right outside by the curb."

Vanessa handed the woman her credit card.

"No charge." The woman handed Vanessa Anna's key ring. "Merry Christmas."

Vanessa cupped the keys in her hand. "Thank you so much. Merry Christmas to you too." She flipped the keys as she walked outside. The car wasn't even cold yet. She started the engine and found a radio station, then pulled out onto the road.

The radio announcer chatted about the weather between songs. "It's an icy-cold one out there, folks. Things here lo-cally? Snow has subsided. Roads are passable and we're at a balmy twenty-seven degrees. Keep an eye on the forecast if you're traveling this weekend, though. The whole county is getting blasted right now. They should have four to eight inches of fresh snow for us tomorrow. Even more at the higher elevations. Who else will be packing up to hit the slopes this weekend besides me? How about this one to get us in the mood."

"Let It Snow" began to play.

She sang along, glad the precipitation had slowed down a

bit, and that the deejay hadn't mentioned Fraser Hills in the snow-blast alert. It was still early; if all went according to plan, she'd be back by midafternoon.

She picked up her phone to call Anna, but at the last moment decided to surprise her instead.

The first hour of her drive back was nice. The radio station stayed clear, and the snow had held off, but then the bright sky suddenly became milky gray.

Heavy clouds now hung like a cloak over the landscape, and sleet spattered against her windshield. She leaned forward, focusing on the road, letting the taillights ahead of her lead the way.

The sleet turned to slushy snowflakes the size of Ping-Pong balls that smashed against the windshield as if she were under attack by a thousand angry elves with slingshots. The windshield wipers slung them from the glass in clumps to the hood of the car.

She slowed as the cars on the highway became fewer and fewer. The radio station had fizzled out, not that she'd be able to hear it over the messy weather anyway.

Her GPS showed that the next turn was twenty miles away. Her stomach clenched at the thought of driving those back twisty roads that were beginning to cover with snow. She moved to the left lane to pass a slow-moving salt truck.

Her hands clutched the steering wheel. When she finally reached the turn toward Fraser Hills, it didn't look as bad. This road had already been scraped. Tall piles of snow had been pushed to the sides of the road.

"Almost there." She patted the dash. "We've got this, old girl."

The sprawling acres of green grass were now blanketed in snow. Like in a picture postcard, smoke puffed from the chimney of a farmhouse. A single white candle shone from each window. She could picture a family inside gathered around the warm fire.

Finally, she passed the WELCOME TO FRASER HILLS sign in the median.

She let out a breath, rolling her tight shoulders from the death grip she'd had on the steering wheel. She slowed to a consistent forty miles an hour. *Keep moving. Slow and steady.*

It was only about three o'clock, ahead a bright yellow snow scraper rumbled along pushing the snow from the roads into town. The sound of the heavy metal blade scratching against the pavement below made an unpleasant screech. She turned right, taking the side road to avoid getting stuck behind it.

Ping. Her eyes only left the road for a split second to check her phone, but when she looked up there was something in the road.

Panic pushed her foot to the brake; the car slid to the right and twisted on the icy asphalt. A deer with big antlers bounded across the windshield as if flying, never touching the car as it continued to swerve. *Turn in to the skid.* The car made a slooshing sound and everything from there was as if she were in slow motion. She caught a glimpse of the bright white tail of the deer disappearing into the woods in front of her, and then, *thud!*

No.

She was more out of breath than had she jogged through the deep snow herself. She clutched her chest, trying to collect herself. The windshield was white. Covered in snow.

The airbag hadn't deployed.

Probably a good thing. She'd heard of people getting pretty banged up from those things.

The car was catawampus, making it hard to sit up straight. She tugged on the door handle and pushed against the door, but it didn't budge, and neither would the seat belt when she pressed the button.

Her purse and phone had slid from the center console into the back. She reached for her phone.

"Seriously?"

It was just out of reach. She pulled her feet up closer to the seat to try to gain a few inches, but the seat belt tightened as she moved.

"Now what?"

She was only a block or two away from Main Street. There had to be houses not too far from here.

She honked the horn. *What's "SOS"? One long. Two short?* She used to know, but right now she couldn't think straight. "If I could reach my phone, I might be able to Google that. Or call for help and not need to honk an SOS."

She blasted the horn then waited a couple of minutes, to try honking again. She looked up at the rearview mirror. In her own car she had emergency assist at the touch of a finger.

Buy Anna a car with emergency assist.

I'll probably owe her a new one after this anyway. At least the deer got away unharmed.

She pictured Bill Campbell with an Elmer Fudd outfit on hunting down the deer that made her wreck.

Okay, I'm getting giddy.

She tried to restart the car, but it wouldn't turn over, but at least the "SOS" code came back to her. "Three short, three long, three short. I knew that." She laid on the horn again with the right dits and dahs.

Wishing for the little hammer-and-cutter gadget they

advertised on late-night television, she rummaged through the console and the glove box the best she could from the driver's seat.

Next year everyone gets one of those gadgets in their stocking.

She rubbed her hands up and down her arms. The car was getting cold fast.

Honking three short, three long, three short she hoped someone out there could hear her.

"I'm going to be really mad if I freeze to death. I've got things I want to do." Anna's reminders that there was more to life than work played in her mind.

She pressed the back of her head against the seat and worked her way out from beneath the shoulder strap. *Freezing to death isn't an option.* Honestly, she didn't even know if it was a possibility. It might only be in the teens out there by now, but she couldn't just sit here either.

The edge of the seat belt scraped her cheek as she cleared it to get it behind her.

With the extra freedom from moving the seat belt, she was able to grab her phone.

"Lilene. It's Vanessa. I've had an accident. I'm in a ditch a half-block away from Main Street. At least I think that's where I am. I can't get out of the car. Can you get me help?"

"Yes. Are you okay?"

"I think I'm fine, but the door won't budge. I can't get out."

"Those roads are slick. We sent everyone home early so they could salt and scrape the roads. Hang on."

Vanessa clutched the phone until Lilene came back on the line.

"They're on their way to get ya. Don't you worry."

"Thanks for calling for help."

"Want me to stay on the line?"

"No. That's not necessary. I'm fine."

She dropped her phone in her lap and relaxed. *Of course they'll drop everything and come help me. That's what they do around here.*

Chapter Twenty-nine

Mike loved nothing more than being on horseback in fresh snow. You could exhaust a smaller horse in no time in this kind of snow, but he and Big Ben didn't mind taking it slow. Mike hitched the light sleigh to Ben and headed out. Nothing demanding, just man, horse, and nature. He inhaled the fresh smell of snow.

When he was showing the hitch, the sound of the equipment and bells made his heart pound with excitement. This was the opposite. The only sound was the quiet slice of the sleigh rails in the snow, and the squeaky crunch as Ben pushed his weight into the icy snow.

Occasionally the heavy air would trap the smoke like a flying carpet afloat above his neighbors' houses.

Less than a week before Christmas he was certain there were some people in a panic that they'd lost one good shopping day today. He could picture the piles of shiny wrapped gifts under the trees of each house as he took the slow ride through the neighborhoods surrounding Main Street.

Most of the houses on this street had a Christmas tree with twinkling lights in the front window. Some white, some colorful. An old soul, he favored the big old glass bulbs of years gone by.

He and Misty loved stringing lights in the barn and on the house. It never got old, and the thought of her outgrowing that made him a little sad.

This year some people had those puffy blow-up air figures. That dadgum Amazon put just about anything at the fingertips of people all over the nation. He'd rather see those big plastic candles from days gone by or a nativity scene than a blowup of a Santa-hat-wearing dinosaur. What was Christmassy about that?

The roads through here hadn't been scraped yet. As Mike rode by his buddy James's house, the eight-foot inflatable Santa driving a bright red monster off-road truck full of presents pretty much fit James to a T, though.

Big Ben's ears flicked back and he took a quicker step, raising his nose into the air. Alert.

"I heard that too, buddy. Whoa." Mike stopped and listened for a long moment. The only sound was the occasional groan of a pile of snow slipping from a branch to the ground, and tiny branches breaking under the weight of it. "I don't know what that was."

Honk. Honk-honk-honk.

Big Ben turned his head back toward Mike.

"Yep, let's go." He clicked his teeth and Ben began plodding with purpose through the deepening snow toward the sound.

A moment later he heard the heavy rumble of the diesel fire engine rolling up Main.

Mike stopped Ben near two pickup trucks already there. A car had run off the road into the ditch.

Mike crunched through the snow over toward the guys. "What happened?"

"Vanessa ran off the road," the fire chief said. "Lilene called it in. She's in there good."

"She okay?"

"Yeah. She can't get out with the driver door against the ditch bank, and the seat belt mechanism locked on impact, so she can't crawl out the other side."

Two of the firemen were working from the passenger side to get her out.

Mike retrieved the heavy wool blanket he'd been sitting on from the sleigh, and jogged over to the car.

A moment later he was standing there when they helped Vanessa climb free of the car.

She was shaken, but fine.

He walked over and gave her the blanket from the carriage. "Here you go. This is warm already."

"Mike?"

He wrapped the blanket around her. "I was out riding. I heard you honk the horn. I'm glad you're okay."

"You and me both."

He wrapped his hands around her arms and rubbed them briskly.

She tightened the wool blanket around her.

"Come on, get in the truck." He led her over to the chief's red pickup and helped her inside, where the heat was cranking.

"What happened?" he asked.

"I looked down a half second when my phone beeped, and when I looked up there was this huge deer standing there. I panicked."

"It happens."

"On a positive note, the deer got away. Jumped right over the car like one of Santa's flying reindeer. Swear to goodness."

"Bump your head?" he joked.

"No. Seriously."

"You and Big Ben need to quit meeting like this. He doesn't like me changing up his routines."

"Send him my apologies."

"I will." He couldn't take his eyes from hers.

"What about you? Do you mind?" She gulped.

"Not at all." He pressed his lips together. "I like running into you."

"You know you've already proven how cool this town is to me. You don't have to go to all this trouble."

"I didn't send that deer to run out in front of you."

"Are you sure?"

"Yeah. Guys around here wouldn't risk losing good venison."

"Ah. Well, that's good to know," she said playfully.

"You know if you'd been even an hour later they'd have had all the roads cleared and you wouldn't have had any problem at all."

"Timing is everything."

"Yes," he said. "It sure is." He cleared his throat. "I'm going to use Ben to help them get your car out of the ditch. We'll take it to James's Pit Stop down the road. He can fix anything. The chief will give you a ride home."

"Thanks, Mike."

"Glad you're okay. You scared me for a second there."

She nodded slowly, her eyes wide. *Thank you,* she mouthed, but the words didn't come out.

He closed the passenger door and then patted it twice before he went over and unhitched Ben and walked him over to the car.

This wasn't Ben's first car pull. He'd pulled cars from ditches for years. It was like a hobby for him.

They made quick work of getting the car out of the ditch; then Mike pulled out his phone and called James. "Hey man, car in the ditch. We're going to leave it at the shop. More job security for you."

"Like I need that."

"Let me know what it'll take once you check it out. I'll take care of it."

"Sure thing, man."

When Mike turned around, the chief had already pulled away.

Mike rehitched Ben to the sleigh. "A hero again," he said to him as he got back in the sleigh. "You're a good horse, Ben."

He gave Ben the signal and they went silently off toward the house. Mike put everything away and checked on things in the barn before going up to the house. When he led Big Ben to his stall, Scooter was curled up in the middle of the stall waiting on him. Ben leaned down nose-to-nose with the little guy.

Scooter scurried off to safety under the hanging corner water system until Ben came in and slurped three full bowls. The water seemed to disappear as soon as he drank. Fresh water swirled back in, refilling it quickly.

Mike closed the stall door and leaned over the side watching him. "Good job today, Ben."

Ben lifted his head, his soft eyes looking pleased with the day as well. He leaned back down toward Scooter, who then shook the water from the top of his head that Ben had just dripped on him.

Mike watched the two together. Like old buddies. He left them be, pausing as he exited the barn, wondering what Vanessa had thought when she'd walked through here the other day. He hoped she'd come to the open house. It looked pretty all lit up at night.

He slid the door closed, and walked up to the house.

He stomped the snow from his boots and left them at the back door. "Hey, Misty. I'm back."

He peeled off his jackets and hung them in the mudroom to dry.

In the kitchen, he grabbed a sausage ball and popped it into his mouth, then walked into the living room expecting to see Misty sprawled out on the leather couch watching television, since school was out until the first week of January.

Clicking through the channels, he stopped on the weather channel to see if the storm system was finally about past. It was supposed to be a fast mover, and it had been dropping two inches an hour for several hours. Faster than anyone could keep clear. Tomorrow would be a busy day of digging out.

After about forty minutes he got up to go check on Misty. Her door was closed. "You good in there? I'm home."

"No. Go away."

He stepped back. He hated the mood swings that seemed to steal his sweet little girl from him some days. "You know that's not going to happen. Open the door."

She walked over to the door. Eyes red and puffy, she looked

like she'd been stung by bees, her lips were so swollen. He tried not to laugh. "What's the problem?"

"My dress for the dance. Everything. I can't go."

"Why?"

"Leave me alone. I'm not going."

His phone rang. "Hello?"

"Mike? It's Vanessa. I wanted to thank you for helping me tonight. I've got your blanket."

"Yeah, okay. Right. Good. I'm sorry. I'm trying to deal with a meltdown here."

"What's going on?"

"My daughter is in her room crying over a dress, and frankly I'm out of my comfort zone on this one. Part of me hopes it means she'll never go out on her first date. She may hate life, but I'll have a happily-ever-after."

"You know what. I'll be right over. I think I can repay the favor on this one."

"But the snow—"

"I know you and Ben just had to pull my car out of a ditch, but I do know how to drive in the snow. Don't call me, though. I won't be checking it while I drive in this."

"Good idea."

*

Vanessa hitched her suitcase in her hand. Everything she needed for a fashion rescue was right in this bag. Thank goodness Anna had also uncovered several things at the cottage that would help out, like needle and thread and all kinds of lace and stuff. She'd go back for more resources if needed. Buck had kindly offered his truck to get here.

She walked up to Mike's front door and gave it a hearty knock.

Mike pulled the door open before her hand hit for the third thump.

"Thank goodness you're here. I don't know what to do. I told her I'd get her another dress, but she says there aren't any other dresses. She's hysterical."

"It's her first dance. This is a big deal." Then she dropped the serious act. "How bad is it? Did you see the dress?"

"Let's just say it doesn't look like I got my money's worth. Kind of looks like those Halloween costumes we wore when we were kids. The kind that was made out of that really shiny material and came with the plastic mask you could never see out of."

"That's not good at all."

"Apparently."

"Where is she?"

"Upstairs in her room. Last door on the right."

She playfully pushed her hand against his shoulder. "You go on out to the barn and do cowboy stuff or something. I'll let you know when to come back."

"I—"

"We're going to be just fine."

He opened his mouth, but she shook her head. "I promise."

"Fine." He grabbed a heavy coat from next to the door and walked outside. "You call me if she needs me."

"You're on speed dial."

"Now you're just pacifying me."

"The sooner you let me handle this the sooner she'll be off to that dance. Go!"

He walked out and she regretted how much she enjoyed

seeing him rattled. It was sweet. She looked at the staircase, then at the bag of gear. She should've made him carry it up before he left. *That's what I get for being so bossy.*

With both hands on the handle of the overnighter, she hoisted it up the stairs one step at a time, steadying it on each tread as she went. At the top of the stairs she dropped the rolling bag to the floor and then rolled it down the hall.

She tapped lightly on the door. "Misty?" When there was no response she tapped again. "It's Vanessa. Are you in there?"

A wimpy "Yes" came from the other side.

"Can I come in?"

"Why?"

"It's the night of the big dance. We have to get you ready."

"I'm not going."

"You can't miss the dance."

"I can, and I am."

"Does your date know yet?"

"I can't call him. I'm cry-y-ying."

"I can hear that. Will you please let me in?"

A meager "Yes" followed. Vanessa opened the door. The light was out, but she could see Misty lying on her bed in a heap. She flipped the light on. "Get up."

"It's a disaster."

"It can't be that bad."

Misty thrust her hand out from under the covers. "Yes, it can. Look." She thrust a picture of the dress she bought online at her.

"This is an adorable dress."

She ripped back her comforter and hopped to her feet.

"Oh. No?" Vanessa knew that she was standing there mouth agape, and that that was not going to comfort Misty, but she was right. It *was* a disaster. The dress looked about three sizes too big, and what was left of her eye makeup was on her cheeks. For the most part. "What in the world?" She tugged and pinched at the fabric.

"See!"

"I do. This is horrible." She tried to look for a bright side. A couple of quick darts, a belt, or tweaks would snazz up the dress. "Well, maybe if . . ." She dropped her hands to the side. "Nope. You're right. This is the pits."

Misty started laughing. "You suck at making me feel better."

Vanessa joined her in the amusement, and they both started laughing. Misty's tears rolled down her face, but at least she wasn't in a heap on the floor.

"I brought in the big guns, but girl, I'm not sure I can rescue that dress."

"It doesn't even look like the picture when it's on the hanger."

"I don't doubt it. You need to take that off right now. We're going to get your money back on that thing." Vanessa turned her back on Misty and retrieved the suitcase from the hall. She plopped it on Misty's bed and unzipped it. If nothing else it would keep Misty from crawling back in it.

"What time is it?" Vanessa demanded.

Misty looked toward the clock on her dresser. "Six twenty-two."

"What time is your date picking you up?"

"Luke is supposed to here at seven forty-five."

"What's our focus? The dream? Or the fear?"

"The dream. Always," Misty said.

"We've got plenty of time. Go! Get that dress off, and wash your face. Bring a cold rag for your eyes. We've got this."

Misty pulled the parachute of material over her head and

tossed it on her dresser as she headed to the bathroom. When she returned, her face was scrubbed clean, and she no longer looked like it was the end of the world.

"Put this on." Vanessa handed Misty her favorite little black dress. Chanel, it was timeless in cut and had enough stretch to flatter just about any figure. She prayed it wasn't going to be too short. Misty had a good couple of inches on her, and the last thing she needed was Mike having a heart attack over the length.

Misty had no idea that this dress cost nearly two thousand dollars at the consignment shop. It had been Vanessa's first real splurge on a dress, but this little dress had paid for itself time and time again over the years. Then again, it wasn't a jewel-tone or shiny fabric like the dream dress in Misty's photo. She remembered how important those formal dance dresses had seemed to her when she was Misty's age. She tried not to take exception to the not-so-impressed look on Misty's face.

It slid right on, and fit just right. The length wasn't bad either. Certainly respectable.

"It fits way better," Misty said with a half nod.

"Very flattering." Vanessa came around to her side, then took a pair of heels from her bag. "Try these."

Misty took them then stared back at Vanessa. "Really?"

"Try them on." Vanessa watched her set the shoes side by side on the floor and step into them.

Misty visibly swallowed and then looked over to her. "Oh my gosh. I can't believe this."

"Oh yeah. Much better. Next, we conquer that hair. Add a little makeup, and you're going to be the prettiest girl at the Winter Festival Dance."

"You really think so?"

Vanessa stood behind her and straightened Misty's posture.

"Look at yourself. You look amazing. The dress is Chanel. The designer who invented the little black dress. Seriously, you'll blow the socks off everyone at the dance. Hands down."

"You're really going to let me wear this?"

"Sure as I'm standing here." She clapped her hands twice. "Time's a-wasting. Go get a chair. I've got less than thirty minutes to get this done."

While Misty went in search of the chair, Vanessa texted Mike to let him know things were in progress and to be ready for Luke's arrival at seven forty-five, and that he might have to stall if they weren't quite done.

Before she put her phone down, she picked it back up and added to the text, And be nice to him.

Maybe, he texted her back.

She knew it had been too much to ask. Fathers lived for the day to scare boys away from their little girls.

At 7:45 on the nose, a bright swath of light fanned past Misty's bedroom window. "He's here!"

"Calm down."

"Oh my gosh. I'm going to be sick."

"No. You're not. Take a breath." Vanessa swept the fluffy powder brush over Misty's face one last time. "You look perfect. Come." She snapped her fingers and pulled her in front of the mirrored closet door. "Seriously. Even if that other dress had looked like the picture, you can never outdo a perfect little black dress. That's all you need, forever. Accessorize up or down, throw a jean jacket on, or pearls and do tea with the queen."

"I've never looked this pretty."

"I'd give a million dollars to see those girls who teased you about not being girly enough tonight."

Misty blushed. "How am I ever going to thank you?"

"Be nice to your dad. He was worried to death. He had a tough day. He had to rescue me, then came home to you in a hot mess."

"Wait a minute. He what?"

"I'll tell you another day. Right now, your nice young man Luke is downstairs. Alone. With your dad."

"Oh, no. This is not good." She spun and practically fled from the room with Vanessa at her heels.

"Coming," Vanessa announced. "Sorry we got hung up. Girl talk. You know."

Luke blanched. "Mist? Misty? Wow."

Mike stared too, only it appeared that he couldn't utter a word.

My work here is complete.

When Misty hit the bottom stair, Luke walked straight over to her and handed her the clear box he held in his shaking hand. "I thought you said your dress was blue."

"It was, well, now it's black. But black goes with everything." She took the box from him. "It's beautiful. Thank you."

"Want me to help you with that?" Vanessa asked.

"I was hoping someone would help." Luke wrung his hands, shifting nervously from foot to foot. "I don't know what to do with that thing."

Mike clapped him on the shoulder. "Been there."

Vanessa pinned the corsage to her dress, and stepped back.

"It matches your eyes," Luke said. "You look pretty."

"Come on, you two," Vanessa insisted. "We need pictures." She took them through no less than a dozen poses before she finally let them get ready to leave.

Mike rolled his lips in, pressing them together, but the glint of those tears was unmistakable. He patted his heart with his two fingers.

"I love you, Daddy." She wrapped her arms around his neck. "Thank you. And you too, Vanessa. Thank you so much."

"You two have fun," she said.

Luke turned and looked at Vanessa as if it were the first time he'd noticed her standing there. His face paled and then his cheeks reddened as he muttered, "Ooh, man."

She watched him visibly gulp.

"I think I owe you an apology," he said to Vanessa.

"Me?" Vanessa was completely confused. "I don't understand. I don't think we've met."

"I didn't know you were staying in town when we met."

"We haven't met."

"Not formally, but . . ." He raised his arms out to the sides and squawked.

The falcon! "You!"

"I was kind of poking fun with you a little. Okay, well, a lot. I thought you were just some out-of-towner passing through."

"Mm-hmm."

"Sorry. Sometimes I get carried away," Luke said. "I didn't mean anything by it."

"That is not what a father wants to hear. In fact, have I shown you my gun collection?"

"Sir?"

Misty grabbed Luke's hand. "I think Vanessa will forgive you sooner than my dad will."

"I'll be a complete gentleman, sir."

Vanessa nodded to Misty. *Every daddy's job.*

Chapter Thirty

Mike watched from the door as Luke helped Misty into his Carolina-blue Ford pickup. "Never did like UNC blue," Mike said.

"Be nice," Vanessa said.

"That was me being nice. At least he's driving a Ford." He swept at a tear on his cheek, pausing when he realized she was watching him while sweeping a tear from her own. "Must be contagious."

"Highly." She dabbed at the corner of her eye. "She really looked beautiful."

"Exactly like her mother." His voice grew quiet. "Man. It's not easy to see her grow up."

"I can't imagine. I'll say this, though: If I'd ever had a daughter, I'd be awfully proud to have one as bright and caring as yours. You're doing something right."

He shrugged as he walked back inside and closed the door behind them.

"Thanks for letting me help her. I was kind of like her when I was her age. I was a little awkward."

"That's hard to believe."

"Oh, I was. I had this whole fashion business and it was pretty successful too for a fourteen-year-old, but even though people thought I had great fashion sense and bought things from me, they made fun of me."

"Kids can be mean."

"Don't I know it," she said. "You never forget that stuff."

"Misty looked so grown tonight. I take it that was your dress she was wearing."

"It is."

"You always pack a fancy dress no matter where you're going?"

"Of course I do. It's a little black dress. You can dress it up. Or down. Never mind. You don't need to understand. But it saved you tonight."

"It did. I owe you for that. Thank you so much. I don't know how you did it. She was a mess when I was trying to talk to her."

"Yeah, she was pretty upset, but she was right. That dress was a disaster."

"That situation needed a woman's touch." He lifted his hands in front of him. "I don't have that. When I first lost my wife, I knew I was in over my head. The women of this town helped me like you wouldn't believe, but that was a long time ago now. I thought I had everything under control. We have routines. But now, dances. Boys. Working. It's a whole new game."

"It's got to be easier here, though. I mean, Fraser Hills. It's Americana. The wide-eyed American dream without all the complexities and drama of the city."

"We get our share of drama here, too," he said. "I don't just mean tonight's meltdown either."

"You mean like big bad corporate lady coming to town?"

"There's that." He looked up at the ceiling and shook his head. "But you're not really that big and bad. I'm glad you're here."

"Thank you."

"Still can't believe it. Thanks for taking all those pictures. If I'd have made Misty stop and pose for all of those, she would've killed me."

"Yeah, figured I could take that one for you." She followed him into the living room. The house was clean and comfortable. The only personal photos in the room were of Misty and horses. Nothing with Mike and his late wife in them.

"I guess you're not seeing someone, else they'd have been here tonight. For all this."

"Yeah. No. I don't date. Haven't. Not even once since Olivia died."

"You said that was a long time ago."

"It was." He pushed his palms together. "No one could ever love me like she did. I'm not always that easy to get along with."

"I find that hard to believe."

"Oh, it's true. I like my way."

"I can understand that."

"No one serious in your life either?"

"Nope."

"Never married?"

"Nope." She tilted her head. "Someone did almost ask me before I left to come here, but we both knew it wasn't for the right reasons. It wasn't love."

The word "love" seemed to hang there between them.

"Love is the only reason to get married," Mike said. "You deserve someone special."

"I never experienced that. Well, not until this small-town guy took me to a parade. Made me chicken stew. Even made me wear some of it."

"That was an accident."

"Rescued me from the snow. Maybe it wasn't in that order. He was nice. I really like being around him. He's not like anyone I've known before."

"Sounds like the perfect man." He stood there smiling for a long moment. "I'm glad you're here." He rubbed his hands together. "Would you like something to drink?"

"You mean, like water?"

"Or hot chocolate? A glass of wine? I've been told I have some very nice wine."

"Yeah. I'd like that." She sat down. "Wine would be nice."

He went to grab a bottle of wine from his stash, and came back carrying two. "I don't know much about wine. Thought I'd better let you pick."

She took them both, then tapped her fingernail on the label of one of them. "This one for sure."

Over a glass of wine, Vanessa listened intently as he talked about Misty and how she'd grown up with the horses, and how he'd gotten started working with the giant Percherons.

"I've been meaning to ask you about the sponsorship. I noticed it on the side of Santa's wagon."

"Porter's?"

"Yeah, I don't know that we'll be able to continue that unless it's already set aside and funded somewhere that I don't have access to. I looked into it earlier this week and there's nothing on record as being paid out for a sponsorship of any level."

"I've been getting them every year."

"May I ask you to pull an old check for me so I can track it back to the right accounting?"

"Yeah. That's no problem. You've done a good thing here in Fraser Hills. I'm sorry I misjudged you at first."

"Just doing my job."

"I don't know. I got the feeling that maybe what you came to do, and what you've done, might be two slightly different things. I'm usually a pretty good judge of things like that."

"Let's just leave it at things worked out the way they should have, and I'm really glad I was the one sent here for this project."

"Fair enough."

She took a long sip of wine. "How's Scooter?"

"That is the strangest puppy we've ever had, and we've had our share of pups around here."

"Can I see him?"

"Sure. Let's go get him. That's assuming he's where I left him." They walked outside. The night was clear. A million stars shone across the inky black sky.

"It's beautiful out here."

"It is." He liked the way her hair shimmered. "I can't imagine living anywhere else."

She took in a deep breath. "I understand that more now. It's like my heart even beats slower here."

"That's good," he said. "Right?"

"I don't know. Maybe?"

He caught her hand, and held it as they walked to the barn. He opened the side door, and flipped the switch. "I love being out here at Christmas. The colored lights dress up this old barn. It's my favorite place."

Something skittered around the corner, and Scooter came running out like Tom Cruise in that iconic dance scene in *Risky Business.* He slid to a stop, then let out a yap.

"Scooter!" He ran right over to Vanessa. She stooped down and he climbed into her arms and started kissing her face. "Oh my gosh. They should have puppies in every office across the country. There'd never be a stressful day." She hugged the puppy and stood up with him in her arms. "I love this wittle guy," she said while rubbing noses with him. "So cute."

"He's a mess. I think I've finally figured out why he keeps getting out. He and Big Ben are practically inseparable."

"The horse?"

"Yes. Crazy, right?"

Before she could answer, she turned to look behind her. "What's all that ruckus?"

"Laying hens."

"Oh, yeah. Eggatha Christie and Oprah Henfrey? I heard about them."

"To name a couple." He started walking down the alley toward Ben's stall. "Follow me."

The puppy wriggled out of her arms and ran ahead of Mike.

"What'd I tell you?" Then Mike put out his arm to stop her and they watched as Scooter climbed up onto a bale of hay, then onto the equipment box and into the stall through the feed-access door, dropping in to the floor. "I've been wondering how he was doing that."

"That's crazy." She followed Mike to the stall. He opened the gate and went inside, then led Ben out into the alleyway.

"This is the first Percheron I ever bought with my own money. Until Ben, all the horses I owned had been bred through the horses on our farm."

"He's so big. Aren't you intimidated?"

Mike shook his head. "No."

Scooter sat in the doorway watching as Mike told Vanessa about the horses. "My family once owned about all this town," he said. "Porter's. The horses. We had quite a carriage business for years. Ran most of that out of the warehouse where you're staying. Slowly family members died, their craftsmanship not carried on by the next generation. Everyone wants what's new, I guess."

"Not you?"

He shook his head again. "Give me the simple life. A comfortable home. Honest day's work. A town full of people trying to do the right thing. Family has always been everything to me."

"So, Buck? How does he fit into all of this?"

He jerked his head around. "What do you know about that?"

"I don't. I mean I know he and Misty are related, but I haven't figured out how all the pieces fit together."

He turned and walked Ben back into the stall. "They don't." Mike stroked the side of the horse's neck with the flat of his hand. His back still to her. He really didn't want to get into that tonight.

A chill rushed in.

Suddenly, repeated barking broke the awkward moment.

"That doggone puppy. He's going to get his fool self killed."

Mike muttered under his breath as he marched toward the big barn door. The barking continued, and Vanessa caught up to him when he got to the barn door.

He raised a hand in the air to keep her quiet as he stepped outside. The group yip howl was unmistakable. He ran back inside and grabbed a rifle from the top of a rack. "Get back. Stay right there."

A long drawn-out growl preceded the next bark.

"Coyote," Mike said over his shoulder. "That must be what had the hens acting up earlier."

Mike had his rifle up and aimed when he heard the familiar heavy footsteps coming from the barn. The coyote took off.

Inside, Vanessa was backed up to one of the stalls, and Big Ben was standing in the doorway. He let out a loud whinny and pawed his foot.

Scooter ran past Mike inside the barn covered in mud. He ran a lap around Ben and then saw Vanessa and crouched as he raced for her like she was the finish line.

Mike put the rifle away, then led Ben back to his stall. "He's lucky Ben scared that coyote off."

"Is it just me or does Scooter look awfully proud of himself? I think he thinks he single-handedly handled that situation."

"He's covered in mud." Mike watched the puppy place a muddy paw on Vanessa's coat.

"Aren't you proud?" she said playfully.

"He won't be proud when he ends up being that coyote's dinner."

"Don't listen to Mike," Vanessa teased. "Seems like this little guy did okay with the help from his friends. I think you've found Rein's replacement. She loves these horses, and at least one of them is very fond of him."

"You actually might be on to something." He looked at her all covered in mud. She'd never looked more beautiful. "I guess it's a season of change in Fraser Hills."

"The good kind," she said.

He'd never been a real fan of change, but he wasn't about to argue with her.

The sound of a truck in the driveway broke the silence between them.

"I think Misty's home," Vanessa said.

"Bring that little guy with you. He's going to need a bath." He grabbed a hand towel from a stack next to the work sink and tossed it her way. "I think I'm going to owe you another dry clean on that coat."

"You do seem to always be making a mess of me." She wrapped the towel around the puppy as she walked toward the house.

They watched quietly as Misty and Luke said their good-byes. Mike felt the vein in his neck pulse. Thank goodness that kid hadn't tried to kiss her good night. He wasn't sure he could've taken that tonight. There was way too much going on in his head right now.

She went in the front door and Mike and Vanessa snuck in the back. Mike started the water in the mudroom for Vanessa. "You can give a puppy a bath, right?"

"Might as well. I'm as muddy as he is," she said with a laugh.

*

Vanessa managed to get Scooter clean, but she got soaking wet in the process. By way of reward, she got about a thousand kisses so she wasn't about to complain. She towel-dried him, which he thought was a big game.

She wasn't sure if Mike would appreciate her giving Scooter free run of his house, so she carried him from the mudroom back to the living room. As she stood in the hallway, she overheard him and Misty speaking.

"You didn't have to worry one bit about Luke. You know he's just a big clown. There'll never be anything like that between us. We've been in every grade together. He's more like a brother, only nicer."

"I'm your father. I'm supposed to worry about things like that."

"For the record, it wouldn't hurt my feelings if you decided you might be a little attracted to Vanessa. Why don't you come up with a reason for her to wear this little black dress with you one night? You're so busy helping me live my life you're forgetting to live yours, Daddy. I'm a big girl. I'm going to be okay."

"Don't you worry about me."

"But I do, Dad. And I like Vanessa. She's nice. And smart. And I saw the way you look at her."

"She's going back to Chicago soon. I'm glad she came into our lives, but, Misty, everyone does not come into our life forever. Sometimes they just come through when we need an extra hand. I'm glad she was here for you tonight."

"Me too, Daddy." She put her hand on the handrail. "Good night."

Scooter took Vanessa's pause as a cue to spring for freedom, which he did right into the middle of the hall, leaving a wet skid across the wide-plank hardwood floor.

"Scooter," she called, pretending to have been chasing him from down the hall. "I'm sorry. He's slippery."

"It's okay. Let him run. I'm not putting him back out in the barn damp. He'll find somewhere to snuggle down in here for the night."

"I guess I'd better get going too. It's late."

"You okay?"

"Yeah. Long day. The drive to Greensboro. Canceled flight. Crash. Dog rescue."

"Daughter rescue."

"That part was my pleasure."

"Thanks for coming."

She started down the walkway.

"I'll see you tomorrow?"

"Of course. Small town. Right?"

"Yeah. It is."

She drove home with nothing on her mind except what it would be like to live in this town. To be a part of its fabric. She'd miss these people. She parked Buck's truck and sat there for a moment in her thoughts.

From here, she could see Buck and Anna sitting across from each other in the chairs in front of the fireplace. Anna was laughing, and the tree twinkled through the front windows, giving off its own kind of joy.

"Joyful. That's what I feel. Joy."

She got out of the truck and walked to the house. She tried to slip in the front door quietly, hoping not to interrupt Anna and Buck's evening.

"Vanessa? Is that you."

She stopped in midstep. *Busted.* "Yes. Disaster averted. Misty looked beautiful in my Chanel. She had no idea how snazzy she looked. I think Mike almost had a heart attack she looked so pretty, but she came home happy."

Buck nodded heartily. "I'm so glad you were there. Olivia is looking down here on this. I know she's thankful for you tonight."

Olivia?

"I'm glad I was able to help."

"Come sit," Anna called out.

"No. I smell like wet dog. The puppy almost got eaten by a coyote. I had to give him a bath. Long story. Anyway. I'm beat. It's been one long day."

"Are you sure you're okay? You didn't hit your head in that crash, did you? I don't think you're supposed to sleep if you might have a concussion."

"No, Anna. I'm fine. I had my seat belt on. All I hurt was my pride—and your car, which I will take care of pronto."

"No worries about the car," she said, placing a hand on Buck's arm. "Buck said he has a car I can use while we're here. It'll all work out. Our time together is all that's important. I'm so glad you ended up in Fraser Hills for Christmas this year."

"Me too. It seems to have all worked out just as it should."

CHAPTER THIRTY-ONE

M onday morning Vanessa sat in her office at Porter's.
The warehouse was ready and waiting on the new
team to come and start unloading inventory from the trucks that
had lined up behind the building over the weekend.

The new processes were shifting on schedule under Misty's
watch, and the whole team was getting acclimated to the new
daily routines. Once she talked to Edward, she'd be done here,
and that bonus was all hers.

Unfortunately, Kendra had sent her a message on Sunday
letting her know that once again Edward had moved their
meeting. This time he'd suggested Thursday, and instructed Vanessa to issue the status on the project via email.

She hit Enter on the final reports. It lacked the shock and
awe she'd imagined when telling him face-to-face that not
only had she done the near impossible early and on budget,

but she'd also saved Porter's and improved the following year's forecast by a not-so-meager 19 percent.

A month ago, she'd have been spitting nails over Edward being so unavailable throughout this project when she was the one doing him a favor, but today . . . it didn't even matter. Her priorities were to do some shopping for the special people she'd met here in Fraser Hills, and spend a merry Christmas with Anna.

This might be the merriest Christmas I've ever had as an adult.

Not getting the Paris project had been a blessing. She hadn't even been here long enough to gather any personal items. With her laptop in her tote bag, she gave the office one last sweeping glance and walked out, closing the door behind her. She could take any follow-up calls from the carriage house.

She walked across the street. People filled the sidewalks as if it were a weekend.

The sign in front of The Stalk Market read 3.5 SHOPPING DAYS UNTIL CHRISTMAS. WE HAVE GIFTS FOR THE GARDENERS ON YOUR LIST.

Strolling down Main Street, Vanessa exchanged pleasantries with passersby carrying colorful packages, even recognizing some of them as employees helping with the changes at Porter's. Across the street in the park next to the library, kids tossed snowballs at each other, and delighted squeals of excitement hung shrill against the icy chill.

She ducked inside a boutique. Warm air welcomed her into the space with the aroma of mulled apple cider being served to every shopper. She sipped on a cup while perusing the variety of gift options. Colorful angel ornaments would make such a cute adornment on a box. She tucked her favorites into a handbasket and picked out a beautiful picture frame for

Kendra, then bought matching holiday pajamas for Anna and herself. They'd open them on Christmas Eve like they always had at her grandparents' house. With three bags in her hand, she made her way into each shop, trying to get a little something from each one, spreading her spending across all of the retail shops.

Loaded up with gifts for everyone on her list and three extra-tall rolls of wrapping paper, she slid into her favorite booth at the Blue Bicycle Bistro.

She was getting ready to swallow her first bite of chicken and dumplings when Lilene marched in and stood next to her booth, her arms folded and her lower lip trembling.

"Lilene? What's the matter? You look upset."

"Upset?"

"Sit." She scooted over in the booth, but Lilene took the seat across from her. "I can't believe you'd stoop so low. Just days before Christmas."

The words came out like hornets, stinging with each syllable.

"What are you talking about?"

"Don't pretend you don't know. Corporate left a very detailed message for me to give to you." She shoved three pink message-pad sheets across the table.

Vanessa read them. "There's some mistake."

"He seemed pretty clear to me."

"No. They have the warehouse. That's what they needed. Did he not get my reports?"

Lilene reached over and flipped the second pink note over to the back. "Indeed. He did." She glared at Vanessa. "How could you pretend to be our friend? You're a wolf in sheep's clothing. That's what you are, or worse, like the wolf that pretended to be Red Riding Hood's grandmother. Mean, just downright mean."

"Lilene, I promise—"

"Do not give me your empty lines," Lilene said. "I've delivered the message. I'm sick about it. I need the rest of the day off." She got up and swept out of the diner like Jack Frost on a tailwind.

Vanessa stared at the messages. There was no reason to return Edward's call. Everything was pretty clear. Edward knew what he'd done. He left those details with Lilene on purpose, so there was no way anyone in this town would ever trust her again.

She stood up, did a half turn, and saw Buck sitting there behind her. "Buck. Can I sit?"

"Sure."

"You heard?"

"Every word."

"You don't believe that about me, do you?"

"Two sides to every story. Always is," he said.

"What's your story?" she asked. "Why are you and Mike estranged?"

"That's a long story."

"How about the log-line version?"

"I'm the one who owned Porter's. All of it. The store, the factory and warehouses. Even Fraser Hills Percherons."

"Why didn't you say something sooner?" Vanessa couldn't believe no one had told her.

"I was the mayor of this town for a long time. My family ran businesses in this town from the time it had a population of less than a hundred."

"You used to do all that stuff with the horses too? Like Mike?"

"Not nearly as good as him, but yes. My family initially built carriages for draft horses. We dabbled, but it wasn't until recent years that Mike really made something big out of that. I carved out that part of the business, and all the land it sits on, and gave it to Mike before I sold to AGC."

"That sounds like a pretty sweet deal. Why was he mad?"

"It's not just business, Vanessa. It's family." Buck looked tired. "I had my reasons for selling, but all Mike noticed was that the legacy he thought would always be there had been torn apart."

"I guess I can see his point. You got a good deal on it."

"I had to. I sold for a reason."

"I know it's none of my business, but why did you sell?"

He looked her straight in the eye. "I used the money from the sale of Porter's to fund the hospital. I tried for years as mayor to get a good hospital to come to this town, or even to the county, but I couldn't make it happen. Then Olivia died. Mike believed if we'd had a hospital closer maybe she could have been saved. I guess we'll never know."

"That's so sad."

"It was. Olivia was a wonderful mother and wife. Mike loved her so much." His eyes softened. "We all loved her." He pressed his lips together. "It tore Mike apart when she died. There was nothing I could do to soothe my grandson. Nothing. That's a bad feeling."

She nodded.

"Then, my wife had a heart attack."

"I'm so sorry."

"Thank you. We'd been married so long I could barely

remember life without her. Frankly, I was tired of seeing people I love die."

"So, you gave up your business to fund a hospital?"

"Yes. Sort of. I couldn't solely fund it, but I made the deal very enticing."

"Mike didn't understand or agree?"

"He didn't know. Still doesn't. It didn't matter. I'd do anything for this town, and these people. I did what I thought was right. It hurt some folks, but in the long run, I'm happy with my decision."

"I know what you mean. These people. This place. They take up residency in your heart when you're not looking."

Buck let out a hearty laugh. "Never heard anyone put it that way, but you're right."

"I thought I was giving everyone what they wanted. Corporate is not happy with me right now." She shook the phone messages in his direction. "It doesn't matter that I was able to increase the profit model for Porter's by nineteen percent, or that I was able to meet the warehouse goals—on time and under budget. They want to sell off Porter's. Building and all. Shut it down."

"Is that bad?"

Vanessa couldn't believe her ears. "It's horrible."

"Everything can seem very different when you look at it from a different perspective." He cocked his head. "Maybe you're looking at this the wrong way."

"I can't fix this."

He sipped his coffee without a word, then simply said, "Can't you?" He dropped a five on the table and walked out.

"No." But he'd already walked away. It seemed as if the whole world was closing in on her. She placed a twenty under the still full bowl of chicken and dumplings, grabbed her bags, and left. She wasn't even sure where she was headed until she got there.

In the bleachers, on the bottom row, she stared out onto the empty football field. School had been out since last week. The bright sun had melted a lot of the snow, leaving it looking like a patchy mess.

She rested her elbows on her knees. The sun tucked itself behind a cloud. A drizzling rain began to fall, splattering against the glossy shopping bags.

"The wrong perspective"? What did Buck mean by that? It was pretty cut-and-dried.

Suddenly she could see herself at ten years old, wearing bright red rubber boots, walking and kicking through piles of leaves just to hear them rustle and crunch beneath her feet.

Marching like a nutcracker in a parade, lifting her heavy boots high with each step. The leaves fluffed into the air, scattering around her, leaving a wake behind her as she kept moving through them.

Nature at its best. When was the last time she'd kicked through leaves, or walked with no expectations? Even her daily runs had purpose, and she kept on task by watching how far and fast she was going to meet the goal. Maybe the goal should be to just enjoy nature and run as the mood dictated. It was exercise either way, but couldn't her mind use a break?

She opened her arms, daring the raindrops to hit her. Closing her eyes, she let the rain surprise her. The simplest of things.

"They're selling." She patted her pockets, looking for her phone. "They're selling." She grabbed her bags and ran on the track all the way out of the schoolyard to Main Street. She headed for the library, and tucked herself in a corner at a table. She opened her laptop and connected to the Wi-Fi. She pulled up the responses from Edward in her email, and the attached sale sheet for Porter's spelled it all out. Because the value of the warehouse sites was so strong, the remaining older building wasn't outrageous. The valuation of Porter's wasn't based on the numbers she'd forecasted, but rather the old revenue.

She did some calculations and then jogged straight back over to the carriage house. She was sweaty despite the cold by the time she got there. She knocked on Buck's front door.

"Thought you might stop by."

"I need your help. I need you to help connect me with the local banker here."

"Come in."

She stepped inside, and paused at the opulence of his house. Neat. Precise. As if it were a museum where no one lived. Which was odd, because he was so laid-back.

"Do you have a connection at the bank here in town? I'm going to buy Porter's myself. I'll make it work. I'll do it with Misty at my side. She's the rightful heir of Porter's, isn't she?"

"What I did, what I had to do, when I sold Porter's was allow someone else to breathe new life into what I'd started. Those buildings were dying. No one wanted to take it over. Now they'll have new jobs. The town will grow again. And now people in this town are ready to fight for Porter's."

"It's worth fighting for."

"Is that what you want? To stay here in this little town and run that old factory?"

"Yes, but bring it into the current times. Add a couple fresh new products. Have you ever had Lilene's cookies made from the fruitcake seconds?"

"Oh, yes."

"Me too. I think they'd be a hit. Especially if we don't call it fruitcake. Not important. The bottom line is, yes. I want this. I want to be a part of it."

"You'd be happy here?"

"I don't know. I think so. I have to try." She sucked in a breath. "It'll be different, but the risk is low. If I don't like it, then I adjust."

"Perspective."

"Exactly like you said. I was listening." She pulled her hands together. "There's something about Fraser Hills. Look at you and Anna. I've never seen her so happy."

"I like her. She's a real good lady."

"She likes you too."

"I think you like my pigheaded grandson."

"I'm going to stay out of your feud, but I'd recommend this as being the right time to get it all out on the table. I'm looking forward to grooming Misty to take over Porter's one day. She's a brilliant young mind." She ran her hand through her hair. "Look. A few weeks ago, I was madder than fire to be sent down to do the dirty work, but something has happened here. It's like all of these unanswered prayers brought me something bigger. Better." She smiled. "I have a new perspective."

"You think this town is big enough for you?"

"You're not going to challenge me to some kind of country gunslinging duel, are you?"

"No, ma'am. I'm going to do you one better."

CHAPTER THIRTY-TWO

Mike still couldn't believe the rumor, although Lilene was never one to assume. If she said she heard Porter's was closing with her own ears from corporate . . . it was the truth.

He couldn't stop shaking his head, though.

She really snowed me.

And what ticked him off the most was that he'd been fine, perfectly fine, before she came along. She interrupted the flow that he and Misty had perfected. Tossing all these new emotions into the mix.

He rested his forearms on the steering wheel as he sat at the stop sign staring at the dark red building that had been Porter's as long as he'd been alive.

Across the way, coming out of the attorney's office, Mike saw Vanessa walk out to the sidewalk.

His heart lurched. How could he have actually thought he

might spend time with her? Share personal parts of his life with her?

A moment later he saw his grandfather walk out and join her. The two stood there talking.

He had no idea what he was going to do or say. All he knew was he couldn't stop.

He swerved his truck into a parking spot, and abandoned it right there still running, and marched over to the two of them.

Squaring up to his grandfather, he said, "I should've known if there was something bad going on in this town that you were behind it."

Buck leaned back at the power of the words, but he didn't argue.

"Mike. Wait," Vanessa said, placing an arm between the two. "You don't have the whole story."

"I know this story. Lies. Deception." He raised his hand to his head and turned his back on the two of them. "Selfish," he stammered. "Selfish decisions that impact others."

"Stop." Vanessa stepped in front of him. "Let me explain before you say something you're going to regret. It's time all of this ended."

"You're darn right it is." He stabbed a finger in the air toward his grandfather. "You're going to run me out of my own hometown just to get away from you and your bad decisions."

"We're not doing this in the middle of Main Street," Vanessa said calmly.

"How can you be so calm?" He glared at her.

"Come on. Both of you." She started walking toward the attorney's office. "Now."

Buck held his ground.

Mike followed her inside.

"Sit."

"Don't tell me what to do. Who do you—"

Vanessa put her hand up. "Mike. I promise this isn't what you think it is. Please. Please, give me ten minutes to fill you in. I promise you on everything I hold dear, it will be worth it."

He sat. "Your promises don't mean much around here." His knee bobbed up and down. He couldn't even bring himself to look her in those deceptive brown eyes.

She took the seat next to him. "Mike, I did the right thing. Yes, AGC sent me here to close down Porter's to make space for the sports warehouse. During my due diligence, I realized we could provide the warehousing, and not negatively impact Porter's."

"Closing? That's not a negative impact? Making Misty think you were going to help her make this big career. You don't do that to a kid."

"Stop. Hear me out. My intentions were good. I had no idea AGC was set on eliminating that part of the portfolio. I proved an uptick in the forecast for the next twelve months at Porter's with no negative impact to the full picture. Selling part of Porter's footprint was a good business decision. They have the right to sell it."

"You should have been up-front from the beginning."

"I bought it."

"You drank the Kool-Aid. 'It's just business.' Is that what you're going to tell me next?"

Buck leaned his shoulder against the door jamb. "Son, you are not a good listener. She bought Porter's. The whole blessed thing. And if you hadn't picked up on it, this town is getting an influx of revenue from a really substantial warehouse and jobs. I couldn't have done that. I was watching this town slowly dwindle away."

Mike's jaw twitched. "You put it all at risk."

"It was a calculated risk, and it's working out for the best. Can you just move past the past?"

"Porter's isn't going anywhere." She laid her hand on his arm. "I'm not going anywhere. Misty will be groomed to take over leadership of that company one day."

Mike blinked. "You knew about all this?"

Buck shook his head. "No. It would have all worked out fine if AGC hadn't pulled the plug on Vanessa's plan. They wanted to take the loss. Which actually worked in our favor. It was a steal."

"I didn't know Buck was your grandfather," she said. "I didn't put it all together until the other day. Misty didn't fill in those pieces. She let me figure it out on my own. She loves you both. You two need to find a way to set these differences aside. For her."

Mike lifted his chin. "All I wanted was for the family businesses to stay connected. The way it had always been."

"You didn't want to run Porter's," Buck said.

"I know." *I was selfish too.* "I assumed the business and farm would always be connected—the family legacy—but when you let that conglomerate buy you out with no discussion with me, it was like our whole family tree had toppled."

"But it didn't. I made sure you and those horses were separate. You'd stand alone."

"I didn't want to be alone. I wanted our family to continue to build on what we had."

"Times are changing, Mike."

"Tell him the rest, Buck. It's time." Vanessa stared at Buck.

Buck shifted his weight. "I used the money from the sale of Porter's to persuade the hospital to come to our town."

"You what?" Mike looked incredulous.

"We couldn't attract a good hospital no matter what we'd tried, so I made it a very attractive deal with good perks to get one here. Maybe, if we'd had a hospital right here, we wouldn't have lost the people we loved. Maybe we would have, but I couldn't sit back and take the chance on letting it happen again."

He stared at his grandfather, and then at Vanessa. "You did that?"

Buck nodded. "It was the right thing to do. I'm getting a very nice return on it too, so don't feel too bad for me."

"I'm sorry I wasn't willing to listen."

"I could have handled it differently, but that's the past. Now Porter's has new breath bringing it back to life, and Vanessa is the new owner."

Vanessa straightened. "But the whole town is up in arms with me. The gossip has already swept through this town like a wildfire."

Mike turned to Vanessa. "What do you need me to do?"

"Believe in me. Help me." Her lashes lowered. "Please?"

"Come here."

She went into his arms, and he pulled her in close. "Together, as a team, we can make this easy work."

"I like the sound of that," Buck said.

"I'm so sorry, Grandpa. I probably wouldn't have understood at the time. It was just too close to Grandma dying. It was like losing Olivia all over again."

"I know, Mike." He cuffed his hand on his grandson's shoulder. "I know."

CHAPTER THIRTY-THREE

Vanessa stood in the concession building at the high school waiting as the town flooded into the seats on the evening before Christmas Eve.

Snide comments peppered the conversations as people speculated what was to come next for Fraser Hills.

Anna walked over to her and pulled Vanessa's hands into her own. "You're going to be fine. I'm so excited about the prospects of our future here in this town."

"I know," Vanessa said. "Don't make me cry."

"I'm sorry. I'm just so happy. For the town. For both of us. Your mother would be beside herself. You are such a remarkable young woman." She dipped her hand in the quilted tote bag she had hung over her arm and pulled out a shiny red box. "I hope you like this. It's not fancy, but it's the most precious memory I have of you and your mother together. I want you to have it."

Vanessa's brows pulled together as she took the box in her hand. "This can wait until Christmas."

"No. I don't think it can. Please. For me," she said.

Vanessa turned and set the box on the counter, and lifted the lid. "Is this . . . ?" She pulled out the old tin. The rattling sound was like a whisper from heaven. "Mom's button tin?"

"You would sit and sort through those buttons for hours with your mother."

"I remember when Grandpa died and we took the buttons from his favorite sport coat and put them in here. They were leather. I thought they were the most precious things in the world."

"I know. Those are the leather buttons I used on your scarf."

Vanessa placed her hand on the fine details, her finger tracing the overlap of the leather pieces on the buttons. "I loved them as soon as you gave me that scarf, but I didn't for a second . . ."

"I know. I should've given this to you a long time ago. It was just so hard for me to let go of. It was the only thing I asked your dad for. He thought I was an idiot. He had no idea how much the memories stuffed into that little tin meant."

"Thank you, Anna." She clutched the tin, then gave it a little shake. "I love the strength of that sound. One by one they are nothing but buttons. Light. Worthless. Together they sound like a symphony. Strong. Creative. Continually shifting to fill the space."

"Like you. You're doing a good thing here. You've changed so many ideas about your future in just a couple of weeks. The opportunities are endless."

"It's not entirely unselfish, you know." Vanessa reached for

Anna's hand. "I can't wait for us to both make our lives in this town."

"And Mike and Misty?" Anna tilted her chin.

"Mike's great. He's a good man, and a wonderful father."

Anna bobbed her head. "I always said there's nothing sexier than a good father."

"I think I finally understand what that means. It scares me at the same time, though. Do you think he has enough love for me too?"

"Loving a wife is different from loving a child, Vanessa. It's not a contest. It's not like he has to divide the love. There are adequate amounts for both. And Misty will refill your wells threefold over and over."

"It's terrifying. It's like I just put my whole life on red, and the roulette wheel is spinning."

Lilene came rushing over to Vanessa. "It's time."

"I'm ready," Vanessa said.

"I'm sorry again for everything I said. I still feel horrible."

Vanessa hugged Lilene. "Please don't. Let's step forward. I can't wait to put the new Porter's cookie on the map together."

"I still can't believe my cookies are going to be available across the country."

"They'll be famous," Anna added.

*

Vanessa had spoken for five minutes straight. Not a peep from that stadium of people had interrupted her. Not one smart-aleck comment or doubt had been flung at her.

She looked to her left, where Mike and Misty, holding Scooter, stood at her side, and to the right, where Buck was flanked by Anna and Lilene.

"In closing," she said, "I look forward to taking Porter's into the future. A long and prosperous one that is agile so we can guarantee Fraser Hills will continue to foster the kind of hometown everyone wants to live in. We're going to bring that small-town family feeling into everything we do. Own it. Share it."

Bill Campbell was the first one to stand up and clap. It wasn't even a second before others joined him.

She turned to Buck, her guardian angel in all of this. Who would have thought the old gray-haired man of few words could have set all of this into motion with one single hope?

In that Sam Elliott voice, Buck grabbed the microphone. "This town just got a Christmas miracle, with a new family at the helm." He looked over toward his great-granddaughter, and then his grandson. "This is the best Christmas gift I've ever known."

"Love you, Grandpa."

Vanessa took the mic back from Buck. "Porter's will reopen on January second. Until then, merry Christmas and here's to an amazing new year . . . together." She handed the microphone off to Lilene, and Mike grabbed her hand and whisked her behind the building, out of the way of all of the townsfolk heading home to celebrate.

"Thank you."

"Stop. You don't need to thank me."

"No, thank you. For believing in Misty. For your belief in this town and its people. For opening this man's heart again. You've given me back my family. It's like a hundred pounds have lifted from my heart. It's beating again. For you."

She placed her hand on his heart. "I'm so glad."

"Vanessa, I will always be there for you. I want to make

you breakfast with fresh eggs from Henny, Penny, Jenny, Oprah Henfrey, Sophia Lor-Hen, and Eggatha Christie. Take you on carriage rides in the snow, and the rain, and on sunny days too."

"And always kiss me good night?"

"And good morning too."

"That sounds amazing."

"You're amazing. A combination of strength and beauty and kindness. You were the missing piece to this all along. I don't want you to leave."

Her heart fluttered, and her mouth went dry. Scooter ran between them, pawing and clawing at Vanessa's pant leg for attention. "And this guy." She picked him up and held him close. "I think we need to change his name to Porter. What do you think? A new face for the company?"

"It couldn't hurt."

"Ahhh." She could barely contain her surprise. "So, there is such a thing as good change."

"Apparently so."

EPILOGUE

In the tiny church up on the hill, only family gathered together on the eighth of August.

With the temperatures hovering in the high nineties, unusually hot for this part of North Carolina, the old air conditioner couldn't cool the dressing room Vanessa and Anna stood in, much less the whole chapel.

Vanessa had opened a hymnal and was fanning Anna with it. "You good?" Vanessa asked.

"Yes, but I'm wishing now we'd gone to the marriage commissioner." Anna placed her clammy hand on Vanessa's arm. "My hands are sweating. I don't know why I'm so nervous. I didn't think I was nervous. Buck's a good man."

"The best. Absolutely. I'm sure your hands are sweating because it's like a hundred degrees in here. Thank goodness you chose to go with the simple sundress rather than that dressy skirt and jacket."

"You were so right about that." Anna turned to her. "Is this crazy? It's crazy, isn't it?"

"No, Anna. You and Buck love each other. Everything is right about this."

"But I'm so old. I never thought I'd ever marry after—"

"That was the past. You need to live and believe in the here and now. Besides you had no way of knowing Buck was going to come into your life. What is it you always told me?" She tapped her finger on her lips as if she were trying to remember, but she knew the speech by heart. "Things happen for a reason. Sometimes you just have to open your heart, and let things happen the way they are supposed to rather than trying to manage every detail."

Anna laughed. "I did say that. About a hundred times."

"Enough that I can repeat it verbatim."

Anna blushed. "I meant it. For you, at least."

"It goes for everyone."

"Thank you. You're right. Buck and I really love our time together. This is right. I have you to thank for it."

"No you don't."

"None of this would have ever happened had we not come here last Christmas."

"If I remember correctly you were the one enforcing the get-together. And as I recall I had hopes we'd spend it in Paris. But that's not what happened. Neither one of us had any control over this. And here we are." Vanessa hugged her. "If you'd told me that the two of us would be living in a tiny town like this and finding our best lives, I'd have never believed it."

"We're so lucky."

"Blessed," Vanessa said.

A double knock sounded at the door. "We're ready when you are," the minister said.

"Thank you." Vanessa took something out of her pocket as she lifted the simple bouquet of wildflowers. "Okay, the flowers are new." She handed them to Anna, then tucked a pick with a flower made of blue buttons into the arrangement. "This button flower was made from buttons in Mom's button tin." Then she lifted her gold cross necklace over her head and placed it over Anna's. "This was Mom's. I know she'd want you to wear it today so she could be a part of this. That's the borrowed."

"Sweet Vanessa. Thank you." She fondled the cross. "This is perfect."

"You're set." She opened the door and reached for Anna's hand. "We're ready."

They walked out of the dressing room and joined Buck, Mike, Edna, and Misty in the church.

The minister didn't waste a moment.

Buck and Anna stood before him.

He rolled right into the ceremony, and it wasn't long before all the "I do" and "I will," and rings were placed upon the bride's and groom's fingers; then the couple turned toward the guests and the minister pronounced them to be husband and wife.

Vanessa dabbed at her eyes with her handkerchief.

Mike walked over to her. "You always cry at weddings?"

She nodded.

"I guess I better get used to it. Right, Misty?"

She nodded in a hurried response. "Yeah."

Vanessa smirked. "You better not be thinking of marriage anytime soon, young lady."

"Not me," Misty said. "Not for a long, long time. I've got things to learn. A business to run."

"Yes, you do." Vanessa was thankful Misty wasn't the type to rush off and do something crazy like marry before she was even out of college. She had a bright future.

Buck stood right behind Mike, holding Anna's hand with a huge grin on his face.

"Yeah," Mike said. "But if you're going to cry like that, you might have a real problem on December twenty-first."

"Why?" She sensed something was up, but she had no idea what it was she was supposed to be remembering. "Is that the tree lighting? Who's getting . . ."

Mike lowered to one knee and took a ring box from his jacket pocket. "Vanessa Larkin. Will you marry me?" He nodded toward Misty. "Help me make sure this girl has someone to always talk to when the going gets tough? Be a part of our family? For as long as we both shall live?"

Her mouth dropped open. Her eyes flitted from person to person. "I didn't. I—"

"It's a yes-or-no question. I've talked about it with everyone here in this room, including the minister. I want to marry you during the holidays."

"Oh my gosh. Really? That's so fast. Are you joking?"

"This is not a joking matter. If it's one thing I learned the hard way, it's that life is unpredictable. Don't make me wait. I don't want to miss a single day with you in my life. I love you."

"I love you too," Misty said. "Both of you."

"I love you both too," Vanessa said. "I already feel like part of the family. I can't believe this."

"I might even teach you my secret chicken-stew recipe," he said with a wink.

"Can we serve it at the reception?"

"Absolutely."

"We'd get married here?" Vanessa asked.

"Well, I'm afraid we're going to need a much larger place. We aren't going to be able to get away with a private ceremony like my grandfather and your cousin. I was thinking in the barn. Or the big church over on Main Street if you prefer a church wedding."

"As long as we have a minister perform the service, I don't care where we get married." She knelt down on the floor next to him. "I can't believe this. Yes. I love you. I love this town. Misty, you're okay with this?"

"More than okay!"

"You'll be my maid of honor," Vanessa said to her.

"That's so exciting. You have to order my dress. You know I'm a disaster at that, and Porter. He has to be the ring bearer. Wouldn't that be so cute?"

"Absolutely. We can buy him a little bow tie." They all laughed. "Oh, Anna. This is your day, and I'm hogging all the excitement. I'm sorry."

"No way. I'm so delighted." Anna giggled, squeezing Buck's hand. "It was so hard to keep a secret from you. Mike's been planning this for a while. That ring is gorgeous."

"You knew?"

"I did, and I'll save the blue button flower for your bouquet. You can borrow it from me to cover old, borrowed, and blue."

"That'll be perfect," she said to Anna. She turned and looked into Mike's eyes. "Yes. I can't wait to be Mrs. Mike Marshall." Tears streamed down her face. "I can't promise I won't cry, but

I do promise I'll be the happiest bride in the world. I'd marry you anytime. Anywhere. I don't have one hesitation."

Mike leaned in and kissed Vanessa as if no one else were in the room.

She might have never seen fireworks from a kiss in her whole life until she met Mike, but this kiss . . . this kiss had her floating on air.

ABOUT THE AUTHOR

Adam Sanner

USA Today bestselling author NANCY NAIGLE whips up small-town love stories with a dash of suspense and a whole lot of heart. Now happily retired, she devotes her time to writing, antiquing, and the occasional spa day with friends. A native of Virginia Beach, she currently calls North Carolina home.